BOOKS BY HORST BIENEK

Earth and Fire

Horst Bienek

Earth and Fire

Translated by Ralph Manheim

New York **Atheneum** *1988*

MAI 2016808

English translation copyright © 1988 by Atheneum Publishers, Inc.
Originally published in German under the title *Erde und Feuer*
Copyright © 1982 Carl Hanser Verlag München, Wien

ATHENEUM
Macmillan Publishing Company
866 Third Avenue, New York, N.Y. 10022
Collier Macmillan Canada, Inc.

Library of Congress Cataloging-in-Publication Data
Bienek, Horst, 1930–
    Earth and fire.
    Translation of: Erde und Feuer.
    I. Title.
PT2662.139E6913   1988   833'.914   88–16641
ISBN 0–689–11992–5

10 9 8 7 6 5 4 3 2 1

PRINTED IN THE UNITED STATES OF AMERICA

The author wishes to thank Rudolf Ziesche, custodian of the Gerhart Hauptmann papers in the Berlin Staatsbibliothek, for his assistance.

We can no more see to the bottom of the next
few hours than we can see to the bottom of
this river.

Charles Dickens
Great Expectations

Earth and Fire

1

IN THE LATE AFTERNOON, as night was falling, Valeska Piontek would sit by the window doing nothing, thinking of nothing, just sit there waiting, looking on as the things around her slowly lost their contours and colors, melted into a shadowy gray, and little by little were swallowed up by the darkness. Occasionally a melody would run through her head, come back again and again, and sometimes she would sit down at the piano and play it hesitantly with one hand, as though to hold it fast. In the end she herself would be no more than a part of the motionless darkness out of which a gentle melody flowed—or could it be that she had fallen asleep in her chair and that this wisp of melody had blown through her dream? On quiet Sunday afternoons, when no pupils came for piano lessons and the others in the house were taking naps, she often sank into this strange state of weightlessness, in which her will was suspended and she lost her awareness of herself.

It hadn't always been like this. Formerly, as soon as it began to get dark outside, she had pulled down the blinds and switched on the light; at that time she had favored sharp transitions. She had gone about the house with a firm step, joked with her little granddaughter, passed the time of day with the Schimmels, and if one of her pupils at the piano proved obtuse, she was quite capable of rebuking him in a firm voice. And later in the evening, if she had invited guests, she needed no urging to sit down at the piano and play an impromptu or a nocturne with brio.

Now all that seemed far in the past. Was it because the house had become so empty? Now there was loneliness all around her, her movements had become slower, her touch gentler, her voice softer. A glass bell seemed to have descended on the city with the first snow, which had come in October this year. There had been times when the house seemed noisy and cramped; now she longed for sounds that said something about life. She had few pupils left, all beginners; after struggling to teach them Czerny Etudes, she had no sooner got them to the point where she could start them on an easy Clementi sonatina or a Chopin prelude, when the girls would be called away to their "duty year" and the boys to their Labor Service, if not the army—nowadays they were taking them straight out of the schoolroom.

The Schimmels had gone back to Berlin before Christmas. With mounting alarm they had followed the advance of the Russian armies to the bend of the Vistula and into East Prussia; they had spent less and less time walking in the woods and more and more studying the big map in the entrance hall, and one fine day they had packed their bags because, as they put it, they would rather be bombed by the British in Berlin than wait in Gleiwitz for the Russians to march in.

She herself seldom looked at the map; when the British and Americans had landed in Normandy, her brother Willi had shown her exactly where and how far away it was—since then she had merely glanced at it in passing now and then, and though hardly a comfort, it was reassuring to see that the little blue flags were still where Josel had put them just before going back to the army.

Perhaps she had no desire to know exactly how close the Russians or the English were to the borders of Germany. Be that as it may, the Schimmels' fears struck her as exaggerated; Gumbinnen, yes, that was far in the east, a place of large estates, great forests, empty swamplands, hardly worth fighting for. Gleiwitz was different; now that the Ruhr was all but destroyed, Upper Silesia was getting to be the arsenal of the Reich; it would be defended; if Upper Silesia were left to the Russians, it would soon be the end of Germany and of the war.

She remembered well how she had taken the Schimmels to the railroad station with their three suitcases and two cartons on the sled, though they had arrived with only two carryalls when their house in Berlin had burned down, and all their worldly goods consisted of what they had taken with them to the air-raid shelter on Savigny Platz. Since the newspapers at the time were full of the Ardennes offensive and reported that the German troops had made

considerable gains on the very first day, she had made one last attempt
to persuade the Schimmels to stay. She had got used to them in the
two years they had spent in the two little rooms upstairs; and after
Halina, the maid, was arrested, Frau Schimmel had helped her in
the kitchen now and then. More important, Frau Schimmel had
always listened attentively to her; in the end there was no one else
with whom she could discuss everything, not even her brother Willi.

Frau Schimmel had walked more and more slowly beside the sled,
burying her face deep in her fur collar. But her husband had hurried
her on, as if this were their last chance of escaping. On the way, he
had told Valeska in a whisper what he had heard from a reliable
source: Hitler was aiming at a separate peace with the Western
powers and the sole purpose of this new offensive was to obtain
better conditions. Then—and here Herr Schimmel spoke even more
softly—the Western armies would join with the Germans to fight
the Bolsheviks, the whole East would be one great bloody battlefield,
and if the Pionteks knew what was good for them, they too would
start moving westward. Meanwhile Frau Schimmel had buried her
face even more deeply in her fur collar as though for protection, not
only from the cold, but also from the terrors of the future.

Herr Schimmel's whisperings had struck Valeska as absurd; such
talk was possible only for people who had lost everything and didn't
care where they would end up. She did care; her possessions were
intact, they had even increased a little during the war, she would
never leave Gleiwitz. Once she had moved a little farther
westward—that was in 1922, when the new borders were established—
but she had been young then and had begun a new life with Leo
Maria.

Now she was too old for that kind of thing, she wanted to stay
where she was and to be buried beside Leo Maria. She hadn't gone
into the station but had quickly taken leave of the Schimmels outside.
She had hurried home, determined to forget Herr Schimmel's whisperings as quickly as possible.

But since the start of the Russian offensive they had been constantly on her mind. Sometimes after the radio news she would go
out to the map, locate the towns that had been mentioned in the

Wehrmacht communiqués, and wonder whether the Russians or the British would get to Gleiwitz first. And once while her brother, for the first time since Josel's departure, was moving the little blue flags on the map, she had discussed it with him. He removed the flags from western Tunisia and put them back on the Dutch-Belgian border; in Italy he placed a flag near Pisa and another near Florence, and in the East he moved the flags from the Black Sea coast, from Kharkov and Lake Ilmen to Kielce, Radom, and up at the top to Insterburg.

"If we manage to maintain a stable front here," piped Willi Wondrak with several little flags bobbing up and down between his lips, "the winter may be over before the Russians get here." And he put in a flag near Kalisch.

Inferring from his tone that he had difficulty in believing his own words, Valeska decided to tell him what Herr Schimmel had said as he was leaving. She didn't know exactly how to put it, but her brother seemed to have understood her instantly, as though he had had the same idea and had even discussed it with Herr Schimmel, for he replied without hesitation: "I'm afraid it's too late for that." And with his last little blue flags he fastened the truth to the map. Now Valeska could see at a glance how close the Russians were and how far away the British, but she still preferred to consider the map as a game played with little flags and to disregard the reality they stood for.

It was dark in the room now. The window was a pearly white rectangle floating in darkness. Valeska Piontek pulled herself up with a start. Had she heard a door closing? She listened, but all was quiet outside. The blanket had fallen from her lap; she bent over, picked it up, folded it with exaggerated care, and slowly set it down in the chair behind her. She moved as in a dream; it seemed to her that she was still sitting motionless in her easy chair, staring at the shimmering window, while another woman was crossing the room, groping her way past the furniture in the darkness, putting a briquette in the stove and poking the grate until a flame shot up, casting a yellow flickering light into the room. For a long time she watched the dancing flames, the darting play of light and shadow, which kept projecting new figures on the wall and as quickly effacing them, a quivering phantasmagoria, which she watched as though spellbound. The way back to her chair seemed twice as long; several times she stopped and listened; she hoped to hear some sound from outside that would bring change. But all remained still; she didn't even hear Irma's children running through the hall. She would just sit there in the dark, put a fresh briquette on the fire from time to time, and wait for her brother or his wife, Rosa.

Willi always brought the latest news; what came over the radio was usually a day or two late. Yesterday the radio had spoken of vigorous defensive action near Radom, but today he had learned from a reliable source that Russian armed spearheads had already reached Tschenstochau. For the first time the question had come up between them; ought they to run from the Russians? But they spoke of it as of something remote, one possibility among many, and had quickly dropped the subject, because they all suspected deep down that in the end they would be left with no other possibility. On the radio someone was singing *"A bunch of roses in Tirol, carries a message from the soul"*; Rosa had brought in the proof of tomorrow's paper announcing a supplement of one-quarter pound of meat or meat products on sections B1 and B2 of the ration cards, and Irma was worried because little Roswitha had a temperature of a hundred point six. And the Russians were in Tschenstochau. From there to Gleiwitz it wasn't far.

As a child, Valeska had walked from Lublinitz to Tschenstochau on a pilgrimage, and from Gleiwitz it was only about twice as far. She didn't remember how long it had taken, only that they had spent one night in a little village church, she was sure of that. For a moment she was transported back to her childhood in the small town on the river. She remembered her father's dry goods store: it smelled of mothballs and the mirrors sparkled and the bolts of material were piled high on the shelves. Once when she was alone in the shop with her brother, she had tried on the cloth like dresses—Willi had kept picking out new bolts, even from the upper shelves; she had had to try them on, more and more of them. He had commanded her to dance and she had complied. When their father came back, bolts of material were spread out all over the floor, and she got a beating; it was the only time her father had ever beaten her.

Suddenly the door was flung open, and the hall light cut a bright rectangle in the darkness. Startled awake, Valeska heard Irma shrieking: "Halina is here! Mother, think of it, Halina is here!"

Valeska saw Halina's face silhouetted in the doorway. Yes, it was really Halina, but her baggy jacket looked so strange; she didn't know that jacket. "Halina, is it really you? *Moja siostrzyczko!*"

She stood up and started toward her, but the shadowy figure came running and fell into her arms; she had to brace herself or she would have been bowled over. "Halina," said Valeska, "Halinko," and now, in her embrace, she really felt Halina's body. "Yes," she whispered, "it's you, it's you," as though having to convince herself that it really was Halina, who had been arrested in her house more than a year ago and dragged away.

Halina said nothing. Her body gave out groans and sobs that were eloquent enough; Valeska understood them better than any stammered words. She passed her hand over Halina's face and felt the tears on her rough skin; she passed it over the eyes and forehead and over the short, hard hair stubble under the head scarf. "Halina!" she screamed. "*Bozhe muy*—what have they done to you? Your hair is all gone!"

2

KOTIK OSSADNIK WAS on his way through the world. Even if he was only walking down Klopot and Breslauer streets, past the engineering school, and across the Klodnitz bridge to the old customhouse. He liked to roam the city streets without any particular destination, and he always discovered something new. In winter he loved the quiet, snow-covered paths along the Klodnitz, which in places was frozen almost to the middle. He would teeter a short way on the ice and hear the water gurgling below him. That could be dangerous during the spring thaw. Ice floes had been known to break off from the shore and to carry playing children away.

If the frost held, the river would soon be frozen solid. That didn't happen every year; when it did, in the old days, they had held an ice carnival under the Wilhelmstrasse Bridge—after getting permission from some government office. This winter Kotik had only been to the river two or three times, there had been so much to keep him busy; and altogether, the older he grew the less time he had for his expeditions.

Today he'd have preferred to stay home reading *The Mauritius Case*; after all, he was already fifteen, and sometimes he wondered how he would ever, as long as he lived, finish so many books—the ones he had seen yesterday in the Jüngst villa, for instance. He had gone into town today only because he hoped for another adventure similar to the one he had had yesterday. So many things had been happening in the last few days, of the kind that ordinarily occurred only in books; but now you could actually be there and not just read about them.

Yesterday, for instance, on his way through the old town, he had passed the Jüngst villa; everyone knew the house because it had belonged to old Herr Jüngst, who owned the steel mill. A crowd had formed outside; he had mixed in and found out that the villa had been broken into and looted during the night, probably by

ostarbeiter, who were becoming more and more uncontrollable now
that the eastern front was coming closer. The present owner had
moved to the Reich some days ago with his family. The police had
been notified immediately, but so far no one had appeared—and a
wag had wondered out loud whether the police had moved out too.
Of course the people had been curious; a woman said why not go
and see what damage the burglars had done. She had marched right
in—the others had expressed admiration for her courage—and come
out a little later, saying: "They've behaved like *khakhars* in there, like
monsters!"

Then a second woman had gone in and many more followed.
Kotik joined them, and they all went up the stairs to the rooms.
With curiosity tempered by fear, they examined the gutted cupboards
and drawers, the broken china and costly carpets. And everyone
picked something up, looked at it, and tucked it way, furtively at
first, then more and more openly, a cup or a vase that was still intact,
a coffee mill, a wristlet, a bathing cap, a pair of shoes—anything
that might come in handy.

One room was full of books from floor to ceiling. Kotik had never
seen anything like it. He had walked along the shelves in amazement,
trying to read the titles on the spines of the books. He would never
have dared to take one out. There were piles of books on the floor,
in such confusion that he hadn't hesitated to slip two of them into
his knapsack. One was *The Mauritius Case* by Jakob Wassermann,
the other *The Magic Mountain* by Thomas Mann. He had never
heard of either author. He wondered why he had taken these rather
than something else. Probably because they were so impressively
thick.

Shortly after Christmas he had found some books in a garbage
can on Niederwallstrasse and taken them home. Yes, people were
even throwing books away these days—mostly about politics, which
didn't interest him. But there were others, such as *The Romanian
Diary* and a novel about Paracelsus; he had taken them home and
put them in the new bookcase. Another was *Students, Love, the Cheka
and Death*, by Alexandra Rachmanova. He had read it in two nights;
the beginning was exciting, he thought, but then it got repetitious.

Mamotschka had got her hands on it, and before long he was sorry he hadn't hidden it from her, because after that she took to shuffling around the house, wailing in front of every crucifix or holy picture.

"*Muy Bozhe*, they smash all the crosses and burn the holy pictures and use the churches for garages."

The Russians, she felt sure, would be just as the book described them as being during the Revolution. Now that the Russian front was coming closer and closer, she armed herself against them in her own way.

One day Kotik surprised her nailing some boards together.

"What are you doing, Mamochka?"

"Can't you see? I'm making a crate. When the Russians come, I'm going to take all the crosses and holy pictures off the wall and put them in this crate and bury them in the cellar under the coal."

"What gave you that idea?"

"That book by the Russian woman, you've read it. The Russians are against the Christian religion. And it's our business to keep it alive. The Church will become a cave church," she said almost triumphantly.

"A what? Where did you get that?"

She had found the word in *The Miracles and Acts of the Saints*. She hadn't paid attention to it before. Now the term evoked images, it appealed to her and nourished her imagination.

"If you ask me," said Kotik, "we'd do better to burn those Hitler Youth magazines and father's Labor Front stuff. They're more likely to look for that kind of thing."

"The Church will survive underground," said Anna Ossadnik. "Even in Russia they haven't been able to suppress it completely."

With her own eyes she had seen the *ostarbeiter* praying in the Church of Sts. Peter and Paul, and crossing themselves, though they did it from right to left and touched their shoulders instead of their chests.

Maybe, Kotik thought, I'd better hide the Paracelsus book from Mamochka, he's that wonder-working doctor in the Middle Ages; if I don't, she'll start doctoring us with his recipes.

On top of their churches they have a red star instead of a cross,

Frau Ossadnik said in a whisper, because she didn't want her husband, who had just come home from work, to hear her. He'd just start asking more questions. And aloud she said to Kotik, "Give me a hand with the crate."

"You packing?" Franz Ossadnik asked suspiciously.

Anna shrugged her shoulders.

"A lot of people are leaving," said Kotik. "Our HY leader says the industrial zone must be defended. We're waiting for a shipment of bazookas, then we're supposed to guard the roads leading into the city."

"I haven't seen a single one of our top men today," said Franz. "And they keep telling us that no one must leave his place of work, it's as good as desertion."

"Maybe we should clear out too before the Russians get here," Kotik suggested.

"Never!" Anna Ossadnik said that as resolutely as if she had thought it over and made up her mind once and for all. She couldn't just drop everything here. The rich leave, they're at home wherever they go. We poor people stick to our home ground. And anyway, where could we go?

"The truth," said Anna darkly, "is that the Antichrist has won out. The Russians are the Antichrist. But the Church will live, it will be a cave church for a while."

"The truth," said Kotik, "the truth! What's truth? There isn't any truth. There's a spoof, that's all there is."

From then on he said spoof instead of truth.

Kotik had bundled up warm. The other kids made fun of him for wearing thick, hand-knitted earmuffs under his cap. As usual, he had his knapsack. His expeditions often took him to out-of-the-way places, and he always found things he could make use of; almost anything could come in handy these days. Once he had found some bent, rusty nails, taken them home, soaked them in machine oil, and hammered them straight—Mamochka couldn't have made her crate without them. And a mangled doll without arms or legs; he had smoothed out the dents and made new limbs out of cloth—a perfect present for Bronder's little sister. And sometimes after the harvest he would

find a few potatoes that hadn't been dug up, or some little sugar
beets that Mamochka would make syrup out of, or a peasant would
sell him some *kapusta*—so it was a good thing that he always had
his knapsack.

He used to go off on bicycles with Bronder or with his brother
Andy; they would go a long way out of town, to the ruined Tost
Castle or even as far as the old Castle Park at Ehrenforst or to
Schakanau, where Paulek had spent some time in the reformatory,
or they'd ride along the Klodnitz Canal to Stauwerder, where they
could watch the barges, which moved so slowly that the boys could
observe the family life of the Oder boatmen. But then Bronder and
Andy had been drafted, though they were only a year or two older
than he was. Boys his own age, his classmates, bored him, they were
so childish—he had always sought out older boys, because he wasn't
interested in wasting his time with friends; he wanted friends he
could learn from.

What books were they reading—if any; that was the crux. Except
for the primer and the prayer book, or perhaps in a pinch *Heidi*,
few had ever opened a book, so naturally he despised them. Others
were still on fairy tales or knights and heroes; the really bright ones
might be reading Rolf Torring or the German West Africa series
or Karl May, or Dominik's science fiction or Paul Rosenhayn's
crime novels—but he had read all those at the age of twelve or
thirteen. His classmates had never even heard of the authors he
was now reading, Theodor Storm or Rudolf G. Binding or Jakob
Wassermann.

He was fifteen now, that meant he'd be called up before Easter
—first to the territorial antiaircraft. Since October, when the Russians invaded East Prussia, his HY duty had consisted almost entirely
of digging antitank trenches outside of town or drawing terrain
maps; in the last two weeks they'd been trained in the use of the 98
rifle and the bazooka, but there were only two rifles for the whole
platoon, target practice had been merely simulated, and their sole
bazooka was a dummy. The only opportunity to see what a bazooka
could do was in a training film, which if true was pretty impressive.
The only hope now was that the promised bazookas would arrive

in time to stop the Russian tanks in the outskirts—he himself wasn't very optimistic.

Kotik probably knew the streets of this town better than any other boy of his age; exploring them was enough for him. He had never longed for the big city, which to them all meant Breslau—Berlin was too far away. His city had plenty of adventures to offer him, he had only to wander around, to keep his eyes open, and to wear a knapsack to carry his finds in.

In the Huldschinsky housing development, for instance, all the windows were wide open, and in passing you could watch a family eating mashed potatoes and the sour soup known as *żur*, or a woman in her petticoat ironing her only Sunday dress, or you could see some drunken lout come home and start beating his wife. It was different on the Ring, on Oberwallstrasse or Miethe-Allee, where the upper crust lived. There the windows were shut on summer evenings and the curtains drawn. In that part of town there were children who didn't even know how to whittle a watermill, blow up a frog, or blow their nose with their fingers. In Port Arthur he had once seen a stabbing and in Ellguth-Zabrze he had seen some teenagers cut the udder off a live goat. His friends, who were always playing stupid games like checkers, mill, and halma, had no idea. Sometimes he wished he were a little more grown-up. He'd seen his brother wetting his hair and combing it smooth, thrusting his hands in his trouser pockets and clenching his fists to make his pockets look interesting, dandling his hips and winking when he passed the girls. When he felt especially bold, he would display that unmistakable sign, thumb between pointer and middle finger, and the girls would guffaw; sometimes he'd even follow them a short way.

When Kotik did that kind of thing—and he had tried in Port Arthur as well as the Huldschinsky housing development, where in the evening the girls often stood outside, watching the swallows and longing for something, they themselves didn't know what; he had sauntered past, baring his white teeth, for he was as proud of his teeth as Tonik of his hair—the girls would snarl and shake their fists at him and spit. Perhaps it was because these girls were older than he was, but it would never have occurred to him to try it with girls of his age, who giggled like simpletons if he so much as pinched their arms.

Kotik remembered how once that spring he had followed Tonik. It was a beautiful afternoon, the Klodnitz was steaming, and the birches were putting out their first green. Tonik was walking along the river with a shopgirl from Barasch's; Kotik had followed them for a while until Tonik noticed him and told him to run along home. He had merely fallen back a little until Tonik in a rage had started throwing stones at him and threatened to kill him. After that he had stood on the old wooden bridge and seen the two of them disappearing behind the trees in the dusk. In that moment his most fervent longing had been to grow up and to walk along the Klodnitz with a girl, even if it was only a shopgirl.

sometimes I wish I were like you, but then I despise you

you struck me, I'll never forget it,

you don't see me, you have eyes only for her

why are you going away stay here I have something to say to you

I won't stand for it keep your hands off her you're taking her, the way you take them all, and the very next day you forget her, and when Mamochka asks who you were with at the Café Loske, you can't remember the name I hate you you don't know how unhappy they are they cry keep your hands off her it was me I tripped you up because you were in such a hurry because you don't listen to me you don't take me seriously I'm only Hoppek little Hoppek the nerve of you disappearing with that girl, no really that's why I tripped you up no don't touch me you'll be sorry

you're a pig a rotten *pyerunnish* pig

One of us is going to get it so help me one of us will kill the other and it'll be me.

I'm not little Hoppek anymore I'm fifteen how I hate you well I don't know if I really hate you I despise you I despise you don't touch me brother of mine.

At the end of Miethe-Allee, where it ran into Parkstrasse, a man and a woman came toward him, pulling a sled piled high with suitcases; a little boy was pushing it from behind. The snow was fairly deep, only a narrow path had been stamped down, and Kotik had to squeeze past them. They went by without noticing him, but Kotik looked at the little boy; it seemed to him that he had never seen so much sadness in a child's face. He stopped at the garden gate and looked after them for a while. It was some time before he realized why: because he had missed the dog, a beautiful, slender brown dog. He remembered the house on Miethe-Allee, he had often passed it on summer days, and this little boy would be playing in the garden with a big long-haired dog—an Afghan, as Kotik had later found out. He had pressed his face to the fence. More than anything in the world he had wanted to be friends with that little boy and to play with that dog. After a while the boy had noticed him; he had come over to the fence and looked Kotik up and down. "What do you want?" he had said. "We don't give to beggers. Father says there's a job for anyone who wants to work." It had taken Kotik a moment to understand; then the blood rose to his head. The fence wasn't very high; he could have climbed over it, but he was afraid of the dog. He hung his head, he didn't want the little boy to see his burning cheeks; he was barefoot and his trousers were patched —it was September, and at that time of year he never wore shoes if he could help it. He had hated that little boy ever since; nevertheless, on the way home from school, he had sometimes gone out of his way to pass that house. He had wanted desperately to look inside.

Now the house would be empty. Kotik walked back and forth outside it, undecided what to do. He pressed the doorbell, and hearing no sign of life, climbed over the fence. He trudged through the deep snow, and banged on the door; he shouted, tried to look through the lower windows, and listened for sounds—in particular, the barking of a dog—but all he heard was his heart, pounding for fear, excitement, eagerness. Once he looked in the direction of the street—there was nothing to be seen or heard—then he went around to the back of the house. He made a hard snowball and threw it with all his might at one of the windows. The glass shattered. In the distance he heard the muffled thunder of a winter storm, or was it gunfire from the front? In the garden shed he found a ladder, leaned it against the back of the house, and climbed through the window.

3

No, SHE WASN'T CRYING; it was just that she'd been trying to make a fire in the disused kiln and so much smoke had got into her eyes that the tears were streaming down her cheeks. She would have preferred—while putting magazines, catalogs, and drawings into the fire—to have an honest-to-goodness cry, but she only felt a weight on her chest and a queasiness in her stomach. Traute Bombonnek had wept enough when Prohaska went away—that had been quite some time ago, but she hadn't forgotten, far from it. Then she had wept all night; her face had been so bloated she couldn't go to school the next day. After that her supply of tears seemed to be exhausted, she had taken on the look of a mournful dog (as rector Konopka had whispered behind her back, but loud enough for her to hear) and kept it ever since. When she laughed, which wasn't very often, her features merely shifted.

Choosing the things she wanted to burn had cost her a hard inner struggle, but no one watching her would have known it; now and then she would hold a picture or a book in her hand for a long while, or even turn the pages, but in the end she'd toss it onto the great mound. And so the morning passed. She knew this was a last good-bye. She had decided to go to Bergkamen, where Prohaska had gone; and if he wasn't there anymore, she would pick up his trail and keep looking until she found him.

Deep down she was glad the Russians were coming, because otherwise she would never have summoned up the courage and strength, she would never have found a pretext for leaving Gleiwitz. And yet there had long been nothing to hold her there. Neither her colleagues at the school, whose attitude toward her had been one of spiteful envy ever since she had won the city's cultural award, nor her pupils; those for whom she had conceived a certain affection had gone off to their Labor Service or their Farm Year. Not even her little workshop in the yard with the kiln had anything to offer her. She wanted to begin a new life, with Prohaska of course. That made it easier for her to part with her possessions. Up in her apartment she had hesitated from time to time, but now she threw papers into the fire with a certain satisfaction; she even surprised herself now and then running upstairs for new things to burn. It was high time she made a fresh start, and what was there to stop her? Wherever she went, she'd be able to support herself as an artisan or a teacher of applied art. If the wild hope she had been cherishing for some time were fulfilled even in small part, things were sure to come out right. She tossed issue after issue of *The German Pedagogue* in the fire and looked on as the flames shot up and the covers buckled in the heat before charring. The very thing that had made her so sore at heart in the first weeks and months after Prohaska's departure—the fact that she hadn't received a single letter or even a postcard from him—was now a source of new hope. Now she was able to indulge in the most delightful fantasies, and no shadow of reality could darken them.

When she returned to her apartment, she was surprised to see the women standing on the stairs; they looked strangely embarrassed as she passed and deliberately averted their eyes. Only Frau Pandelczyk, who occupied the basement apartment, functioned as a kind of janitor, and always made trouble when Fräulein Bombonnek fired her kiln, claiming that the smoke seeped through her windows, looked her straight in the eye with surely insolence.

Traute Bombonnek kept her distance from the other occupants. She made it plain to them that she was different from them, though perhaps no better. She was always first to come out with a greeting, adding a few meaningless words, to which the others could think up no answer, or, if they did, it was only long after she had passed. For a moment she thought of engaging them in conversation, after all the situation was most unusual; but for months and years she had neglected to do so, so why should she now, when she was getting ready to leave this ill-assorted community forever? While closing the door behind her and leaning against it for a moment to rest, she wondered whether these simple people had any comprehension of what was happening out in the world and only a few miles from the city, or whether they just accepted war and peace as they did the wind and the rain.

Her suitcase was packed. She wouldn't take any more than this one suitcase and a carryall. That morning she had gone to the post office with a carton containing her best work, embroideries, small enamel pieces, a hand-woven wall carpet, and her table silver, all neatly packed, and mailed it to herself at Bergkamen, general delivery. She'd probably get there before the package. At first the post office clerk hadn't wanted to accept it, there hadn't been any mail trains for days and his storeroom was full, but she was so determined not to drag the carton back home again that she managed to win him around in the end. In any case, it was too heavy to take in the train with her, and if she left it in the apartment, she'd probably never see it again. What really mattered for her new life would fit in her one suitcase and her carryall—all the luggage that was permitted. She had read in the paper that the Russians had burst into the Gumbinnen region so suddenly that the people had grabbed a coat off the hook and fled in all haste, and when they returned a few days later with the German troops, their houses had been burnt down and the people who had stayed behind lay dead in the snow. So this one suitcase and a warm blanket would have to do. The more things she took, the more memories she'd be dragging around with her.

Her colleague Fräulein Widawka the biology teacher, whom she had called on the day before, had packed three suitcases, a crate on rollers, four shoeboxes, and a knapsack. And she had kept taking something out, putting something in, exchanging one dress for another, one pair of shoes for another; she had been so bent on taking the picture from her bedroom, a reproduction of a Raphael Holy Family, that in the end she had removed it from its frame and rolled it up. The necessity of choosing tore her to pieces—a heartrending sight.

When Traute Bombonnek made it clear to her that no one with a job was allowed to leave town, that, though teachers were permitted to travel because the Christmas holidays had been prolonged until the end of January, they were restricted to a radius of seventy kilometers, and she would not be allowed through the station gate with her three suitcases, four shoeboxes, crate, and knapsack, Fräulein Widawka burst into tears and started to repack. When she finally had to recognize the fact that she would never be able to take all her belongings, she stood up, wiped away the tears, and announced calmly and resolutely that she would stay in Gleiwitz come what may, she simply couldn't part with the things for which she had slaved these last forty years, she would rather be knocked dead by the Russians in the midst of her possessions. She had forced this out between clenched teeth and without getting up had reached for a bottle of schnapps, which she had actually meant to leave behind.

Traute Bombonnek heard the sound at her door. Wasn't that a shuffling and whispering? When it stopped, she went to the kitchen and washed her face under the faucet. She looked in the mirror, but only for an instant; it really didn't matter now how she looked. All the same, she couldn't go about with soot on her face. But she reknotted her turban, which had slipped out of place. Then she rubbed her hands with Vaseline which she herself had slightly perfumed; there hadn't been any proper skin cream for a long time, and her skin was very dry, especially her hands.

That sound again! Then a scratching at the door, then a knocking. She stuck the pin in her turban and went to the door. When she opened, she was surprised to see so many women assembled on the landing. They must have come from all over the house, possibly even from the house next door, for there were some she had never seen before. Their numbers seemed menacing, but perhaps only because they stood there in silence, looking at the floor, and she hadn't the faintest idea what to say to them. It was Frau Pandelczyk who finally moved. She thrust out her head in its black cap until it was almost inside the apartment, making it impossible for Traute Bombonnek to shut the door.

"Shoving off, is that it? I suppose you're scared."

"I am not scared," said Traute Bombonnek. "I'm giving the house a thorough cleaning, now that there's a little time. And," she added pointedly, "certain things have to be thrown away."

Frau Pandelczyk moved nearer and put one foot in the doorjamb. "You've been packing," she said. "Going to beat it, aren't you? Going to clear out, just like the Party bosses. A little gunfire, and away they go. And what are we supposed to do? Nobody asks us."

Traute Bombonnek was bewildered; this Pandelczyk woman, whom she had always seen down on her knees scrubbing the floor, was coming inexorably closer.

"It's true that I'm going away"—she couldn't deny it, her suitcase was out on the landing for all to see—"but not far, only a few miles to my aunt's in Cosel. School is closed for fuel saving until January 29. I'll be back . . ."

Why, she wondered, did she justify herself to this woman?

"By then the Russians will be here. Can't you hear the gunfire? . . . Oh yes, you'd better get away quick, Fräulein Bombonnek, before it's too late. But let's hope"—with that she gave the other woman a sign, pushed the teacher out of the doorway, and invaded the apartment—"let's hope you've packed your pictures of the Führer and the bust . . ."

Fräulein Bombonnek went pale. And then red. The corners of her mouth trembled. She pressed the door handle so hard that her knuckles turned white. She couldn't think of anything to say.

"You burn a couple of notebooks and beat it. Just like that. When the Russians come and find a bust of Hitler, they'll burn the whole house down. Our house. See what I mean? That Hitler bust has got to go before you do. The bust must go!"

The women pushed past her into the entrance, into the kitchen and the two rooms.

"What do you want of me?" At last Fräulein Bombonnek recovered her voice. "Have you taken leave of your senses? You have no business in my apartment. Get out of my apartment this minute or I'll call the police. You have no right . . ."

"There ain't no police. The police are pulling out." Suddenly she began to scream. "Everybody's pulling out. But we've got to stay here. We've got nowhere to go. I've been scrubbing stairs for three years to buy myself a little kitchen cabinet. Do you think I can pack up and leave it all? We're simple folk. We didn't want this war. But we've got to stay here and face the music, *pyerunnye* and double *pyerunnye!*"

It wasn't just anger. There was fear in it too.

A woman came out of the living room with a framed document; the watermark figured an eagle and a swastika. She threw it on the floor and stamped on it. The glass splintered under her shoes. Traute Bombonnek looked on. The document certified that Fräulein Bombonnek had been awarded the Gleiwitz Cultural Prize for 1943. Yes, she had forgotten that.

"How about the Hitler bust?" Frau Pandelczyk asked the woman. "Have you found it?"

Traute Bombonnek held her breath. She had hidden the terracotta bust under a pile of sacks in a corner of her workshop, because she herself couldn't bear to look at it.

"We want that bust out of here. Or we won't let you go."

The other women, who had come back, nodded their heads in agreement. Apparently they had been discussing the matter for some time, and this invasion was the result.

"Oh my God!" was all that Traute Bombonnek could say.

"Give us the key to your workshop," said Frau Pandelczyk. "Or we'll break down the door. We're going to find that Hitler bust and smash it . . . We don't want the Russians burning the house down . . ."

Later, on her way to the station, Traute Bombonnek could still see those women barging into the little workshop, upsetting and smashing the shaped but not yet fired bowls and jugs, sweeping the terra-cotta vases off the shelves, ripping the photographs and newspaper clippings and sketches off the wall, turning the potter's wheel and knocking it over, and finally, with a triumphant roar, discovering the terra-cotta bust under the sacks. They dragged it out and battered it with logs until nothing was left but reddish-brown shards offering no clue to its original form.

Traute Bombonnek had hurried back to her apartment, the door of which had remained open, taken her suitcase, changed her coat, double-locked the door behind her, and fled.

She was on her way to the station. The women had torn the turban off her head, she hadn't even been able to rescue the pin. Now she pulled her woolen cap down lower. Her hands were cold, she had forgotten her gloves. She wound her shawl around the hand that was carrying her suitcase. She made a fist with the other and buried it in her coat pocket.

That Frau Pandelczyk, she thought as she walked, that no-good *zygana*, how insolent she had been, how shamelessly she had looked her in the face without lowering her eyes, that filthy *kachka*, how rudely she had spoken, that worthless *ogura*, daring to shout at her, that ignorant *chapla*, that *zebulla* with her stinking breath, that *hadra*, that *dupa*, that *tuleya*, that *klekota*, that *tepshlag*, that *khakhara* . . .

4

"SHEARING HER HAIR, just like that! *Muy Bozhe*. How could they! The things people can do to people!"

Valeska Piontek couldn't calm down. She kept saying the same things over and over. She stared at Halina, as though trying to get used to the sight of her.

Willi Wondrak had come in. He had stuffed his gloves into his coat pocket and was holding his cap and scarf in one hand. He was so startled by Halina's presence that he kept buttoning and unbuttoning his coat and telling everyone in a loud voice how glad he was to see Halina back again, which no one doubted.

Valeska had waited a long time for her brother, but now she only said: "Think of it. Our Halina has just come in, it's as if she had dropped from heaven. Somebody switched on the light and there she was in the doorway. At first I thought, I've fallen asleep and I'm dreaming, but then she gave me a real, honest-to-God hug, our Halinka . . ."

Willi Wondrak tried to visualize the scene, but he couldn't, he didn't believe in heaven. But he believed what he saw. And there was Halina, his sister's maid. A little thinner, looking a little unfamiliar, because her head scarf had slipped, revealing her shorn skull. "Where have you come from, Halina? Did they let you out?"

Valeska answered for her. "She says she was in a camp near Tschenstochau; the guards disappeared during the night, and the inmates all cleared out. Some soldiers gave her a lift as far as Königshütte, and from there she took the streetcar, she says."

Halina couldn't have answered for herself; it was all she could do to stop sobbing.

"I sent in several petitions," said Wondrak; "we kept hoping to get you out. But in the end we didn't know where you were. Did we, Valeska?" He sat down on the footstool and began to undo his shoelaces. "Your last card came last . . . that's right, it was last summer, quite a while ago, from some place none of us had ever heard of, we looked all over the map and we couldn't find it. Maybe it was a code address."

Some muffled sounds came from where Halina was sitting. Wondrak didn't know whether to interpret them as a reply.

"She had to work in a munitions factory, and to keep her from running away they cut off her hair and branded a number on her arm," explained Irma, who had helped her take off her coat and shoes and had brought her a warm knitted jacket. That was as much as she could do for her now.

"Has she got any papers, a certificate or an identity card or something?" Wondrak asked in a businesslike tone, as if he needed the information for his records.

"But you've heard," said Valeska, "she ran away from the camp." And to Halina: "Everything will be all right now. Don't worry, we'll look after you. You won't have to leave again. Even if we have to hide you."

A look at Halina told Wondrak that for the present he would get no answers out of her. Of course the presence of an escaped convict would create problems for the family, but he would discuss that with his sister alone later on. But what, he wondered, could his wife be doing? "Where's Rosa?" he asked.

"Rosa is digging ditches," said Valeska.

"What?!" said Wondrak in amazement.

"Yes," Irma explained. "They assigned her to digging tank traps. Frau Jelinek came and told us. Every day half the staff have to dig tank traps. First one half, then the other."

"Out of doors? In this cold? All day?" Willi had heard about it. But he couldn't conceive of such things happening to Rosa. She wasn't exactly built for digging.

"It's out of town," said Irma. "Near Gröling. It seems they're preparing some sort of defensive position."

Willi opened the stove door and tossed in two half briquettes. "Let's hope it will never be used. Do you know when she'll be back?"

"Oh, she'll be here any minute, I think. They're sure to stop digging at nightfall. But what about you? Have you heard anything new?"

"The situation is becoming critical," said Wondrak. "We must have a serious talk and decide what to do." He wanted to wait for his wife to arrive.

"I was in town," said Irma, "there's a big crowd at the station. But I've heard that no one is allowed to leave his place of work. They call it desertion."

"*Muy Bozhe,*" Valeska groaned.

"We've sent off some of our files," said Willi, "but no one is allowed to leave town until they issue an evacuation order."

"I have no desire to leave," said Irma. "It's almost zero out and terrible scenes are going on at the station, every train that comes in is already full to bursting."

"Women with small children may be forced to go," said Willi. "I've heard of such plans. The Party is taking things in hand."

"My God," cried Valeska, "we haven't even asked Halina if she's hungry. Do you want something to eat?" She didn't wait for an answer. "You must be starving, *moja siostrzyczko*, you're as thin as a rail."

She would have liked to feel Halina's waist under the knitted jacket to see if it was really so. You couldn't tell by looking at her, but if a person had been in a camp, they must have gone hungry. So everybody said.

"Maybe she should take a bath before eating," said Irma. "She stinks. Her clothes smell all musty. In such cases, I always recommend a bath, it makes you feel brand-new."

"I'll light up the bath boiler," said Wondrak. "Then I'll take a bath too. In times like this you never know where the next bath is coming from." The joke fell flat and Wondrak made a glum face.

"I'll make Halina some bouillon," said Valeska, "a cup of good strong broth. And there's still a jar of chicken in the cellar." Valeska stroked Halina's forehead and pulled her head scarf lower; she couldn't bear to look at that bald skull. "I'm sure a cup of broth will do you good. It will give you strength."

"I wonder if Halina has any papers," Wondrak put in. "If only an old health insurance card."

As Halina hadn't said a single word, he didn't dare address her directly. She would speak more readily to his sister. In any case it would not be so easy to hide Halina, especially at a time like this when the block warden dropped in almost every other day. A bald-headed woman who had escaped from a camp—that could mean trouble for them all.

"We'd better wash her clothes," said Irma. "There's always vermin in a camp. Everybody knows that."

It made her sick just to think of it, and she moved a little further away from Halina.

"In my opinion," said Valeska firmly, "what Halina needs first is food and then rest." With that she left the room. Always practical, she picked up Willi's coat on her way out, and hung it up in the entrance.

"See what the children are doing," Irma called after her. At the moment she was incapable of standing up and looking after the children herself. Something held her fast. The soft sofa, the warmth, the diffuse light of the standing lamp with the green silk cloth over it. But probably it was only curiosity about what would happen next.

Halina leaned back on the sofa and closed her eyes; with one hand she held her head scarf to keep it from sliding off. She let the warmth seep into her and believed in the miracle (for which she had prayed to the Virgin Mary) that had come to pass. That gave her enough to do. Voices had been pouring in on her from all sides, so many voices and so many sounds, she would never have been able to answer. She pursed her lips and hummed something, but broke off immediately. Although she had shut her eyes, little colored explosions kept flaring up in front of her. Her body seemed as heavy as lead, yet she felt she was floating; she felt she was close to the others, and yet she couldn't have touched any of them. She thought this would go on forever, anyway for quite a while, and that was all right with her, she certainly wouldn't do anything to change it, she just wanted to pull her head scarf down lower so the others wouldn't see her shorn skull.

She didn't realize that something had changed until she opened her eyes and saw the Pani's face above her in the green light and someone slapped her cheeks and she heard the Pani scream: "Halina, *muy Bozhe kokhany,* do you hear me, wake up!"

She looked around, she looked into the face of each one; little by little her cheekbones softened and her skin smoothed out, and she smiled, Halina Gwiozda smiled for the first time in many days. Smiling made her beautiful, Valeska saw it, and after that the bald head didn't bother her anymore. Good God, what they had done to her! Cutting her hair off like that, how awful!

Halina took the cup of broth in her hand and sipped until the cup was empty. Then she said: "That not the worst. But main thing I keep my teeth. Hair grow again, all by itself, *naturalnie*. But I keep teeth, which I thank God and *Matka Boska*. Teeth still beautiful."

She took them out and showed them. They were indeed flawless. "I all time worry about teeth," she said with her slightly sunken mouth. Then she put the teeth back in place and beamed.

"Those teeth!" Valeska clapped her hands. "Oh, my God, those teeth!" It all came back to her. It had all begun with those new teeth and that Ukrainian.

By that time Rosa Wondrak had come in and heard the whole story from Irma. "Did they beat you?" she asked. She took off her coat; there was a second coat under it.

"There's no point in asking her that," said Valeska.

"Anyway not so soon," Wondrak added. "We'll get the whole story out of her later on." He helped his wife out of her second coat. "It's getting colder," said Rosa, pressing her knuckles to her cheeks, which were still cold.

"You've brought the cold with you," said Irma, who suddenly felt chilled.

Halina held her empty cup tight. To her it was something more than a cup that had just had hot broth in it; it was an object belonging to the world of the living, the world she had longed for and which, up to a few days ago, she had had little hope of ever seeing again. And now everything had changed.

"I every day pray święta Maryja Matka Boża. She proteck me."

Ever since they took her away, she had been passing through a long tunnel of ice; little by little she herself had turned to ice, all except the warm heart deep inside her, which she heard beating like something that didn't belong to her.

"No hair, no lice," said Irma brightly, as though coming up with a conclusion arrived at after serious thought.

"Where were you digging?" Willi Wondrak asked his wife.

"Out at Gröling. The ground is as hard as stone. We had to make a little fire." She took off her shoes and massaged her feet near the open stove door. "I hear the Russians have taken Tschenstochau; they're making a beeline for Lublinitz and Gleiwitz."

A muffled cry escaped Valeska: "Holy Mother of God! That's only two hours away by train."

"The Russians won't be coming by train," Willi tried to reassure her. "They have to fight for every inch of ground, and they're having trouble with their supply lines. Even so, Tschenstochau is less than sixty miles from here, and there are no natural barriers, no mountains or rivers in between. We'd better be prepared for the worst."

"Do you really think the Russians will get here?" Rosa asked incredulously. "Do you really think we'll have to defend the city?" All this was too much for her. A week ago the Russians had still been on the far side of Warsaw, today in Gröling she had heard gunfire from the front, tomorrow or the day after they could be in the outskirts. How was she to take it all in?

"All I know," said Wondrak, "is that they're supposed to be putting up antitank barriers on all the main roads. The Russian offensive has broken through our lines in many places. I hear that it's only armored spearheads that have advanced so far; supposedly their main force is still far behind, and strong German units are still fighting in between. We can't let this industrial zone fall into the hands of the Russians."

Willi Wondrak was saying what he had heard in the courthouse. There in the midst of so many people he had believed it. Here that was no longer possible.

"Do you seriously think Gleiwitz will be defended?" Valeska asked.

"It's madness," Irma muttered, "sheer madness."

Wondrak stationed himself in the middle of the group. "I don't even think the Reich border can be defended," he said. And added helplessly: "But somewhere the Russians must be stopped."

That silenced them all. Even Valeska with her penchant for wild hopes.

"Lots of people are leaving," Rosa ventured.

They exchanged looks as though suspecting one another of wanting to run away.

"Where will they go?" Irma stood up. She thought of the little blue flags on the map in the entrance, which kept coming closer and closer. "Whatever we do, there's no hope."

She had felt that way for some time. More precisely, since she had stopped hearing from Skrobek. Just that she hadn't imagination enough to form an exact picture of the end. An existence without the children and Skrobek seemed inconceivable, and more than anything in the world she wanted Skrobek back. She would never leave, whatever happened, she would wait for him here. The catastrophe, the terrible end, would overtake her wherever she went. So it might as well be here.

"Don't say such things," said Irma. "Think of the children."

"We employed people can't leave anyway," said Rosa firmly. "They told us again today. Anyone who leaves his place of work is running out on the fatherland. It's not quite the same with Irma and the children . . ."

Muttering something to himself, Willi Wondrak crossed the room to the other lamp and switched it on. Valeska looked at him in surprise: at such a time, when everyone was trying to save electricity! When he turned to her, she fell silent. She realized that after long reflection he had decided to let them in on a terrible secret.

"My dear ones," he began solemnly. "I must beg you to listen to me. Let's not delude ourselves. We must expect the worst. Rosa is right. The Russians are heading straight for Gross-Strehlitz and Gleiwitz. All day they've been burning files at police headquarters. It seems that the mayor and all the top officials have flown the coop. I don't know if it's true, but the city administration has lost all authority, the Party has taken over. An evacuation order is ready, but it won't be put into effect until the Russians are actually here. If they did it now, there'd be chaos."

Halina cried out as in a nightmare: "Holy Mary, pray for us."

"So," Wondrak went on, "I think Irma and the children should leave tomorrow with Valeska. I'll make the arrangements and take you to the station. Tonight we'll pack what's most urgently needed . . ."

"But where can we go? The trains are overcrowded, little Hannelore will die of the cold . . ." Irma really had no idea where to go. To the Schimmels in Berlin? Why, she wasn't even sure they'd ever got there. To stay with Uncle Prohaska or the Kumiaks in the Ruhr? They didn't even have a proper address.

"But I can't just drop everything here," said Valeska with a deep sigh. She went over to the piano and rested her hand on it.

"Rosa and I will stay here for the present and do what has to be done," said Willi Wondrak. "But the rest of you must leave."

Rosa nodded and gathered up her things.

Valeska Piontek reached for her eau de cologne. "No, I can't leave all this for the Russians. I'm staying right here. Irma should go, yes, of course, she and the children should go. When I think of how the Russians treated the women in East Prussia, in Gumbinnen . . . But I'm old . . ."

"Travel with the children in this freezing weather!" cried Irma. "I'd rather turn on the gas right away." She looked out the window, she didn't want the others to see the grim look on her face.

Valeska sank down on the piano stool. "*Muy Bozhe!*" she sighed, "How at my age can I leave house and home for the second time and lose everything that Leo Maria and I worked so hard for . . ."

She looked slowly around the room as though to accustom herself to the thought of leaving all this.

"What about Halina?" Rosa asked. "What will we do with Halina?"

"Me not leaving this house," said Halina. "Only feet first."

"Halina had better stay here," said Willi Wondrak. "It will be easier to hide her in the house. And when things calm down, I'll get her a ration card, with my connections."

Willi was amazed at his own courage. He turned to Halina:

"Did anyone see you come in? Any of the neighbors?"

"No, no. Nobody. I keep head down, I keep scarf down over face." She acted it out.

"I must have her old health insurance card," said Valeska. "It says she's German, Ethnic Group III. That's all the identification she needs."

"Maybe in the present juncture," said Wondrak half to himself in an undertone, "it would be better for us to have her Polish."

"Whatever happens you won't get me to leave here," said Irma vehemently. "I'd rather die on this soil, on my black Upper Silesian soil. This is where I belong, me and my children and my Skrobek, regardless. Let it be Polish or Russian or Chinese. Here I stay."

She left the room. She had the feeling that the others were deciding her fate and that her mere presence would be interpreted as consent.

"What a wicked thing to say!" Valeska whispered. Torn and bewildered, she looked helplessly from corner to corner of the room.

Suddenly Halina jumped up from the sofa. "Excuse, Pani, can I see vase with strawflowers? You know, tin vase with beautiful dead flowers?" And her eyes searched all the places where the vase might have been.

"Oh yes," said Valeska, slowly beginning to remember. She hadn't noticed the pewter vase with the immortelles in it for a long time.

"It's gathering dust in the kitchen," said Rosa.

Halina rushed into the kitchen and came back with the vase. She carefully removed the immortelles and turned the vase upside down. A piece of amber fell on the table.

"From Kolya," Halina whispered, staring at it as if the amber were pure fire. "I always pray stone be in vase when I come back, then Kolyechka come back too."

5

THE PORTALS OF Sts. Peter and Paul were closed; only the little east door was open. Anna Ossadnik slipped in. Without taking her gloves off, she dipped her fingertips in the stoup. They met a sheet of ice. She was so taken aback that she forgot to cross herself. Her breath turned to white smoke. She glided through the resounding silence and vibrant darkness. Rather than light the nave, a single candle accentuated the darkness. She knelt at the main altar and beat her breast, but quickly put her hand back in her muff. As far as she could see, there was no one else in the church, she could hear no sound but her own shuffling steps on the stone floor. Maybe they had taken to closing the church on weekdays, and the sacristan had merely forgotten the east door. Then she remembered how before Christmas she had read a notice signed by Father Pattas in person, announcing that because of the coal shortage the church could be heated only on Sundays and holidays, and begging the indulgence of the congregation. She had seen certain women taking bags of coal to the presbytery, and more than once she herself had wrapped two briquettes in newspaper and deposited them in the entrance to the church. She was a member of Holy Cross parish but on Sunday she preferred Peter and Paul, because of Father Pattas's beautiful sermons and also because at Peter and Paul she met more friends to chat with after mass on the square outside. She only went to Holy Cross for the Stations of the Cross, which were more impressive there, and because in its narrow side aisle the Stations of the Cross didn't make you feel as lost as in the enormous church of Peter and Paul. It was a long time since the church had been heated for the early weekday mass that she sometimes attended, and during this severe winter it had not been possible to keep the church decently warm even on Sundays. You had to wear a heavy coat to mass, preferably fur if you had one; she herself anyway could only afford an imitation lambskin, and actually there weren't very many people with fur coats in the parish. At All Saints, it's true, you could even see sables at midnight mass, and Frau Lohmeyer, whose husband owned the soap factory, had caused a sensation with her ocelot.

Anna herself never failed to stuff a bit of rabbit fur in her shoes before going to church, because the worst of the cold came up from the stone floor, and in early childhood she had learned the Silesian saying: Keep your feet warm and you won't feel the cold.

Anna Ossadnik couldn't have said why she had gone to church on this particular day. Certainly not to confess, she had confessed as recently as Christmas, and once a month was plenty at her age. Probably she was impelled by the secret hope of seeing Father Pattas, with whom, it was generally known, you could discuss other things beside sins, if you came to him for confession. Or at least Father Jarosch, the curate, who sometimes conducted an intercession service in front of the statue of St. Anthony. She would have liked to ask him about the cave church; she would so much like to know if he had prepared a hiding place for the crosses and sacred images. The Jews had often had to hide their scrolls of the Torah, and their faith had grown stronger and more fervent as a result.

Anna Ossadnik went over to the confessionals and made sure the light wasn't on in any of them. Though she had not come to confess, she felt somehow disappointed. She couldn't dispel the thought that the church might someday be converted into a warehouse or a garage—no, she must try not to think of such things.

Suddenly she caught sight of a woman at the side altar. How on earth had she got in? Anna had just passed this same altar and hadn't seen anyone. She sat down at the other end of the pew, looked at the black statue of St. Anthony, bowed low, beat her breast three times, and whispered: "O Lamb of God, who takest away the sins of the world. O Lamb of God, who takest away the sins of the world. O Lamb of God, who takest away the sins of the world. Have mercy on us."

Now there could be no harm in turning and looking directly at this woman. and though the woman's face was pretty well hidden by her hat and shawl and turned-up collar, Anna had no difficulty in recognizing Frau Wieczorek. "How glad I am to see you!" she said; she seemed really glad.

"My goodness, Frau Ossadnik," said the other slowly, as though emerging from a dream. "You've given me a fright. I've been praying for quite a while, and I didn't see anyone come in. The whole town seems to have emptied." Frau Wieczorek sat back in her seat. In one hand she held her prayer book; with the other she rubbed her knees, trying to warm them, first one, then the other. "Isn't this emptiness amazing? All the portals were closed. I haven't even seen a priest. Can they all have left town?" Frau Wieczorek blew on her hands.

"Run away, you mean?" Anna asked incredulously. "Our Pattas run away? That can't be. A captain stays with his ship to the last. And a priest stays with his congregation." That seemed an incontrovertible truth. There weren't many truths left these days. But that was one on which Anna Ossadnik chose to rely.

"I also believe in him when I'm with you," said Frau Wieczorek.

When alone, she preferred to believe in God or Saint Anthony, whom she had been imploring to intercede for her missing son Adalbert.

"So many have cleared out, even my best friend Verena, who would have thought it? You know, Frau Schimitschek. She came to see me a week ago, she brought me her featherbeds and her thirty-six-piece gold-rimmed dinner service. She said I could keep it all if she didn't come back. She was in tears."

To hold back her own tears, she said: "Saint Anthony, protector of the poor, pray for us."

"Do you think . . . do you think the worst will . . . ?" asked Anna Ossadnik, staring at the life-size wooden statue of the meditative Capuchin, who looked down on them from his pedestal.

"The very worst!" said Frau Wieczorek as though it were quite impossible to think differently.

"Holy Mary, Mother of God, then why are you still here?"

"I will stay here whatever happens," said Frau Wieczorek grimly. "I put my trust in the Virgin Mary . . . Where would I go? My husband has been killed and my sons are all scattered in the war.

Adalbert has been missing in the East since last summer, and I haven't heard from Klaus in three months. I don't know who will be left to me in the end . . . When they come home after the war, they'll need an address, won't they, and that's Ziethenstrasse 25, Gleiwitz, and nowhere else. We'd never find one another without it."

It was plain that she lived only for the day when her sons would come trooping into the little apartment on Ziethenstrasse, in as rapid succession as possible, on a Sunday afternoon. She'd bake a cake and brew coffee, and put her friend Verena's beautiful thirty-six-piece gold-rimmed dinner service on the table, and she'd gaze and gaze on her children, marveling at how they had grown and the gravity the war had stamped on their young faces. That would be the day, the one thing she was waiting for.

Anna Ossadnik thought the same way; she felt vindicated by Frau Wieczorek's words.

"It's the same with me," she said. "I don't want to leave. This is my home. I can't just drop everything here. We haven't got much, but my husband has worked thirty years for it. And you know how attached a body gets to her belongings."

Come to think of it, she wasn't attached to so many things; only the little cupboard with the colored glass panes, the books and magazines she and Kotik had collected, and the philodendron it had taken her so long to raise and which had just begun to flower.

"But you must leave, Frau Ossadnik. You have children."

"There's only one left at home." Anna sighed. "The others are all off in the war somewhere like yours. Only one out of six left. The youngest is fifteen, and I'm worried sick that they'll take him for the Flak or the Volkssturm."

"Have mercy on us!" said Frau Wieczorek, beating her breast.

"What will the Russians do to the church?" said Anna. "Those people don't believe in God. Do you think they'll close the church?"

Before Frau Wieczorek could answer, they heard sharp footfalls in the nave, coming rapidly closer. It was an unaccustomed sound, loud and obtrusive enough to arouse their curiosity. The woman coming toward them was wearing a white fur coat and a thick fur hat; her collar was turned up to cover her ears. She genuflected

before the saint, crossed herself with ostentatious slowness, and greeted
the other women as matter-of-factly as if she had been fully expecting
to see just them in this chapel.

Heavenly saints, thought Anna at the sight of her.

"*Muy Bozhe*, is it cold out there!" Erna Dolezich gasped. "It must
be fifteen below, it'll go down to twenty tonight." She rubbed her
gloved hands together, rubbed her cheeks and forehead, and lowered
her fur collar.

Frau Wieczorek stared at her friend Erna. She had never seen that
white fur coat on her. Where had she got it from? She had to admit
that it was becoming to her, it made her look really smart. But this
was a church; perhaps it wasn't the right time or place to be thinking
about such things.

"This is perfect weather for the Russians," Frau Dolezich went
on. "It won't bother them in the least, they're used to Siberian
winters; they'll get through in no time."

She wanted to sit down with the two others, but neither showed
any inclination to move from her well-warmed seat.

"Get through to where?" Anna Ossadnik asked. She made herself
thin and took her feet off the prie-dieu, giving Erna Dolezich access
to a place in the pew.

"To here," she said. "To Gleiwitz."

Anna thrust her hands into her muff, took them out, and put
them in again. These women, she thought, talked as if the Russians
would burst over the town like a thunderstorm any minute, like a
natural catastrophe that nothing could stop.

"But don't you think the borders will be defended? The industrial
zone can't just be abandoned. After all, we're the arsenal of the Reich,
as my Franz is always saying."

"That's what I used to think," said Frau Dolezich. More than a
head taller than the others, she looked like a great furry animal. "I
changed my mind yesterday when I found out that the Party bosses
are leaving."

"We've all been kidding ourselves," said Frau Wieczorek.

"The Russians are coming from the north, or rather from the
northwest," said Frau Dolezich. "That was unexpected. They're sur-

rounding the industrial zone. They want to occupy it in good condition. Luckily for us."

"Blessed Lord Jesus!" Anna Ossadnik was aghast. "You mean you've given up hope? You think we're going to be occupied? You think it's inevitable?"

What incredible naiveté, thought Frau Dolezich. "Where have you been living? We've been at war for five years. The whole world is against us, we're surrounded on all sides. Now the war is coming to us. We left scorched earth behind us in Russia, now they're doing the same to us. But nothing much will happen to us here. They need our industry, and they need the local work force. Without our workers they can't produce. So they'll see to it that we're fed. After all . . ." Here Frau Dolezich adopted a knowledgeable, businesslike tone. "You don't slaughter a cow if you need her milk."

"Maybe we should ask the Archpriest," Anna Ossadnik suggested hopefully.

"Heavenly saints!" Frau Dolezich cried. "You mustn't mention what I've just told you to anyone. Not to a soul. Just forget that I've said anything. I'd be in very hot water."

Frau Wieczorek came to Anna Ossadnik's defense. "But we can talk to Father Pattas, can't we?" She, too, had ceased to delude herself. But she felt that her friend was a little too pessimistic.

"I won't say a word about you," said Anna Ossadnik. "I'd just like to know what the Church will do when they march in. And . . . how it will react to the occupation. Maybe the Archpriest knows. Come, let's go and see him."

After a few more prayers Anna Ossadnik was the first to rise. She looked around to see if anyone else had come in after them. She would at least have expected to see some of the Third Order women. But maybe they had already been evacuated.

The Eternal Light flickered on the high altar. It glittered and glowed and exerted a magic attraction on them. She wondered what would happen if the Eternal Light went out. Had that ever happened? According to the tradition, the Eternal Light had been kindled by the Apostle Peter. Since then it had been passed on from wick to wick. She had once read that during the Civil War in Russia a Red Army man had shot five priests, saying, "Why doesn't your God help you?" But when he had taken aim and fired at the flickering light on the altar, he had fallen to the floor as though struck by lightning; his own bullet had ricocheted from the Eternal Light and penetrated his heart. She couldn't stop wondering what would happen if the city were besieged and shelled and no one was able to rekindle the Eternal Flame.

Anna Ossadnik shuddered. Beside the stoup at the entrance she stopped to wait for the others. Only then was she struck by Frau Wieczorek's girth. She hadn't got fat, she had just spread out.

"Maybe we could get to the presbytery through the sacristy," said the ever-practical Frau Dolezich.

The others agreed. That way they didn't have to go out into the cold. Erna Dolezich went around the high altar and stepped over the low chancel rail. In spite of herself she felt a certain awe. She had never been on that side of the altar. That area was reserved for the priests and servers. But she wasn't going to stay long. She turned to the altar and crossed herself. A moment later she was at the door to the sacristy, which was closed. She tugged at the bell pull, and the little bell, which ordinarily announced that the service was about to begin, rang out. They had often heard that sound at early mass. But now the delicate little bell sounded like a warning.

The Archpriest wasn't there. The sacristan said he'd gone to a conference of the city priests, he wouldn't be back that afternoon, and Father Jarosch had been called away to administer extreme unction. In that case, they said, they wouldn't go to the presbytery, their business was with the venerable Archpriest and was no concern of the sacristan or even the curate. They would come back another time, perhaps on Sunday after High Mass.

Outside, a light snow was falling. Darkness was descending on the square as the three women started home. Erna Dolezich turned up the collar of her white fur coat and sheltered her face behind it. She hoped her two friends would notice what an expensive coat she had on. True, it was only rabbit, but to the inexpert eye it looked like chinchilla. It had been given her only a few weeks before by her friend Verena Schimitschek, who had gone off to the Reich in a sable coat. Frau Dolezich had taken her to the station, which was only fitting and proper, considering that she'd given her a practically genuine chinchilla coat.

The sable, of course, was not her friend's only precious possession. The two suitcases she had been able to take were thought to be chockful of silk dresses, leather shoes, jewelry, and furs. Her husband, who had been traveling around occupied Poland for years confiscating precious metal, was said to have bought luxury articles cheap from Jews wherever he went. Later when the Jews were sent to concentration camps, their valuables were simply taken away, so he was even able to claim that he had done the Jews a kindness. Be that as it may, Frau Schimitschek was terrified of the Russians and had gone to stay with her aunt in Berlin at the very start of their offensive. How Erna Dolezich would have loved to take another look at Frau Schimitschek's apartment. To whom could she have given the keys?

"I got the coat from our friend Frau Schimitschek," she explained. "She gave it to me before she left. Wasn't that generous of her?"

"Oh well," said Frau Wieczorek. "The Party bigshots are the first to clear out."

"Frau Schimitschek's husband wasn't in the Party," said Erna Dolezich.

"But he was traveling around Poland the whole time," said Frau Wieczorek. "Who else can do that?" A terrible suspicion wormed its way into her mind. A thirty-six-piece gold-rimmed Meissen dinner service—the Schimitscheks couldn't normally have afforded that kind of thing.

"Anyway," she said without a trace of envy. "The coat looks good on you."

The dinner service, she reflected, would also look nice in her apartment. And she was glad to accept it as a gift, just as Frau Dolezich accepted the fur coat. She only hoped that Frau Schimitschek wouldn't come back. Too bad she hadn't left her the key to her apartment. She'd have been sure to find something attractive and useful in it. When the Russians get here, they'll loot everything anyway.

"*When shall we three meet again*

In thunder, lightning or in rain?"

"What do you think?"

Anna Ossadnik's old imitation lambskin was worn thin; she felt the cold through it. She gave her scarf another turn to keep her goiter warm.

Frau Wieczorek merely mumbled: "Oh my goodness."

On the corner of Fröbelstrasse the women separated.

Anna Ossadnik went on alone. No one had answered her question. Neither God. Nor the Archpriest. Nor the other women. Nor had the gray January sky anything to tell her. The snow had a dull sheen. The treetops painted riddles in the air. Somewhere a door slammed. A child passed, pulling a sled behind him. One might have thought that nothing had changed. And as she walked along, rubbing her hands in her thin muff to warm them, she actually did think so for a few moments.

6

It was late. Valeska Piontek had no need to look at the clock. The talk became more and more laconic, the pauses longer and longer. They were sitting at the round English mahogany table in the music room. The light diffused by the green silk lampshade softened their faces and slowed their movements, muffled their voices and drew them close together.

They had sent Halina to bed. She hadn't wanted to go at first, she was afraid of the dark and afraid of being alone. But after the mulled wine Rosa had made with the last bottle of red wine and a bit of rose-hip juice, she had fallen asleep at the table, and Irma had laid a mattress on the floor of the children's room for her.

What were they to do if the front came closer and the city was threatened? They had discussed the situation in detail and examined a number of possibilities. However, they came to no definite conclusion, for one thing because they still hoped there would be no need to make a decision that, they were well aware, would change their lives more radically than any they had ever made before. They talked about such a decision as if it were something that concerned other people and had nothing to do with them—at least for the present, seated as they were around the table, carrying on with their habits, sipping at their long-empty glasses, and listening absently to the muted music floating out of the radio. They did not look at one another, because they were dimly aware that their consensus did not go very deep. No one made a move toward going to bed, though they all bore witness with repressed yawns to their weariness and to the lateness of the hour. Somehow they all felt that once they left this circle they would never again come together in such intimacy. There had been too many signs and portents—it was no longer possible to lull themselves in the thought that tomorrow or the day after their world would be unchanged. Just that made it all the more important to preserve the old habits that enabled them to close their eyes to the abyss.

Irma filed and polished her fingernails with such dedication that one might have expected them to sparkle in the greenish light. Rosa stared at the open book she was holding, but not reading, because her thoughts were far away. Willi was holding a weeks-old Berlin newspaper but in fact wondering which files to destroy first. From time to time he went to the radio, turned the knobs, and took a drink from the bottle he had hidden behind it. The knitting in Valeska's lap had begun to shape up as the sleeve of a jacket, but as she didn't have enough wool she unraveled it and started all over again.

"On Sunday I could make prune dumplings with smoked pork," said Valeska. "We haven't had that for a long time, and our Halina is so fond of it. And almond pudding for dessert."

"They're playing *The Woman of My Dreams* with Marika Rökk at the CT Theater," said Irma. "It's a color film."

"I met Frau Gawenda while we were digging today," said Rosa, turning a page of her book. "Her sister definitely has cancer of the larynx. Isn't that awful? On top of everything else."

Willi had stood up and was fiddling with the radio, pretending to be looking for news, but secretly taking a swig from his hidden bottle. After giving up on the news he sat down again. He ran his hand over his head to make sure that in spite of the unusual events he had put on his hairnet as he did every evening.

"Now that Halina is here," he said, "we could clean out the cellar. Then we'll find the knapsack, I'm sure I left it down there, but that was ages ago. It never occurred to me that we might need it."

At the same time, he thought, he could check on the condition of his precious glassware that he had packed in a crate full of sand a year ago in case the house was bombed.

"Oh well," said Valeska. "When spring comes, we'll move everything out. And we'll have to repair the floor of the laundry room, it's crumbling away. Maybe Herr Ossadnik can get us some cement."

She had seen her brother taking swigs from the bottle. If only I knew what's wrong with him, she thought. He never used to drink. What can it be?

"The paper shortage is getting worse," said Rosa. "The paper only has two pages now. Just on Sunday they put in an extra page, the cultural supplement."

Since her marriage Rosa Wondrak had been working at the local office of the *Upper Silesian Traveler*. As she brought the proofs of the next day's paper home with her at night, they were the first to know when there would be a special allotment of ration coupons and who in their neighborhood had died or fallen in battle. But otherwise they were no better informed than anyone else. When it came to news of the front, they now relied on the radio.

"There's nothing worth reading in it anymore," Valeska said. "There haven't been any concerts since last fall." She sighed and noted with indifference that she had dropped several stitches in the last quarter of an hour. She pulled out the needle and with a certain satisfaction unraveled the sleeve.

"The last time I was in Kraków Edwin Fischer was giving a guest performance. When could it have been? That's right, July 1943, quite a while ago. Even Gauleiter Frank applauded . . . To think that the Russians are in Kraków now . . ."

So they went on talking, each for himself. They talked about trifles, because they were afraid to speak of what mattered.

"V-2 rockets are coming down on London every day," said Rosa out of a clear sky. She shut her book. Time to go to bed. All evening she had watched her husband going to the radio and reaching for the bottle. He had never been a drinker, not to her knowledge, at least. But a few days ago she had noticed the liquor on his breath when he came home from the office. She wouldn't have dared to say anything as long as he made a secret of it. She only hoped he'd keep it secret from the others as well. But she couldn't fail to see Irma and Valeska look up every time he went over to the radio.

"If you people want to wait for the late news, don't mind me. I doubt if there will be anything much. I'm going to bed. I've been out all day digging in the freezing cold. I ache all over."

At that moment Willi turned up the volume: ". . . *the enemy is storming the gates of the industrial zone with superior forces. But in the last few days Upper Silesia has become a steel bastion of resistance, a fortress determined to defend itself. The spirit of the Annaberg lives again. The Freikorps of 1919 and 1939 have been reborn in the Volkssturm . . ."*

Wondrak switched it off. For a moment there wasn't a sound to be heard. Even Valeska's knitting needles had stopped clicking.

Wondrak broke the silence. "I didn't want to frighten you," he said. "But you'll find out soon enough. You'll have to get along without me for a while. I've been drafted into the Volkssturm. I'm to report to the Katzler Barracks tomorrow."

The women all started talking at once. They were shocked and bewildered, sorry for him and for themselves. '

Only Irma kept silent. And then, loudly enough for all to hear, she said: "I don't think Uncle Willi should go."

Rosa spun around. Valeska moved the empty glasses to the middle of the table so briskly that they jangled. Willi dropped his silver cigarette holder.

"That's right. I say he shouldn't go. He should keep out of it. He should refuse. He should simply hide. What's the sense in going to war at five minutes to midnight? Now that the war is lost, are you going to get yourself killed for those beasts?"

The others stood like statues. They gaped at Irma as though she were an entirely different person from the one they knew so well.

Valeska was the first to regain her composure. "Irma is right," she said. "You've managed to keep out of it up to now."

"Right," said Rosa. "We'll hide you. When they come for you, we'll say you've been sent to the Reich on Party business."

She herself was surprised at her audacity.

Wondrak looked nervously for his cigarette holder. He had never thought of that. Every time his case was reviewed he had managed to be deferred, first as "indispensable" and later as "unfit for military service." That had been strictly legal. What his niece Irma was suggesting was definitely against the law, it was insubordination. But what kind of a law is that? Will it be valid tomorrow with the Russians in the suburbs?

"You could hide at Aunt Lucie's in Mathesdorf," Valeska suggested. "Or better still, with Aunt Lucie Lanolin in Kalinowitz. No one would think of looking for you there."

"In my father's bookstore—no one would think of that," Rosa suggested.

"It will only be for a few days," said Irma. "It's sure to be over by then."

Wondrak finally found his cigarette holder, it had been on the floor next to the table leg. He was pleased that the women were prepared to disobey the law for his sake and even more so at not having to spend the night in a sweaty, ill-ventilated barracks with nineteen other old men.

"There's a bit of schnapps left in the bottle," he said. He hadn't quite made up his mind, but he was cheered by the turn of events. "Just enough for a sip all around. Let's give ourselves a treat before we go to bed. Who knows what tomorrow will bring . . ."

"Just so we live through it," said Irma matter-of-factly.

Then they drank. But before they had time to enjoy the festive mood, Wondrak jumped up and cried out: "Hush. Be still."

He turned out the light, released the blackout shade and opened an inner window. Then, pushing aside the old rags that were supposed to keep out the cold, he opened the outer window. Cold night poured in, and with it, now louder, now more softly, distant shell bursts.

"Listen to that."

The women approached the window in the darkness.

"Yesterday there was nothing," said Wondrak. "And today gunfire from the front." He leaned out and listened. "It's not far away. I'd say thirty or forty kilometers."

"*Muy Bozhe!*" said Valeska with a shudder.

Rosa groped her way to the table and switched on the lamp. Familiar objects regained their old contours. The green light conferred a sense of security which they knew to be illusory, but it was all they had left.

7

Since little Roswitha's fever had not abated during the night, Irma took her to the City Hospital early in the morning. She had deposited the other two children in the music room, where Valeska did her best to make them forget their mother's absence. She was expecting only two pupils that day, Liesl Bednarz and little Karlheinz Graudenz, son of the brewer at the Scobel Brewery, whom they had formerly known by the name of Garwonczyk. But she wasn't really expecting them to show up, because only Adelheid Mainka had come the day before, and the situation had become more critical since then. On the pretext that the Mainka girl had a slight cold, Valeska had sent her straight home; actually, she had been meaning for some time to drop in on the child's parents and tell them that every pfennig they spent on piano lessons was wasted, because the child was hopelessly unmusical and would never go beyond *The Merry Peasant*, which she had learned to rattle off with a slightly imbecilic smile. But when the bell rang after all and she looked out the window, young Graudenz was standing there swathed in coat and muffler. He brought his music with him, sat down at the piano, and began—at the exact place where he had stopped the last time—to play Schumann's *Album for the Young* (Opus 68). At first Valeska watched him rather absently, while bringing out a last Christmas cookie for little Helga; then she gave him her instructions and hummed the melody with special emphasis on the rhythm in an attempt, supported by the loud ticktock of the metronome, to make the podgy fingers move a little faster. She was rather annoyed with her pupil; he was acting as if nothing in the whole world mattered but this piano lesson. When she became aware of her own irritability, she broke off the lesson ahead of time. Taking the child to the door, she remembered what she had wanted to ask him: "Is your father home?"

The boy replied with a sulky nod. He would have preferred to stay at the piano a little longer.

"Do you know if he's been drafted into the Volkssturm?" she persisted.

"He's gone to work at the brewery."

"And your mother lets you run off to your piano lesson with the gunfire coming closer by the hour."

"I have two piano lessons a week. Everyone in the family knows that. Nothing would make me miss a lesson, Frau Piontek."

"What will your parents do if the Russians keep coming closer? Have they said anything about it to you?"

"Oh, Frau Piontek," said the boy without a moment's hesitation, "where danger threatens, salvation grows apace."

"But child!" Valeska gasped. "What kind of nonsense is that?!" Her nerves were on edge.

"We must vanquish our fear. Then we will overcome the enemy. Our new weapons will soon be operational, the V-2 is a terrible weapon, it will undoubtedly decide the war."

"*Muy Bozhe,* good God, I mean, where did you get that? Do you believe what you're saying?" Valeska asked in a tone of incredulity mingled with horror.

"That's what father says, and I believe it, Frau Piontek," said the boy and without turning strode resolutely through the front garden to the street.

When Irma came back from the hospital, Valeska described the incident. "The child is just eleven. And do you know what he said? When danger threatens, salvation grows apace."

Irma didn't get it. Besides, she had more important things on her mind. Dr. Kluba had given her some Vitamin C tablets to take home to Helga.

"The hospital is full of wounded soldiers from the front. I talked to a few of them in the corridor, they're waiting to be evacuated across the Oder. They say that if an evacuation order comes the city will be abandoned."

Valeska rocked the baby carriage gently. "Abandoned?" she asked suspiciously. "What does that mean?"

"It means they won't defend the city. They'll just move out."

"Oh, you mean we'll be some kind of open city? Like Paris in 1940?"

Good idea, Valeska thought. "Maybe because of our museums? And the big greenhouse in the Botanical Gardens?"

"Certainly not," said Irma. "It's because of the front. Our soldiers are on the run. An officer said something about trying to stabilize a new front on the Oder."

"What does Aunt Milka have to say? Did you see her at the hospital?"

"She wasn't there," said Irma. "She must be on the night shift. I left her a note telling her to come and see us, especially the children. We really ought to be a little closer at a time like this."

Oh yes, Milka, Valeska thought. As if Milka had ceased to be anything more than a memory. She hadn't seen her sister-in-law in quite some time. They had drifted apart since the death of Leo Maria, but that, she had to admit, was all right with her. She had never been really fond of Milka. She had been polite and even friendly, but only for Leo Maria's sake. And besides, Milka had been stand-offish. More than once Valeska had offered Milka her friendship. She had offered her gifts and even money and asked her to go into business with her and Leo Maria. But Milka had always declined and given them to understand that even in the direst straits she would never accept anything from them.

"If Milka and the countess are still in town," said Valeska, "things can't be so bad. They have a sixth sense. The countess has fancy relatives all over the country. They'd have cleared out long ago."

"A lot of people are leaving," said Irma. "They say the trains are jam-packed, but only women with children under twelve are allowed to go, and old people over sixty. The Party has its special police everywhere, they arrest people at the drop of a hat. There have been terrible scenes at the station. One child is twelve, he can go; another is fifteen, he has to stay. It seems that one of these cops has been beaten to a pulp by the infuriated crowd."

Irma tried to give Valeska the gist in a few sentences of what she had heard in the hospital waiting room in the course of an hour. She rattled on without order or emphasis, her way of showing how little importance she attached to such things. It meant much more to her that there was no fresh milk to be had that day. "Frau Janoschka gave me a double ration of dried milk for my coupons."

"I think I'll go to church," said Valeska. "I could drop in on Milka on the way. What do you think? It's true she hasn't been to see us in a long time. But it's not my fault, no, it's definitely not my fault. I've invited her time and again, but she didn't even see fit to come to your Roswitha's baptism. She and the old countess are as thick as thieves. Though actually it's only because of the inheritance, she's only waiting for the countess to pass away . . ."

"Mamusha, don't say such things; she is really sacrificing herself for the countess."

At that Valeska calmed down. "She does have a wonderful voice. I've got to hand her that. It's really expressive . . . If only she didn't smoke those awful cigars. I'll go and see her." And half to herself, "Yes, I'll go and see her right away."

She would have liked to put on her warm winter coat and her genuine sable muff, but if she was going to see Milka, the Persian lamb would be more appropriate, because it was new and Milka hadn't seen it yet.

Valeska took the streetcar as far as the second stop and walked from there. The countess's house seemed strangely deserted, but only because she hadn't met a soul on the street. She rang the bell. When no one answered, she pounded on the door—maybe there had been another power cut. Nothing stirred. She threw a snowball at the window, then another. She waited to see if at least a curtain was lifted. Milka could have gone shopping, or possibly she was sleeping so soundly after her night duty at the hospital that she really heard nothing. But the countess had to be there, peering out from behind the curtains; she was bound to show herself once she recognized Milka's sister-in-law. Valeska waited a long time, then she started throwing snowballs at the upstairs windows.

A woman finally opened one of them, but only by a crack. She was wearing a surgical collar and couldn't bend her neck. She spoke so softly that Valeska could hardly understand her. Still, Valeska managed to gather that the countess and her companion had left two days ago to take the cure at . . .

Surgical Collar slammed the window shut. Valeska hadn't caught the name of the place. But she simply had to find out. What should she say at home when they asked about Milka? She waved her arms and shouted; she saw the woman standing behind the curtains as motionless as a dressmaker's dummy. With one gloved hand Valeska wrote in the snow: WHERE?

The woman opened the window again and screamed: "Marien-bad."

Valeska's feet were frozen. She hurried away. Well, that gave her something to report. Amazing all the people who had gone off to take cures since Christmas. Especially when you consider that the watering places were crowded with wounded soldiers. She herself had never found time for a cure, just once she had spent a weekend with her husband at Bad Kudowa; actually, Bad Kudowa catered to heart disease and his trouble was asthma, but he had wanted to go there for the good air. He had brought home a white wicker chair. When she saw it in the garden, it reminded her of sun, fountains, old trees, open-air concerts, and walks in the woods.

The Church of Sts. Peter and Paul stood dark and massive in the gleaming snow. Never had it seemed so remote to her. When she found the portal closed, she thought it only fitting and proper. Seeing a woman leave by one of the side doors, she went in through it. She was enveloped by the cold and dazed by the muted light. Her steps resounded forlornly on the stone floor. But that was just how she wanted the church to be, immense, sublime, forbidding. A church must never be cozy or familiar, there simply had to be a distance between God and man. In this respect she liked Gothic churches best. Breslau cathedral, for instance; she had once been there. At the foot of those vast pillars and arches you can't help feeling like what you really are: a sinner. Ah, if only once in her life she could see the Cologne cathedral, where everything was said to be even bigger, loftier, more sublime and forbidding; if only she could see it and fall on her knees, feeling nothing but God's omnipotence and the paltriness of humankind.

After crossing herself before the high altar, she went to the little side chapel and turned toward the Mother of God with the wide blue mantle, who had protected the city during the Thirty Years'

War when it was besieged by Mansfeld's army and the Swedes, and who for that reason figured in the city's coat-of-arms. Valeska hoped for a modern miracle. She prayed the Loretan litany, concluding with a plea for everyone she was able to remember at the moment —a goodly number of people—and prayed that she might see them all once again gathered in her home at a great feast comparable to the wedding of Irma and Heiko, who had fallen in Poland a few days later. She opened her handbag, took out a twenty-mark bill, which must have been there for some time because it smelled of Johann Maria Farina, and she put it in the offertory box for Saint Mary, Mother of God, Queen of Heaven, patron saint of the city and of all virgins and all mothers and all the weak and all supplicants; she had never given so much, but this plea, which she now, burying her face in her hands, addressed to heaven, was an enormous one.

On the way home she made a detour to Wilhelmstrasse. Suddenly she found herself outside the Café Loske. This was the only café where she could usually be sure of seeing a familiar face; even her brother had been going there since the Gruban Wine Room closed. There hadn't been any coffee for a long time, but there were various kinds of tea, including one made from rose hips, which was famous. And there was a hot beverage which, though the taste was indefinable, gave one the feeling that a dash of alcohol had found its way into it.

The café was closed, the blackout shades were down, and a sign said: CLOSED FOR LACK OF HEAT. These signs had become more and more frequent outside cafés and restaurants, especially at the beginning of the week. Most were open on Saturdays. She went a few steps farther to one of the Municipal Warming Rooms. She didn't especially care for the place, she thought she'd just look in in the hope of seeing a familiar face. The Warming Rooms were too noisy and dirty for her taste, they were full of old men puffing away at their home-grown and home-cured tobacco, and the smoke was so thick you could cut it with a knife. But they were warm, and that was what mattered most to the old people, who couldn't afford to heat their houses anymore, and sometimes there was an air of good cheer, especially when someone passed a bottle of schnapps around.

Today even the Warming Room was deserted. When Valeska stuck her head in, there were only a few people sitting singly at the tables, each for himself; the place smelled of cold smoke and urine. Way at the back, all huddled up, sat Frau Pietrucha, someone Valeska had completely lost sight of. Always ailing, she had formerly framed her pale face in large, flamboyant hats, all of which she had dyed black when her husband was killed. Her present hat covered her head like a bellflower and was held in place by a thin black veil tied under her chin. Frau Piontek sat down at her table.

"We haven't seen each other in a long time, Frau Pietrucha," she said cautiously. "How have you been? You're looking well." And when Frau Pietrucha shook her head, "Oh yes, you really are, just a bit pale."

"Oh well," said the woman, vaguely shrugging her shoulders. "Life must go on, though sometimes one can't imagine how . . ."

Frau Pietrucha was glad to have someone to talk to.

"You knew my husband," she said. "I just can't get used to living without him. When there are no children, the loss is more painful." She moved closer to Frau Piontek. "You know, my walls at home are beginning to talk. I hear strange voices at night. I'm afraid. You have children and grandchildren, there's always something going on, the house is full, you hear living voices. Am I right?"

"I haven't heard from my son in four weeks," said Valeska. "I'm terribly worried."

"Is he on the west front?" asked Frau Pietrucha. As if it mattered.

"In his last letter he was somewhere near Warsaw. They can't be too exact in letters from the front, but he said he was able to go to Sunday mass at Holy Cross. Of course there are churches by that name everywhere, but the most famous is in Warsaw, and if my Josel mentions it I think he must mean that one. Because Chopin's heart is walled up in one of the pillars . . ."

Frau Pietrucha shuddered.

"People go and pray beside that pillar. It's sacred to the Poles. Anyway the whole front has been disorganized since the offensive, nobody knows what's going on."

"I'm surprised that you're still here."

"What do you mean by that?"

"I mean you should go away with your children and grandchildren before it's too late," Frau Pietrucha whispered in a tone of entreaty.

"You mean because of the war?"

"Yes, of course. The Russians will be here in a few days. Save what you can save, Frau Piontek; most of all, save your grandchildren . . ."

"Do you really believe the Russians . . . you think they'll get this far?" Valeska unbuttoned her coat.

"Of course they will," said Frau Pietrucha, wagging her head and hat. "Nothing can stop them. They'll get a lot farther. The steppes have risen to engulf us, the barbarians have come from the East to destroy civilization. Nostradamus predicted it all for the middle of this century!"

"Nostradamus?"

"That's right," said Frau Pietrucha triumphantly. "I believe it, because up until now all his predictions have come true!"

Frau Pietrucha went red in the face. She'd do better to take her hat off, Valeska thought. "What about you?" she asked. "Why are you still here?"

Frau Pietrucha unclasped her bag and took out a handkerchief. She was a long time in answering.

"I have no one left. Since my husband was killed, nothing matters anymore. Where should I go? What difference does it make whether I die here or a hundred kilometers farther on? It's the end of civilization. The godless are coming from the East, and they'll be followed by the slant-eyes, the Chinese. Just as it says in Nostradamus."

"Oh my God!" was all Valeska could say.

"Haven't you noticed how many people have already cleared out. The rats are leaving the sinking ship. I could pour out a whole litany. But you should leave, Frau Piontek. For the sake of your grandchildren. Nostradamus says the grandchildren will preserve the fire and carry it on. Think of that, Frau Piontek."

A crowd had formed at the Klodnitz bridge car stop. Valeska mingled with the people, peered into their faces as she passed, but found nothing to alarm her, only fatigue, emptiness, exhaustion. Everything looked as usual. And yet there had been so many portents that she couldn't just ignore. She took one hand out of her muff, pushed her shawl down to uncover her mouth, and spoke to a woman softly, for fear of being overheard: "Do you think the Russians will occupy the city?"

The woman raised her face, gave Valeska a look of surprise, and turned away without a word.

A streetcar approached, braking with a decrescendo screech. Lightning hissed in the overhead wire. That reassured Valeska. She walked the short distance to the station. Under a leaden sky, the ugly gray building looked to her as it always had, like an enormous morgue. The station square was as still as a graveyard, not a soul to be seen, not a parking car, not a door opening or closing; for a moment it occurred to Valeska that the station might have shut down. But when she pushed the swing door with her muff, she heard loud voices. The ticket hall was full of people, swarming like so many bees toward the gate.

She didn't go far; the swarm of people with their suitcases, cartons, and bags became a wall. She caught sight of Fräulein Bombonnek not far away and waved to her, glad to have found a familiar face in this crowd. But Fräulein Bombonnek turned abruptly away, as though she felt caught in a dishonorable action.

Valeska Piontek fled. The sky had darkened, the cloud cover lay low over the houses. A few snowflakes whirled through the air, then more and more of them, and soon they were coming down thick and fast; they blew into Valeska's face and stuck to her eyebrows. She raised her muff to her chin and trudged across Germaniaplatz to Kronprinzenstrasse.

Suddenly a procession emerged from the curtain of snow up ahead of her. Long files of men in striped clothing and striped caps, being driven with truncheon blows and shouts by other men dressed exactly as they were. Valeska slipped into a doorway and looked on; she pressed her muff to her face, and what she now saw as through a gunsight made her go rigid with horror.

She couldn't have said how long she stood there. Only when the procession had passed, when nothing remained but a gray curtain of snow traversed by a blue-lit streetcar, was she able to shake off her rigidity. Then she moved, at first slowly, then more quickly, until in the end she was running as though pursued. She went straight to old Herr Apitt's house. In a frenzy she rang the rusty old bell, knocked at the door, and called his name, until Herr Apitt opened. There she stood, leaning against the wall, staring at his green velvet cap and the glasses that she had never before seen him wearing. A strong, acrid smell came to her from inside the house.

"Let me in, Herr Apitt," she panted. "I must tell you what I've just seen."

8

Wondrak went to his office late that day. The first thing he did when he got there was to call his old fraternity brother Dr. Slazak and tell him without beating about the bush that he needed a certificate attesting that he was unfit to travel and would be for at least the next two or three days, though he was far from certain that the draft board accepted certificates made out by private physicians. Dr. Slazak seemed to be in a hurry; in any case he declared his willingness to accredit Wondrak with any known disability, only he must come immediately, because, he, Dr. Slazak, was on the point of leaving town with his family.

Wondrak started out at once. He put on his woolen earmuffs and pulled his hat down low over his face. In this cold he should really have worn his peaked cap with the ear flaps. There were few people on the streets and they seemed to be in more of a hurry than usual. But that could be because of the cold; who wants to go out in such weather if he can help it? He, too, walked faster than usual, at least here on Oberwallstrasse, where the snow had already been tramped down.

Dr. Slazak had managed to wangle a gasogene car in which to move his family and that of his friend Dr. Hanau from Gutenbergstrasse to Neisse. When Wondrak arrived, he was trying to persuade his eight-year-old son to leave his caged canary behind, on the ground that it would freeze if he took it along. But the child was unwilling to part with his bird and was swathing the cage in towels. There wasn't much luggage waiting in the entrance. This mustn't look like an evacuation, Slazak explained, because the Wehrmacht had set up checkpoints on the Oder; it seemed they even sent back some Party bigwigs who had cleared out with their furniture and carpets, and confiscated their cars. An ordinary citizen would do well not to get involved in the friction that had developed between the Party and the Wehrmacht.

"How at this late date did you manage to get hold of a car?" asked Wondrak, who had been toying with all sorts of plans.

"I got it from the medical officer at the Katzler Barracks," said Slazak. "We have a permit to be on the road until twelve midnight today. We have to be back by then. That's why we're in such a hurry. See?"

Wondrak saw. "I have to report to the Katzler Barracks today," he said. "To the Volkssturm."

"Greater Germany's last reserves," Slazak joked, mustering Wondrak from top to toe as if he were a calf ready to be slaughtered.

"If the bird stays, so do I," said the child, and took off his coat to show he meant it.

"What's your view of the situation?" Wondrak asked.

"Shitty would be an understatement," said Slazak, trying with the help of his wife to force the child back into his coat. "The Russians are at Gross-Strehlitz. They've started burning files at Police Headquarters. And I'm told that the Party bosses left their district office in the Upper Silesia House last night."

The child had won out. They were letting him take his bird. He clung to the cage with one hand and dried his tears with the other. It was time to pick up Dr. Hanau.

Wondrak pocketed his certificate without reading it. Perhaps it was no longer necessary to have a contagious disease.

He made a slight detour to see what was going on at Police Headquarters. There he saw prisoners, under the supervision of Inspector Linz, loading files into a truck.

"Pure routine," Linz explained. "Certain secret files are being stored in the Riesengebirge, as was planned a long time ago." He kept shifting nervously from leg to leg. "The news is good," he added. "Our troops have stopped the Russians at Tarnowitz. The whole industrial zone is being turned into a fortress. Every factory, every house will be defended. Just wait until the fresh divisions from the West get here. Then the Russians will be thrown back behind the border."

What an idiot, Wondrak thought. Suddenly he was in a hurry to get out of there.

Back at his office, he sought out the papers that he wanted to burn right away. He didn't hesitate, he had thought it all out on his way home. When he saw the paper burning, he knew he had made his decision. Yes, on the street, just as he was passing the arcades on the Ring, he had decided to leave town. It was not as if he had considered the pros and cons and finally made up his mind. No, at a certain moment he had suddenly realized that everything he was doing tended toward a definite goal. He shoved his license to practice law and a few other documents into his inside pocket and wrapped his two rubber stamps in a handkerchief. He picked up his fountain pen and fingered it thoughtfully. How little one really needs, he thought without self-pity. He went out to the faucet for water and sprinkled the hibiscus that he had already watered that day. He cast a look about the room—a cold, sober, photographic look, and it seemed to him that all this would soon be no more than a photograph to him.

He called up Rosa at the *Traveler*; it was some time before she came to the phone. At last he heard her voice.

"Is the news good or bad?" she asked.

What a question! Wondrak couldn't help laughing. "I'll pick you up in half an hour. Will that be all right?"

After that he sat at his desk for a while. He asked himself when he had last been obliged to make a decision. A long time ago. He had always sidestepped decisions, because he was wary of radical changes and upheavals. His life had been rather like a river, flowing quietly along; when there were barriers, he had evaded them, and when there were mountains he had flowed around them. His father had wanted him to study theology, and he had refused. Then they had agreed on law, though at the time he would have preferred something else, something far out, such as singing or dancing. But he hadn't had the courage to resist. From then on there had been few no's in his career, in any case none that might have changed his life. (With one exception, when his marriage banns were published and he had called the whole thing off.) He preferred decisions that were forced on him. They at least provided him with an alibi—for himself.

He shut his office door. While trudging through the snow past a row of front gardens, he thought for a moment of throwing his key into the snow, where it wouldn't come to light until after the spring thaw. But of course he held it fast in his trouser pocket. He had to think of Rosa. She knew he didn't love her and had reconciled herself to the fact, but she did her best to make herself useful if not indispensable to him. Yet she had never been obtrusive or clinging, on the contrary—her discretion was admirable, and he prized it. She left him alone in his garden house and kept out of his way when he was working. There were times when they didn't see each other all day. He only wondered why she had married him in the first place. True, he had proposed to her, but then his sister had just about forced his hand. He had hoped to the end that she wouldn't hold him to this marriage pact.

In time he found himself taking an interest in the bookseller, though he wasn't quite able to account for it. But when he asked himself who was the most important person in his life, he didn't have to think very long; it was his sister. Whatever he did, the question that confronted him was: what would his sister Valeska say? He imagined that this was a mere habit he had fallen into. Actually, it had been that way since he was a child. When he stole eggs from under the brooding hen, it was because he hoped his sister would praise him for it; he had plaited daisies into wreaths, because she had taught him to; he had broken off his love affair with Jürgen because she had wanted him to. This attachment had intensified after the death of her husband, when Valeska—after the customary year of mourning—had begun to enjoy life again. They had gone to opening nights, concerts, and art shows together, attended illustrated lectures about "Dürer's Late Period" or "The Beauties of the Engadine" so regularly that Irma was beginning to joke about "the charming couple." It was all Willi could do to get away from his sister now and then without hurting her feelings.

The fact is that there was no getting away from Valeska and the other women who dominated the Piontek household. He thought of his sister's husband, Leo Maria, who had fled first into illness and then into death; he thought of Valeska's son, Josel, who while still a child had run away from this matriarchal household, and of Heiko, Irma's first husband, who had been killed at the very start of the Polish campaign. Chance? Willi had stopped believing in chance. And Skrobek, who had stopped writing poems the moment Irma married him, and who had been cursed with begetting nothing but girls. These women were like spiders; they caught every man who came near them in fine golden threads, fascinated them with glittering dewdrops in the morning sun, and at night sucked all the strength and life out of them. Suddenly it came to him that Irma's idea of hiding him to keep him out of the Volkssturm was a subtly sophisticated way of catching him in the spiderweb. Still, he was breaking loose. He wasn't sure of succeeding, he was wriggling and struggling to tear the golden threads.

Gregor would help him. Grzegorz, who had fled from Kattowitz because the Germans had arrested his father, and suddenly appeared outside Willi's house two years before. For a while Willi kept him hidden in the house, but the women were afraid and urged him to send the boy back to Kattowitz. To pacify them, he told them he had taken Gregor to a hostel for Volhynian Germans in Ziegenhals. In reality he had managed to get Gregor into a Franciscan hostel on Hüttenstrasse, where he went to see him every few weeks. Not so long ago, he had learned to his surprise that Gregor had asked to be admitted to the Franciscan order and, as he had just attained the age of fifteen, he was accepted as a novice.

Wondrak had included Gregor in his decision. He would take him along when he flew the coop. Gregor would be safer in another monastery in the Reich—in Dresden, for instance. Willi would speak to the abbot about it. He would also talk it over with Valeska and Rosa; he could see their faces in advance.

Lost in his labyrinthine thoughts, he looked into the printshop. The rotary press was just starting on the Sunday paper. He read the headline: OUR INDUSTRIAL ZONE MUST BE DEFENDED LIKE A FORTRESS.

Rosa was getting ready to leave. She opened her desk drawers and pondered what to take with her. The crimson lipstick, which she seldom used because it was too conspicuous; some 400-gram bread coupons and 150-gram meat coupons, which she had saved up for a special occasion. The letter opener with the ivory handle that an admirer had brought her from Brussels, a bit of money, her little black memo book, the monogrammed silver mechanical pencil, which had never functioned. Lastly, a box of Togal pills that she put in her coat pocket to have on hand if the terrible headaches she had been having lately started up again.

Willi Wondrak was surprised to find her alone, and it seemed even more surprising that he hadn't seen anyone in the corridors.

"The offices seem to be deserted," said Willi.

"Normally half the staff are out digging," said Rosa. "But today there were no cars to drive them out there. So they've simply stayed home."

"And the management?"

"They've been disappearing, one after another. Missions for the Party, or so they claim."

"What about the next edition?"

"I doubt if there'll be one on Tuesday."

"What are the others saying?"

"The same. The Russians are at Gross-Strehlitz. We haven't much time."

"It says in your paper that the industrial zone must be defended like a fortress."

"I wish you wouldn't keep saying 'my paper.' All day we've been discussing what to do about the press if the Russians get here. The Party commissar has ordered us to smash the cylinder and put the press out of commission. The printers refuse."

"What about Herr Neumann, the owner? Is he still around? It's his property after all."

"He's in the army. And the family is afraid of the Party, they don't dare say anything. Our compositor says when the war is over the Russians will give the press back to its former owners. There was a long discussion; at the end the Party commissar screamed that if Gleiwitz is occupied by the Russians printing presses will never be needed again, because, as Roosevelt has proclaimed, the Germans will be reduced to slave laborers and no book or newspaper will ever again be printed."

"You people certainly say amazing things," said Wondrak.

"Yes, and the compositor took off his smock and walked out. Now the commissar is on the phone, trying to have him arrested for sabotage."

"And you personally, what do you think?"

Rosa put *The Uhlans' Patrol* in her handbag. When there wasn't much to do, she had been dreaming herself back into bygone times with it. She still read a good deal, and it grieved her that she hadn't been able to get Wondrak to read—books, that is. He was an avid newspaper reader, but like most people in Silesia, it took him six months to finish a book, and by the time he got to the end he had forgotten the beginning.

"I think when the Russians take over they will put the press to work. They'll need specialists. Whether they'll need me is another question. But Herr Kania, our compositor, definitely. We'll just have to print Cyrillic. I'm told it's not hard to learn. Russian is a rich, beautiful language."

"So you want to stay here?"

Rosa gave a start. "I . . . I'll stay with you, wherever you go," she said haltingly.

"I've decided to clear out," said Wondrak. "This evening or tomorrow morning."

"Good, then let's clear out," said Rosa staunchly and shut her handbag.

9

KOTIK LOOKED AROUND. The avenue lay deserted, and the snow foamed in the darkness. He jumped over the fence and walked in the direction of Reichspräsidentenplatz. The houses on either side of the avenue lurked black, crouching to leap like great fabulous beasts. There was no light in any of the windows and most of those on the lower floors were boarded up. When he came to the intersection, Kotik turned around for the first time and was glad to see that no one had followed him. It had been the same yesterday, he hadn't seen a soul at this hour. Maybe Mamochka was right in saying that the rich were the first to abandon the ship. At the corner of Hauptstrasse it was almost comforting to see smoke coming out of a chimney.

Because what made the houses on this avenue seem so dead and forlorn was the total absence of any smoke. Except for the one he had just come out of. He had put some briquettes in the tile stove and before leaving shut the fire door to make it burn as slowly as possible. He didn't know when he'd be coming back, but hoped it would be soon. He felt the book in his coat pocket. It proved that he had really been in the house. If no one wanted to believe him, here was the evidence.

Yesterday he had taken a cake of soap; it smelled deliciously of hyacinths and it fitted into his hand like an egg. Mamochka couldn't get over it. She had asked where it came from, but to judge by her tone she hadn't really wanted to know, and he had answered evasively. That night he'd had trouble falling asleep, his head had been whirling with images of the house he had broken into to see what it was like inside; he had sat up, held the soap in the hollow of his hand, and breathed the hyacinth scent.

Today he could hardly wait for the HY exercise to be over. They had practiced ground defense in the open and simulated mortar firing in the classroom. Drenched in sweat, he had gone home to get his flashlight and tell his mother there was to be a night exercise, but not to worry, the guns weren't loaded, and he'd be back in the morning.

It was already dark when he turned from Oberwallstrasse into Miethe-Alle, where the house, which now belonged to him, was situated. Yes, in his thoughts it belonged to him, it was his kingdom. The only thing that dampened his spirits was the dead dog, the beautiful Afghan, who lay in the entrance between the front door and the staircase, legs outstretched in an unnatural position, jaws wide open as if he had gasped for air at the end. Kotik had lit a match on entering and discovered him right away. He had gone slowly closer and touched the head with the tip of his shoe. How often he had longed to run his fingers through the dog's coat and stroke his head! But now he couldn't. They must have poisoned him just before leaving, not wanting to be there when he died. That's what Kotik had figured while going from room to room, lighting a match now and then. Everywhere he saw signs of haste, a half-rolled carpet, a suitcase that had been packed but then left behind after all, an overturned chair, articles of clothing strewn over the floor. Finding the tile stove still warm in the living room, he knelt down, shook up the coals, put on wood and briquettes. He left the fire door open, looked around the room, and delighted in the flames which cast reflections on the walls.

He had found a room with nothing in it but a bathtub, a toilet, and a washbasin with a mirror above it. That was something he had never seen before, a whole room for a bathtub. In the light of a candle stub he detected a fine marble shell and in it, waxen and glowing, a cake of soap. He picked up the soap and smelled it; it nestled soft in his hand and smelled of summer and hyacinths, like Aunt Rita's garden in Heidersdorf. After a moment's thought, he slipped it into his pocket; it would serve as proof later on that he had actually been in this house. Then he crossed the hallway and mounted the stairs. At the top a woman stood motionless, her face averted.

It took him some time to get over his fright. Slowly climbing the rest of the way, he saw a white summer dress and a wide-brimmed hat; it was a dressmaker's dummy. He had been so paralyzed with fear that it was some time before he could breathe.

On this floor he found bedrooms and a large workroom. Here there were three more dressmaker's dummies. Two were draped in lengths of cloth; the third was standing in a corner. The long work table, extending from wall to wall of the room, was strewn helter-skelter with stage photos, colored sketches, remnants of cloth, pads of paper. A paint box had been left open, the paints had dried; beside it stood a glass of water with paintbrushes in it, and some thistles in a vase. On the walls hung playbills and sketches of costumes. After making sure that the windows were properly blacked out, Kotik inspected the scene in the candlelight. He imagined the little boy moving through these rooms and wished the boy were here to explain it all to him.

Later this experience had struck him as a fantastic dream; if not for the cake of soap he would have doubted its reality. But now there was a book in his pocket, a thin little volume, he had found it on the boy's bedside table (that at least is what he took the little table to be); it lay open, and Kotik had read a little in the candlelight, not very much, only a few sentences, and the biblical language had appealed to him. It was Nietzsche's *Thus Spake Zarathustra*. He had heard of it or read something about it, he couldn't remember exactly, but anyway it was not completely unknown to him as *The Mauritius Case* had been.

In the cellar he had found that all the fuses had been removed. He let it go at that. A neighbor or someone who knew the family might get suspicious if he saw light in the house. In his thoughts Kotik passed all his school friends in review, but found none worthy to share this secret with him.

He came to Wilhelmstrasse. A streetcar passed, its windows were painted blue and cast a blue light on the snow. A clock struck twice, indicating the half hour. Even if Russian shells reduced the city to ashes, there would always be a smoking church tower somewhere with a clock. The hours pass, the hours strike, the hours punish.

Kotik was feeling the cold. The hand holding the book in his coat pocket was half frozen. He watched the people getting out of the streetcar. Wasn't that Hedel Zock? The girl in the long baggy coat, gathered at the waist with a cloth belt? Yes, it was her all right. Kotik recognized her now by her shape and way of walking. He hurried after her so fast that he came close to slipping.

He had gone swimming a few times with her, and they had skied together on the Autobahn embankment near Gröling, but that had been long ago. He wondered if she remembered. His brother Tonik had made a play for her, with what success Kotik had never found out. Since then he had noticed her a few times at the Italian ice-cream parlor on Wilhelmstrasse; he had seen her standing around with soldiers and even smoking cigarettes.

He walked faster and caught up with her on the bridge.

"Hedel! Do you remember me?"

Hedel looked around.

"I'm an Ossadnik," said Kotik. "I'm the youngest of the Ossadniks, they call me Kotik, but it's not my real name. Don't you remember me? You're Hedel Zock, aren't you? We went sledding and skiing together, on barrel staves, remember?"

Hedel Zock stopped walking. She pulled her shawl aside to uncover her mouth. She looked Kotik over. Her expression gave no clue to her thoughts.

"What do you want?" she said after a while and walked on.

Kotik walked beside her. "I've a book here," he said, taking it out of his pocket. "Do you know it?"

Hedel gave it a passing glance. It was too dark to see much. "I'm cold," she said. "I have to go home."

Kotik put the book away. "It's by Nietzsche," he said. "*Thus Spake Zarathustra*. I'd like to read you some of it."

There was more surprise than annoyance in Hedel's look: "You're the littlest of the Ossadniks, aren't you?"

"I'm the youngest," Kotik corrected her with dignity.

"You must be nuts," said Hedel. "*Chaychay*."

10

"I'LL NEVER FORGET IT," Valeska stammered. "*Muy Bozhe kokhany,* I'll never forget it." Exhausted, she let herself drop on the ottoman which Herr Apitt had moved close to the green tile stove for her, warmed her hands, and discreetly sniffed the air; she couldn't get used to that smell. What could it be? The room was cluttered with furniture. The walls were lined with cupboards, vitrines, and bookcases—hardly a gap between them—and in the middle of the room armchairs, a tall table and a low table seemed to beleaguer an immense bed, which was unmade and covered with books, magazines, phonograph records, and a washbasin.

"All of a sudden this procession appeared from out of the snow, it seemed to come from nowhere, five or six abreast, anyway they took up most of the street, an endless column, they weren't exactly marching, more like staggering. I knew right away that they were prisoners from a concentration camp."

Apitt had sat down facing her, almost hidden from view by the furniture. She leaned against the tiles to warm her back. "Those striped uniforms, I'd seen them before, but never so many at a time. The kapos were along the edge, you know what a kapo is, don't you? They looked exactly like the others except they had sticks, and they kept hitting the others with them—yes, that was how I recognized them . . . And do you know, Herr Apitt, the weirdest part of it, I couldn't hear a thing; the procession moved without a sound, their feet were wrapped in rags tied with wire, they had no shoes, the poor things . . . an army of ghosts staggering through the snowstorm."

Again the gruesome procession passed before her eyes. The high-wheeled carts bearing the dead and the sick, lying motionless all in a heap, my God, had they all frozen to death? "I went to the edge of the sidewalk, I wanted to see their faces, a face tells the whole story, you know, but they were all looking at the ground, as if they hadn't the strength to hold their heads up, and all they could do was drag their feet mechanically, Mother Mary Dolorosa, God knows how long they'd been marching in this cold . . ."

"They've come from Auschwitz," said Apitt almost tonelessly. "You've heard of Auschwitz?"

"Yes," said Valeska. "Father Mikas was there. I once asked him about it, but he only said he couldn't and wouldn't talk about it. I can imagine . . ."

Her thoughts wandered, the light began to fail. Why hadn't she thought of that? Where else could they have come from? Auschwitz wasn't far. A little beyond Kattowitz.

"Anyone who's been in Auschwitz keeps his mouth shut," said Apitt, half to himself. "They're evacuating the camp. Which means they're leaving us to our fate."

He looked at Valeska through his dark glasses. Her expression hadn't changed. He realized that she hadn't understood him.

Valeska's gaze strayed over the furniture and came to rest on a vitrine which attracted her attention with its elegantly curved lines and yellow leaded glass. On the table beside the bed she discovered what looked like a phonograph; she would have liked to get up and examine it, but she remained seated.

"Oh, forgive me," said Herr Apitt. "I haven't offered you anything." He stood up and took a glass from the vitrine. "I never have visitors, you know. I'm not prepared for it. You see what the place looks like." Apitt made a sweeping gesture that took in the whole room. "But I have so much to do that I never even get around to making the bed. I won't apologize to you for that." He produced a bottle from somewhere. "But I do apologize for delaying to offer you my cognac in this cold . . .

"It's prewar," he said while pouring. "I'd been keeping it for special occasions, but I doubt if there will be any more special occasions."

He carefully picked up the full glass and handed it to Valeska.

"This is Hennessy, French cognac. You must swirl it around your mouth for a while to let the taste penetrate," said Apitt in the tone of a connoisseur. "I need a drop of it now and then to deaden my toothache."

Valeska had tasted French cognac only once in her life, on her wedding day, and that was long ago. She took a sip. It tasted like soap and burned her mouth and throat. A trail of fire led to her stomach; from there it spread a pleasant warmth in all directions. She felt it all the way from her face to her feet. Oh, how delightful it was; she took another sip.

"I believe," Apitt resumed the thread of his thoughts, "I believe that if they're giving up Auschwitz, they expect the Russians to break through, at least as far as the Oder. In that case, Gleiwitz hasn't a chance."

"You mean," said Valeska, trying to follow his line of reasoning, "that the Russians can't be stopped. You think they're going to occupy the city?"

Apitt only nodded. He pulled up a chair and sat down beside Valeska.

"I wish it were already summer and we were able to sit together in this room, talking as we are now. The worst would be behind us. But in the meantime . . ." Apitt refilled the glasses.

"What will they do to those poor devils?" Valeska asked.

She felt besieged by furniture.

"Drag them into the Reich as slave laborers. Slave labor is always needed. Humans are the cheapest form of energy. That hasn't changed since the Egyptians. When you come right down to it, the main purpose of the whole penal system is to provide cheap labor. In ancient times wars were fought as a means of acquiring slaves. The same was true in the Middle Ages and it's no different today. The vanquished have always worked for the victors and always will."

Apitt was beginning to pontificate. He encouraged Valeska to take another drop.

"In former days, the conquerors built prisons, towers, and dungeons to hide their slaves in. Today these are replaced by camps. Now all they need is barbed wire, a few shacks, and watchtowers. Humans are cheaper than any machine, and can be adapted to any task. Someday our whole world will consist of camps, and there will be only two varieties of people, the slaves and the slave drivers. Nothing will ever change. The only change will be an exchange: one day the slaves will become the slave drivers, the persecuted will become the persecutors. There you have all history in a nutshell . . ."

Apitt broke off. He had resolved not to pontificate, and here he was doing it again. His old weakness. He probably did it because he was alone so much. He liked to talk and he was glad to have an audience. Sometimes he went whole days without leaving his house or seeing anyone, and then he would talk to himself for the sheer pleasure of hearing his voice.

It was generally known that Herr Apitt didn't admit visitors; even to the priest or the Party people, who came snooping around now and then, his door remained closed. Even Frau Bortel, who lived in the house and was always sweeping outside his door in the hope of getting a glimpse of the apartment when he came home from a walk or a shopping expedition, had never seen anything but piles of old newspapers in the entrance, and these too had diminished since the Party had started its wastepaper collections. The smell coming out of the apartment was a source of wild speculation; everyone noticed it, but it was interpreted in different ways. The most persistent belief was that Apitt hoarded quantities of food, which was gradually rotting. Then one day a commission appeared (Gestapo men, according to Frau Bortel, who was scrubbing the stairs at the time) and soon went away without removing either Herr Apitt or any of the legendary supplies.

Valeska couldn't get her mind off the phonograph. "What have you got here? Could it be a phonograph?"

"Oh, that?" said Apitt. Both stared at the rectangular case, which had suddenly become a magical object.

"I never knew you listened to mechanical music," she said in a tone which revealed that she knew little or nothing about old Apitt. Her own phonograph was much smaller and technically no doubt vastly inferior; she seldom used it, she preferred to play the piano.

"Yes, I often listen to music now. I haven't got very many records, but there are some pieces that I can listen to over and over again. I didn't know how much one can discover in them . . ."

"You never told me you were a music lover," said Valeska, with an air of feeling offended. "I'd gladly have lent you some of my records . . . You never came to my musical evenings, what a shame! And now you're going to tell me that you even play an instrument. The violin, the flute?"

She looked about in the hope of discovering a musical instrument that would confirm her suspicion. "Cello? Yes, the cello. And we were ages looking for a cello after Frau Weinrich went back to the Reich . . ."

"No, no. I don't play any instrument, sorry to say. I can't even read music. I haven't had the phonograph very long. It was left to me by an old friend; I couldn't even play it at first because I had no needles, and there are none to be had nowadays, but then someone sent me a box from Ostrau."

Apitt refilled the glasses. As he was standing between the phonograph and Valeska, she couldn't get by. She would so much have liked to see the machine close up and the records too. Some people inspect the bookshelves of a new acquaintance to get an idea of what he is like; Valeska did the same with phonograph records. Phonographs were a rarity in Gleiwitz, not even the Countess Hohenlohe-Langwitz had one.

"I can't read books anymore," said Apitt. "I need a magnifying glass, and an hour of that gives me a headache. That's what brought me to music. In the old days, when I wore a bandage over my eyes, I had excellent eyesight, I only wore it as a means of avoiding people, and I didn't have to stand in line at the butcher's—there are some advantages in being blind. But in the past year my eyes have really deteriorated, so now I have good reason to wear a bandage. Sometimes I think I tempted fate, committed a sin . . ."

"Yes, that may be," said Valeska thoughtfully.

Apitt was pleased at Valeska's reaction, which he interpreted as recognition of his guilt. Threading his way between table and armchair, he opened the phonograph.

"Would you care to listen to something?" he asked.

"Yes, of course." Valeska could hardly wait.

"Schubert? Beethoven?"

Valeska only nodded. She was too excited to say anything.

"Something from one of the late quartets? I have Opus 130 and

131. I only play the late quartets now. How about the adagio from 130? Or the cavatina?" Herr Apitt's little green cap quivered.

He reached under the bed without looking, took out a record, and set it carefully on the turntable. Then he wound up the machine, tested the needle by passing it gently over the tip of his middle finger, and lowered the arm onto the disk, which was already turning.

Valeska sat silent. The music had melted the ice in her heart. When it stopped, it echoed in her ears and mingled with her images of the prisoners staggering down the snowy street.

"Music is a wonderful thing," she said. "It opens the soul. But do you know, I still see those striped figures before me."

Apitt removed his dark glasses and passed his hand over his eyes. "Now we are dragging our slaves to the Reich," he said in a tired voice. "And when the Russians take over, they will drag us to Siberia as slave laborers."

Valeska's world was tottering.

"Then you think we should run away from the Russians?"

"Nothing can stop them. They're like a flood. Everything will be submerged."

"What are you going to do?"

Apitt had long known the answer. Since Christmas he had considered the possibilities over and over again.

"I'll tell you the truth, Frau Piontek. All we have left is the truth—and art. I shall stay here. Where can an old man like me go? Twice in my life I've had to leave everything; I can't do it again. I'm too old and tired. There's no running away from death. But it's also because the old world that I belonged to is dying; what can I do but die with it? I shall lock myself up in my apartment, play Beethoven's late quartets, drink up my brandy, and listen to the music over and over again. Until a shell comes and blows me to bits. *The Grammar of Pain*, my life work, which has taken me almost twenty years, is finished. I've deposited two copies in different places; some day men will find them and learn . . . and here I have a little capsule that I've been keeping in case the bombs don't finish me off."

They sat in silence, immersed in the music, gazing into the bronze-colored light. Time stood still. It was the hour when shadows appear on the wall, when thoughts grow light and souls take flight. Valeska knew she had better go if she was ever to escape from this labyrinth. She fled the bitter smell, which descended like a curtain behind her, preserving its secret forever.

11

HEDEL ZOCK WAS in a hurry to get home. Chilled to the bone, she was looking forward to the cup of hot mallow tea that her grandmother would brew for her. All day, along with other women, she had been digging a tank trap out near Petersdorf; the ground was frozen solid and they had not made much progress. Luckily there had been an empty shack not far off; they had made a fire in it and stayed there for quite a while. Someone had brought a bottle of schnapps, they had made some sort of grog, and she had drunk enough of it to make her fairly tipsy. Thanks to the schnapps, it wasn't until nightfall, when a truck brought her back to town, that she had realized how bitter cold it was. The continuous rumble from the front, which she had almost ceased to notice, seemed louder on her return to town. Now it seemed to be coming from the west. Two days before, all had still been quiet, and no one was willing to believe that the Russians had advanced as far as Tschenstochau. But now the noise had been going on for a whole day and people seemed to have become as used to it as they had been to the silence.

Now what could this young whippersnapper, who was hopping along in the snow beside her, want of her? She had no recollection of sleigh riding with this babyface. He wanted to read to her from a book, he must be nuts. She could only remember another Ossadnik, a big fellow in a lovely uniform, even if he was only a corporal.

"I wanted to take you home. It's getting dark, and a girl alone . . . There are so many *ostarbeiter* around, anything could happen . . ." Kotik didn't say what might happen, because he himself hadn't the vaguest idea.

Hedel slackened her pace. Come to think of it, she was rather pleased to have an escort, even if it was only this little Kotik. There were getting to be fewer and fewer people on Marienstrasse, and she actually had been afraid coming home in the evening.

"So you're Kotik Ossadnik?" she said. "You've got a brother, haven't you? I remember him all right, I've just forgotten his name."

"Sure, that's Tonik. He used to flirt with you," said Kotik with a giggle.

"He used to what? What did he do with me?" Hedel laughed a cloud of white smoke into the air.

"On his last leave he said he was in love with Hedel Zock from Marienstrasse, said he was going to marry her when the war was over."

Kotik was proud of this invention. He watched her face to see how she would react.

"Who? Tonik? Why, I only went dancing with him once, and I haven't heard a word from him since. Anyway, that was a long time ago."

"My brother Tonik," Kotik went on improvising, "has been severely wounded. Didn't he write you about it? Now he's in the hospital in . . . I've forgotten the name of the place. They've taken out one of his lungs."

Hedel Zock knew nothing about Tonik Ossadnik's wound. She had never received a single letter from him. She had gone to the movies with him once or twice, they had walked along the Wild Klodnitz. And he had kissed her. But nothing more. Her boyfriend Konrad, on the other hand, had written her lots of letters, which he addressed to her friend Angela, because Hedel's mother would be sure to open and read them and throw them in the fire.

"People have two lungs," Kotik explained, "one on the right and one on the left, but they can live to a ripe old age with just one."

He himself was amazed at the things he was saying. He was thinking fast. They would be coming to Miethe-Allee in a minute; how was he to steer Hedel in that direction?

"Wasn't your brother a PFC? In the infantry?"

If only he had been in the tank corps, they had those stunning black uniforms with the dashing caps that made a private look like a sergeant.

"Tonik is a corporal and a candidate for sergeant," said Kotik proudly. "In fact," he added, "he was sure to make staff sergeant, because of all his decorations." Kotik couldn't remember them all at the moment, he tended to get them mixed up with Paulek's, which included the Iron Cross First Class awarded posthumously after his hero's death in Africa. Mamochka kept all these medals in a cup in the kitchen cupboard.

"Anyway, Tonik once told Mamochka, I overheard it by accident, that he was getting engaged to Hedel Zock on his next leave."

Kotik stopped walking. He was confident now that his fantasies were taking effect.

And true enough, Hedel also stopped still. It was all so startling.

"And what . . . what did your mother say?"

"Oh, Mamochka, she always says: If it makes him happy. That's what counts." Kotik was glad this had occurred to him. It was true that his mother sometimes concluded a discussion with those words. With reference to Tonik, she had certainly said nothing of the kind, Kotik was sure of that, because Mamochka was always complaining about Tonik and his girls.

"That's news to me," said Hedel. "Your brother certainly never mentioned it to me. He should have consulted me, shouldn't he?"

"Definitely," Kotik hastened to say. "He's sure to bring it up on his next leave. But now, Hedel, listen to me. About this book I want to read you. And something else. Something real crazy, you won't believe it. But I want you to come and see for yourself. You see, I have this house, a whole house all to myself. It's on Miethe-Allee, two steps from here. With lots of rooms and a whole big one with nothing but a bathtub in it, and a phonograph and dressmaker's dummies, dressed fit to kill like in the movies . . ."

Kotik had talked himself red in the face. He had taken a few steps ahead of Hedel and was barring her way.

"What are you talking about?" she said. "What has this house got to do with me?"

They were standing in the snow under the arching black branches of a locust tree.

"At least come and take a look, Hedel. You've never seen anything like it. Beautiful furniture, soft carpets, and it's warm inside, I've made a fire in the tile stove . . ."

"Yes, but how come? How can you have a house?" Hedel was beginning to get interested.

"The owners have cleared out. Their son is a friend of mine. He made me promise to keep an eye on the place while they're away; otherwise I can do what I please in it. So come on, Hedel, just for a minute, I'll show you around, you'll be surprised, and don't worry, you'll get home on time."

Kotik was out of breath. He had talked as though his life depended on it. Without even noticing it, he had taken Hedel's mittened hand and was holding on to it.

Hedel offered no resistance. She was fascinated by the picture evoked by Kotik's words and curious to see what it was really like. She had nothing to look forward to at home. Her mother did nothing but complain: the times were hard, her sciatica was killing her, and no one understood her. She only left her chair to shift half a dozen hot-water bags from one position to another. And then there was her aged grandmother, who shuffled around the apartment with bent back, putting coal on the fire, while a torrent of incomprehensible words poured from her toothless mouth.

"All right," Hedel murmured. "If it won't take too long, I'll come."

"Let me carry your spade," said Kotik, who was feeling feverish with excitement. "It's not far. Just around the corner on Miethe-Allee."

"Ten minutes," said Hedel, "but no more." This to appease her conscience.

They trudged on side by side through the snow.

"I don't see how you could ever have gotten the key to those people's house," said Hedel with a sidelong glance at Kotik's face. It was a childlike face, whose only conspicuous feature was the prominent lips. He looked sixteen, but probably he was no more than fifteen, because the sixteen-year-olds had been drafted in the fall.

"Hmm," he said. "It was pure chance. Anyway it's a long story . . ." He was walking faster now. He'd be able to explain all that once he had her in the house.

"You see the golden pheasants are all clearing out . . ."

"The what?" Hedel asked.

"You know, the golden pheasants, the Party big shots. They're the first to clear out, they're scared of the Russians."

They turned into Miethe-Allee. Kotik saved his confession for the last moment. He'd probably have to tell her something. He was so excited that he almost stuttered. "We'll have to climb over the fence and squeeze through the toilet window, we mustn't let the neighbors see that anyone's in there . . . that's what my friend said and we've got to do what he said."

If Hedel were to turn back now, all would lost.

Hedel saw the villa in among the tall trees. By then her curiosity was irresistible.

Getting over the fence was easy, and Kotik helped her. Climbing the chicken ladder and squeezing through the window was harder. It suddenly occurred to Hedel that the whole thing might be a trap, that this Ossadnik kid might want to lure her into the house and she'd never leave it alive. What did she know about Kotik anyway? And no one had seen them together in the street. Her throat broke out in gooseflesh. But by then there was no stopping her. She had to see the inside of the house and all the wonders Kotik had promised her.

And then the smell told her everything she wanted to know. She breathed it in: Kotik had told her the truth. The house smelled warm, it smelled fragrant, it smelled of life.

Kotik went ahead. He had taken off his gloves and he held her hand tight. He took a flashlight from his pocket and lit the way, which he already knew. First he led Hedel into the living room to keep her from discovering the dead dog. Tomorrow he would bury it in the snow. So far he hadn't been able to bring himself to move it out of the entrance. If only he knew how to stuff animals like old Miska did, he'd stuff the dog and put him back where he'd found him.

"Take your coat off, it's warm here," he said, leading Hedel to the stove. "I'll light a candle. Where are the damned matches?" He was so excited it took him some time to find them.

Then the candle was burning, and its warm, yellow light made them feel easier. Hedel laid her coat over a chair and put her woolen cap on top of it. She pressed her hands to the warm tiles and looked around.

"It's beautiful," she said. In her embarrassment she felt she had to say something.

"There's everything in this house," said Kotik with increasing self-assurance. "Maybe I'd better make us some mulled wine before I show you the other rooms. To make us feel warm inside."

He brought a bottle of wine, glasses, and sugar from the pantry. In the kitchen he found an iron pot, which he put into the niche in the tile stove.

"Would you have imagined ten minutes ago that you'd be drinking mulled wine in a villa with Kotik Ossadnik and forget the cold outside?" Kotik spoke in a loud voice and laughed, as though trying to make the unusual situation more usual.

"I don't get it," said Hedel earnestly. "I can't believe it's real, it's like a dream."

"You know, we could hold out here till the Russians come," said Kotik, making himself comfortable in the easy chair. How soft it was. Like floating on air.

Here in the house you couldn't hear the shells bursting. Only the crackling of the fire.

"I'd like to stay here and bury myself in the books and forget everything." He gazed at Hedel and her heavy, gray, baggy men's trousers.

"Weren't you going to show me the house?" asked Hedel, her cheeks aflame with the wine.

"Yes, of course," said Kotik, jumping up. "Where should we start?"

"I want you to show me everything," said Hedel with a sweep of the hand, as though to take in the whole world. She spoke softly, trying not to show her excitement.

He poured more wine and handed her the glass. "Follow me," he said. "Take a nip now and then to keep you warm, it'll be cold in the other rooms."

Hedel Zock went from room to room with Kotik; trembling with vague expectations, she tiptoed from silence to silence, broken only by the creaking of floorboards and the ticking of clocks. She wasn't the least bit frightened when Kotik showed her the dressmaker's dummy at the head of the stairs and the three others in the room with the posters; she knew all that from her department store, except that the materials on display in the store weren't nearly as beautiful as these; she felt them, she ran her hands over them, as though to make them more real.

"Heavenly saints," she said suddenly. "I feel sick. I haven't had supper yet . . . everything is spinning like a merry-go-round."

Kotik took her by the waist and led her slowly down the stairs.

"I'll get something to eat. Hell, how could I have forgotten! Maybe you'd better come with me and see what you want. We can take anything we please, my friend said, there's plenty in the pantry and the cellar."

They found potted chicken and picked it up in their fingers; they hadn't found any bread. For dessert they had stewed blueberries, straight out of the preserving jar. Then they looked at each other and laughed. Their mouths were all blue. Kotik stroked Hedel's lips and she playfully snapped at his fingers. He poured her some more wine, which had grown cold in the meantime. He touched her gently on the knee and wondered how he could get her to take off those hideous men's trousers. He clicked glasses with her. He had made pretty good progress. But he still had a long way to go.

"Get me the hat off the dummy upstairs," said Hedel with a giggle. "The pretty white bonnet."

Kotik ran up the stairs in the dark.

Hedel took the hat, put it on, and tied the strings under her chin.

"It's real nice here," she said, taking Kotik by the hand. "Sit here at the table and read me something, like you promised."

"Of course," he said. "I'll read from *Zarathustra*. About friendship. All right?" He moved the candle closer and looked into her bright, expectant face. He opened to the passage; he had put a bookmark in it. While he was reading, his hand moved slowly from her knee to her thigh, but all he felt was the coarse woolen goods.

"You cannot make yourself beautiful enough for your friend, for you should be to him an arrow and a yearning for the superman.

"Have you watched your friend sleeping—to discover what he looks like?

For what is your friend's face? It is your own face in a crude, imperfect mirror.

"Have you watched your friend sleeping? Were you not frightened that your friend should look as he does? Oh, my friend, man is something that must be transcended.

"A friend should be expert in divining and keeping silent: you must not wish to see everything. Your dream should tell you what your friend does when awake.

"Hide your sympathy for your friend under a hard shell and break a tooth on it. Then it will preserve its delicacy and sweetness."

Hedel pushed Kotik's hand away. He went on reading as though he hadn't noticed.

"For too long woman has harbored a slave and a tyrant within her. Thus woman is not yet capable of friendship, but only of love. In woman's love there is injustice and blindness toward all—. Are you still listening, Hedel?" He looked up for a moment. Hedel only nodded. Her face was very pale. *"—all she does not love. And even in woman's conscious love there is always aggression and lightning and night along with the light . . ."*

12

At the Pionteks' they were packing. Willi went from room to room, giving advice, checking weight, admonishing the others not to take too much, telling each one to take no more than she could carry if it became necessary. That, when they tried it, seemed hopelessly little. Irma gave up and flung herself on her bed in tears; in that case, she simply wouldn't go. Rosa decided to wear her fur coat over her raglan, which would be indispensable in the spring and fall but refused to go into the suitcase. Valeska was first to finish; wishing to have one hand free for little Roswitha, she had decided to take a knapsack; and as her one suitcase wasn't even full, she stuffed a light woolen blanket into it for the children. Lastly, she filled her handbag with identification papers, stock certificates, title deeds, savings bank passbooks, and a few photographs. It had occasionally crossed her mind that if the war came to Gleiwitz the impossibility of deciding what to take and what to abandon would prevent her from leaving. She had never given the matter serious thought, it would have broken her heart. But now that the worst had happened, she found it easier to decide. She simply packed what she thought she would need for a short trip; it didn't even enter her head that this trip might be a long one, let alone that she might never come back.

One thing that may have made it easier for her to go was that Halina had decided to stay in the house. They had talked it over at length, and at times the discussion had been heated, because Valeska felt that if they had to run from the Russians they should all run together, that no one should stay behind; they were all one family, even Halina the maid, who was actually a distant relative, and of this Valeska had managed to convince her brother. But then Halina had spoken up and had abruptly announced that nothing would make her leave, that she was more afraid of being sent back to a camp than she was of the Russians. She had burst into tears and said that if the Pani tried to force her to go, she'd run away and hide somewhere. Valeska had pacified her, and in the end they were all glad to have someone who would stay in the house and take care of their possessions. Of course there would be looting, so they decided to bury the silver and some of the crystal and glassware in the garden. In Valeska's opinion her most precious possession was the piano, which they could neither take with them nor bury. It was the only thing that really upset her, for she knew she would never as long as she lived be able to afford another such instrument.

Irma was in tears again; she wanted to pack one of Skrobek's suits, but once she had packed what she needed for the three children there was simply no room in the suitcase. Even so, she had trouble closing it, and it was so heavy she could hardly drag it across the room. Weeping and wailing, she shut herself up with the children. Once again she refused to budge from the house and changed her mind only when Willi undertook to leave one of his summer suits behind and take one of Skrobek's in its place. The atmosphere was tense; as much as possible, they kept out of each other's way. They didn't eat dinner together, and when it was time for the evening news, Willi was alone in the music room. Up until then, Valeska had dispensed a bit of cheer by remarking from time to time that the Russians might still be stopped, but now, as the sound became more and more inescapable, her words of comfort fell flat. Wondrak had tried in vain to call various people on the phone, but then he had somehow got through to his colleague Koziollek, who informed him that an official evacuation order was expected any minute from Kattowitz, but that there were no trains running to Heydebreck-Cosel—no one knew whether the signals had been knocked out, or whether the Russians, who were pushing southwest from Gross-Strehlitz, had cut the line; he himself, he said, was planning to leave the next day with his family, if it was not already too late.

The eastern front was mentioned only briefly in the news broadcast. The gunfire was more informative. Willi tried to tune in on a foreign station. The BBC was almost unintelligible because of interference. He practically crawled into the radio, especially after Valeska came in and started playing variations on a theme by Haydn.

The English commentator attributed the rapid advance of the Soviet troops since the start of their Vistula offensive to the fact that Hitler had withdrawn several divisions from the east front for his Ardennes campaign. This wasn't exactly what Willi had wanted to hear.

Valeska stood up and paced until she noticed that the wall clock had stopped; as far back as she could remember, she had never forgotten to wind it; she had always wound it while brushing her hair before going to bed; it was a ritual with her. She must have forgotten yesterday, and today, with everything that was going on in the house, she hadn't even noticed that the pendulum had stopped moving. The hands pointed to half past five. That's when she had been at Herr Apitt's. She took the key from the top drawer of the chiffonier, wound the clock, and set the pendulum in motion. Would this be the last time?

"It might be better," she said suddenly to her brother, "to stay here and be buried here."

Willi looked at his sister out of tired eyes. The tear sacks under them were swollen. He had forgotten to put on his hairnet. All through the years Valeska had hated this flaky hairnet her brother was always wearing, but now that he didn't have it on there seemed to be something wrong with his face.

"Sometimes I feel the same way, Valeska, but now the war is coming to Germany, and we here on the border are the first to feel it."

They had talked about all this so often and said everything there was to be said.

Valeska steadied herself on the table edge. Now she was all memory, and if she wasn't careful, memory would carry her away. There was a time when she would have been glad to go away, along with Leo Maria, before there were any children. But then every child, every new friend, every new pupil had strengthened her ties with this town and its people. When Leo Maria died, she had begun, if the truth be known, to practice leave-taking; that had continued with a thousand little leave-takings—until now. She had accepted the thousand little leave-takings for fear of the great, irrevocable one, which she had never been willing to envisage.

For safety's sake Rosa persuaded Willi to spend the night at her father's on Wilhelmstrasse. Of course, it was unlikely that the authorities would be looking for Dr. Wondrak (apparently the "authorities" had already cleared out), but it did seem wiser for him to be away from home that night. Only Valeska had been told the details of his plan. The next morning he and his colleague Koziollek would scare up some sort of vehicle, if only a peasant's wagon or a gasogene car to take them and their families to Ratibor on the opposite bank of the Oder. There was no need to alarm old Herr Willimczyk by telling him the real reason why they had come; Rosa concocted a story about some refugees from Gross-Strehlitz who were spending the night at the Pionteks' house.

The old man was delighted with their company and took it as a welcome change. He had been rather lonely of late; his daughter came to see him rarely and never stayed for long. His store had been busy during the Christmas holidays, for books were just about the only presents you could buy without ration coupons, and Insel-Verlag had recently published a few volumes that he could recommend with a clear conscience, Hölderlin's *Letters*, Hermann Hesse's *The Tree of Life*, Hans Carossa's little volume about *Goethe's Impact on the Present*, and *The Insel Book of Birds and Birds' Nests*, which was beautifully printed on wood-free, almost-white paper that made one think of peacetime. He had also bought a job lot of secondhand books, including a fine edition of *The Book of Optics*, which his customers were quick to snap up. But early in the new year, business had fallen off; people no longer came in to exchange books as they had done before, and there were days when not a single customer appeared. He stood by the door looking out; people hurried by, they didn't even stop to look at his showcase. Admittedly, it was no longer possible to keep the shop warm, and there were days when he couldn't even melt the ice on the showcase window. Even so, he had been able to display a few books, such as *The Complete Works of Gerhart Hauptmann* or the Staackmann primers; he had even ordered a copy of *Arno Breker, the Man and His Work*, but in these unsettled times even a member of the Party's district leadership could hardly afford to pay 198 marks for that.

Old man Willimczyk insisted, in any case, on drinking a glass of wine with his daughter and son-in-law; he had a few bottles in the cellar that he was keeping for special occasions, and this was un-doubtedly such an occasion, for the Russians could be counted on to loot his cellar and it seemed to make more sense to drink it up first. Up until 1943 he had regularly received a few cases of wine through a friend and colleague in Freiburg; it hadn't been much, but he had made it last by never offering a guest any, thus honoring the old Gleiwitz dictum: "Good things for your friend, the best things for yourself." Laughing, he took a candle and went down to the cellar for the wine; he preferred to do that alone.

Willimczyk had formerly owned a book and stationery store in Sosnowitz. In 1922 when the area was ceded to Poland he had moved out and decided on Gleiwitz, which was not too far away. At that time you could still take your belongings with you. Actually he had improved his situation by moving, for he had obtained a low-interest government loan, with which he was able to open a new store on Wilhelmstrasse, one of the best locations in Gleiwitz. And while previously his main business had been stationery and books had been more of a side line, he was now able to concentrate on books. The first years had been difficult, first the inflation and then the economic crisis, but in the thirties he had prospered, the engineering school had expanded, and in 1935 Gleiwitz had become a garrison town. Wil-limczyk furnished the army posts with training material, officers' wives came in to buy novels for the winter afternoons, and Rosa found ways of making the shop attractive to journalists and profes-sors. Little by little, it became the city's leading bookstore. In the summer of 1943, when most of the publishing houses were just about forced to stop putting out books, business had fallen off. Rosa had finally married and taken a job as a secretary on the *Traveler*. Lawyer Wondrak, whose name had been Wondraczek when Willimczyk first met him, was a good match. Yes, it was rumored that he took more interest in young men than in young women, but that was no concern of his father-in-law, and after all Rosa was not as young as she used to be. He had secretly hoped that she would never find a husband, because Frau Willimczyk had long been dead and Rosa, in addition to helping in the bookstore, had kept house for him. That had been a comfortable arrangement, but now that she was married she belonged to her husband, and Willimczyk had been managing quite well on his own.

The old man finally reappeared with a bottle of Markgräfler Gutedel 1942, from the Marschall von Bieberstein vineyard, which he opened and served ceremoniously. He was seventy-two years of age and absolutely refused to leave his shop or the city. He was not afraid of the Russians, what interest could they take in an old man like him, he was too old for Siberia, young people were what they needed there, and that was why he thought Rosa and her husband should make themselves scarce. What he feared the most was that the Germans would doom the city to destruction by stupidly trying to defend it. He was convinced that the war was lost, and he only hoped that the capitulation would come soon.

"In the First World War," he said, "the High Command capitulated as soon as enemy troops set foot on German soil. The same is bound to happen today. We are a country of the middle. Germany can only wage wars outside its frontiers—in our own country we destroy ourselves.

"The Russians will march in, it will be terrible. So it's better for you to get away. But they will go back to Moscow. Russia is an Asian country; in Europe the Russians lose their strength."

"But it's not just the Russians that are coming into our country," said Wondrak. "It's the Bolshevist ideology."

"I don't know," said Willimczyk thoughtfully. "Before 1914 I was often in the Russian part of Poland. I saw the Russians marching behind their church banners. And in the war I fought against them on the Bug. I know something about the Russians. They are first Russians and only then Christians or Bolsheviks or whatever you may call it. They will always be alien to us. Our country has often been threatened, it has always been a bulwark against the East. That is its historical mission. In the battle of Liegnitz we defeated the Mongols once and for all, they never came to Europe again."

"That's the whole trouble," said Willi heatedly. "There won't be another Liegnitz. We've become decadent."

"Our mistake," said the old bookseller, "has been to fight the West; we belong to Central Europe and at the same time to the West; when we fight the West, we are fighting ourselves. That is the lesson we should learn from three wars. By joining forces with the West, we'll keep the Mongols out of Europe. There will be a new Liegnitz, I'm convinced of that; it will be a little farther west, but at that point Asia will be stopped."

"I don't give a hoot where the new Liegnitz will be," said Willi, "if I have to run away from my country."

"I don't know either where it will be. But this country can't be defeated; it has always bled and borne its cross. The people who live in this part of the world seem to be born to suffer, but that may be why they love this soil so dearly. We are like the Irish, poor and Catholic; our people emigrate by the thousands—but none of them forget this parcel of ground. It's not beautiful country, no one would say it is. It demands hard work, but there's not enough work to go around. The air is dirtier than in other regions, the forests are darker, the women more pious, the rivers flow more slowly, the church is richer, the industrialists greedier. So what's so good about it? Eichendorff's Good-for-Nothing leaves the warm sunshine, leaves the water dripping from the roof; he takes his fiddle and away he goes, heading south, to Regensburg and Vienna, to the Danube, the Arno, the Tiber—and why not to Warsaw, Copenhagen, London? But how happy he is to be home again; not with the happiness that everyone feels who has a home; no, it's something more—it's a feeling for this parcel of earth that has cost more sweat, more tears, and more blood than any other . . . And when Eichendorff was old and tired he arranged to be buried not far from the Oder. The Oder, not the Rhine, is Germany's river of destiny. Once, long ago, I went farther west, but now I want to stay here and die; perhaps you will have to go farther west, to the other side of the Oder, where Eichendorff is buried."

The old bookseller liked to soliloquize; he often had no one to listen to him.

Willi had draped himself in silence. Rosa sipped nervously at her glass and looked at her father. She felt sorry for the old man. What would become of him when they were gone? Better not think about it.

"They call this a country with a cross," said Willimczyk, opening his hands in a gesture of helplessness. "All his life each one of us carries a cross over his shoulder. And no Simon of Cyrene comes to help us."

13

"I could listen to you for hours," said Hedel. "Even if I don't understand most of it, I could listen for hours and forget everything else in the world. You ought to be an actor. How did you get that way?"

Hedel was dumbfounded. Everything that was happening dumbfounded her. And most of all that she had been here in the strange house with Kotik all this time, when she had only meant to look around for a few minutes. It had been almost two hours, and her mother and grandmother would be waiting for her.

"Well, you see," said Kotik, "I read a lot. My sister played the piano all day and I read all day. It runs in the family. My mamochka reads a lot too."

"I hardly ever read," said Hedel. "But I know a lot of songs by heart. Marian hymns. I learned them at chapel. *Hail, Queen of Heaven, the ocean star; Maiden mother, meek and mild; Look down, O Mother Mary; Oh, who is she who ascends so high* . . ." She could have gone on forever, but stopped when she saw Kotik's faraway look.

Kotik had something very different on his mind. "Tell me," he said. "You and my brother Tonik, what did you do together? It wasn't so long ago. You didn't just take walks and hold hands, did you? What else did you do? I want to know."

"Nothing at all," said Hedel, startled and slightly annoyed at the question. "We went to the movies once or twice, and then we'd go to the Café Loske, and then . . ."

"And then what?" Kotik insisted. "What did you do then?"

"What business is it of yours? You shouldn't ask such questions," she said angrily. "Anyway, I have to go now. They must be worried about me."

But she made no move to go.

Kotik started in again: "You went with soldiers, didn't you? I saw you a couple of times at the Italian ice-cream parlor. I liked you, I

really did. I wanted to speak to you, but I thought I'd better wait
till I'm in uniform. Well, I will be in uniform soon, at Easter, I'll be
drafted into the Home Anti-Aircraft . . ."

"Have you got a cigarette?" Hedel looked around inquiringly.

"No, there aren't any. I've looked all over, and I haven't found
any. But I can roll you one with tea leaves."

"With what?" Hedel shook her head.

"When we were kids we used to make cigarettes with peppermint
tea, they bite your tongue something awful . . ."

Hedel laughed. "Peppermint tea? No, I'd rather eat some more
of the blueberry preserve."

"What must I do to please you?" Kotik asked with a penetrating
look. "Take you walking along the Wild Klodnitz in the summer. I
can promise you that. Take you for a pedal boat ride on the pond,
take you swimming in the lake—you'll be amazed, I dive from the
five-meter board—anything your soldiers do I can do just as well."

"What are you talking about? What do you mean 'my soldiers'?
So a soldier treated me to a dish of ice cream or took me to the Café
Loske and bought me a piece of cake on his travel coupons. What's
wrong with that? I've gone to the movies with this one and that
one, because soldiers always have two weeks' leave, and then they're
off to the front for a year or two. I've laughed with them, I've let
them kiss me. Why not? All day I'm running myself ragged in the
store. At home I have a mother with sciatica, who can hardly get
out of her chair, and a grandmother who says her rosary ten times
a day and spits in the soup, all this in two rooms. So what do I get
out of life? Nothing at all. And soldiers, you know, are different,
they have to go back to the war, they don't know if they'll ever come
home; that's why I like them, they give me the feeling that this hour
may be the last. That's it, believe it or not, I often think that this
may be my last happy hour . . ."

"Couldn't you take off those awful *galoty*?" Kotik cut in.

"You mean these pants?" said Hedel, standing up. She looked
down at her legs and smoothed out the material. "I made them
myself out of a horse blanket. You're right, they look terrible, they're

scratchy too, but for this kind of weather they're just what I need."

Here inside, though, it was warm, very warm. Kotik was right, why shouldn't she take off these bulky pants, especially as she was wearing thick stockings underneath?

Kotik wanted very much to give her a hand. "Oh oh, *hoppek!*" She gave him a playful tap on the fingers. "You're too young for that game."

"What do you mean too young?" Kotik wiped the hair off his forehead. "I'm sixteen. That's as good as a soldier these days."

"You're fifteen, if you're lucky," she said.

Kotik was so excited there was no holding him. "Why couldn't the two of us just stay here?" he suggested. "You quit digging ditches in the cold and I cut my HY sessions. Nobody will look for us here. That's for sure."

The idea had occurred to him a number of times before. His meeting with Hedel clinched it. Now he'd never leave the house, except maybe to scrounge some cigarettes.

"You must be crazy. If I don't go home tonight, all hell will break loose. I've been racking my brains for an explanation to give them."

"Same here," said Kotik in a conspiratorial tone. "My mother will sound the alarm if I don't come home . . . Let her. There are plenty of explanations these days. You've been called for hospital duty. Me, it's night exercises, courier service, guard duty, etcetera."

"Yes, but . . ." Hedel was flabbergasted. At the scheme Kotik had thought up and at the sudden presence of a hand on her knee. ". . . but we should have notified them in advance." She pulled her knee away.

"I'll attend to it," said Kotik. "I'll go see your mother, I'll tell her I've been sent by So-and-so . . ."

"Boy, you think of everything!"

She saw the table with the wine bottle and empty glasses, she saw the plate full of chicken bones, she saw the shoes on the carpet, she saw Kotik, and she saw the wall partitioned between light and shade.

Suddenly Kotik went down on his knees in front of her, laid his head in her lap, and hugged her thighs. Speechless with amazement,

Hedel waited to see what would happen. But nothing happened, because Kotik didn't know what he was supposed to do next. He just rolled his head back and forth in her lap.

Hedel Zock didn't get it. Everything had been so weird that day, so very different from any other day. The ride in the open truck to the Tarnowitz highway, digging the frozen ground, the sound of gunfire from the front, the refugees she had seen passing with sleds and hand carts. And then Kotik had turned up and brought her to this house; they had climbed a fence and squeezed through a window, she had eaten off strangers' plates and warmed her back against these people's stove. Kotik had read her something out of a book, and she had listened and thought about all sorts of things. And now this boy, who had been a total stranger to her a short while ago, was down on his knees, burying his flushed face in her lap and mumbling incomprehensible words. Slowly Hedel let herself slide to the floor and threw her arms around his trembling body. And in a long, slow movement, the two of them surrendered to a wild, confused dream.

14

THEY HAD SLEPT only a few hours. Shortly after seven Willi knocked at Rosa's door and they exchanged a few whispered words. Then he had gone out and made his way to his garden house; it had suddenly occurred to him that some letters he was bent on destroying were hidden in certain of his books and that his private files also included documents that he preferred to burn rather than let them fall into the hands of curious neighbors. Once that was done, he would go and get Koziollek, who had evidently, so he had assured Willi over the phone, got hold of a peasant's wagon.

Still groggy, Valeska staggered into the kitchen and put her face under the cold water tap. Halina was on her knees, lighting the fire in the kitchen stove, opening the fire door from time to time to make sure it was catching. Then she put on more and more wood, impatient for the rings to heat up. She had put on Irma's knitted jacket but she was still shivering. She would have liked to crawl into the stove.

Rosa checked her suitcase one last time for items she might have forgotten and items that had best be left behind. As she lay awake during the night, it had come to her that she had forgotten something of the utmost importance, but now she couldn't remember what it was. Irma, immobilized in the toilet, was wailing that the flush water had frozen. Halina prepared to heat water on the kitchen stove.

Valeska was brushing her hair, which she had been letting grow for the past year. While brushing from her forehead to her shoulders, she looked at herself, half in the oval mirror and half in the glassed dial of the wall clock. She tried to visualize the Russians marching in over Tarnowitzer Landstrasse or Bergwerkstrasse, but the picture wouldn't jell. No, the tanks, she felt sure, would come bursting out of Makoschau Forest. To her way of thinking, there had always been something sinister about that forest; someone had told her that it extended without a break all the way to Poland and Russia. She had walked in it now and then with her husband and children, but always on the fringe, fearing to get lost and never find the way back. Even in recent times (the people who lived near it were full of tales) a blackberry picker or mushroom gatherer had been known to disappear, and once when two lovers went for a stroll in the woods there had been no sign of them until a year later when their skeletons were found. By the time her braid was finished, she had pretty well convinced herself that the Russians would indeed come bursting out of the woods near Makoschau. "We'd better get to work in the garden before it's too light," she said. She had decided to bury the silver under the gooseberry bushes.

As in a dream, Rosa checked the hot water, put the cups on the table, and began mechanically to grind the barley coffee.

Valeska raised the blackout shades; the dawn was spreading over the eastern sky like a white undercoat, you could see it clearly through the veranda door. She opened a window; cold air and silence poured in—the only sounds were the bubbling of the kettle and the grinding of the coffee mill. Taking a pick and a spade, Rosa and Halina went out into the garden, where they shoveled the snow off the gooseberry bushes and broke the frozen ground. Valeska wrapped the silver in newspaper, each knife, fork, and spoon singly, the sauce boat, two goblets, the fish platter, and the cake slicer—which was only silver plated—stuffed the lot in an old pillowcase, and wrapped it in tarred roofing paper.

When she came into the garden with her bundle, Rosa was digging up a jar of the kind used for preserving fruit or vegetables. But in it there was something different, something that looked like paper. Valeska knelt down in the snow to look at it more closely. Yes, it was paper, evidently pages torn out of a copybook; and there was writing on them.

Cautiously Halina dug out more earth and a second jar appeared.

"Careful," said Valeska, her voice trembling with expectancy. She took the jar from Rosa's hands, removed one glove, and pushed away the metal clasp that secured the lid. She took out a rolled sheet of paper.

"It looks like the district magistrate's handwriting," she said, turning the page. "Yes, I'm pretty sure it's his writing." She caught sight of a date. "It looks like a diary," she said. "I must show this to Willi." She took her find to the garden house, where she surprised her brother pulling papers out of the desk drawers and throwing them into a laundry basket, which was already half full.

"Look," she said, winding her way between pieces of furniture and potted plants. "Look at what we've found in the garden, under the gooseberry bushes where we're going to bury the silver . . ."

In one hand, she held the preserving jar, in the other a few of the pages she had taken out. She spread them out on the desk.

"Papers in Herr Montag's handwriting. I'm sure of it, I know that handwriting. All in this jar, hermetically sealed. Rosa and Halina are digging up a second one. What do you think of it?"

Wondrak took one of the sheets, sniffed at it, held it up to the light, read the first sentences: "*Adalbert (Wojciech) Korfanty was born on April 30, 1873, the son of a miner and smallholder in Zawadze (which means barrier), a suburb of Laurahütte, close to the Russian border. He came of a German-minded family . . .*"

It was a disciplined, easily legible handwriting, the letters pressed closely together, with long flowery downstrokes.

"Looks like pages from a diary," said Valeska, who was paying closer attention to the expression on her brother's face than to the writing.

"Torn out of a notebook. Probably because the cover was hard cardboard that couldn't be bent," said Willi. He was in a hurry, he had no time, and yet he read the whole page through and then the next.

"Herr Montag," he said, still reading, "seems to have been writing a book about Korfanty, a biography. Have you any more of it?"

"About Korfanty?" said Valeska. "Yes, he told me once about some letters he was expecting from Kattowitz. But why Korfanty of all people?"

Rosa and Halina had dug a little deeper, but found nothing more. And there wasn't time enough now to dig up the whole garden. They lowered the silver into the hole they had dug and shoveled earth and snow over it. Rosa smoothed the snow with an osier broom, but it was obvious that the earth had been disturbed. She consoled herself with the thought that there would soon be more snow. The sky looked like snow, the air smelled of snow, but the cold would have to let up a little, then it would snow.

"What will you do with it?" Willi asked.

Valeska only shrugged. There was still so much to attend to. She wanted to look through Josel's room; perhaps she would find some little thing she could save for him. She had already packed his Rotring fountain pen, his white summer cap with the green tortoiseshell visor that he had been so fond of. And lastly a volume of Dostoevski that she had taken from his bedside table; nearly every page of it was scribbled with his notes and underlinings.

Montag's papers were his legacy, she couldn't just abandon them. "What can he have had in mind?" she pondered out loud.

"He must have buried them just before his death," said Willi. "Look, here's an entry dated August 30, 1939." He read aloud: "*The tragedy of the Upper Silesian is that he is neither a Pole nor a German, but an Upper Silesian, and that it would be an injustice to attach him either to Poland or to Germany. There should be a Free State of Upper Silesia. Korfanty was a Pole because he wanted to be a Pole. I have never felt myself to be a half-Jew, I don't even know what a half-Jew is, I was baptized a Catholic and I attended Catholic mass. But the more the Jews are persecuted in this country, the more I feel the Jewish part of me growing. I have always identified with the suffering part of humanity, and now I belong to the sufferers, to the Jews. I want to be like them. But getting back to K. No politician of that time, not even in Berlin, used the press so deliberately and consistently for his purposes as K. Certainly not in Prussia. The first thing he did when he decided to run for the Prussian Diet was to build up a broad propagandist base with the help of the newspapers. He bought and sold newspapers . . . he infiltrated his men into editorial offices; often he himself, under different names, was the responsible editor of three newspapers—*"

"To think that I knew nothing of all this," Valeska interrupted.

"I believe," said Willi, "that we should leave these papers where they were. They weren't meant for us."

Valeska gathered up the sheets and put them in order. "I am sure," she said firmly, "that he didn't want these notes to fall into the hands of the Russians. I mean to take them with me."

"But your suitcase is full, and so is your knapsack."

"I'll make room," she said calmly. "I'll just take out a pair of shoes. Something tells me we'll run into Montag's daughter one of these days—remember, she was living in Paris when he last heard from her. Then I'll be able to give her something to remember her father by . . ."

Rosa came rushing in. "Irma suddenly says she's not coming. She's locked herself in with the children, she says she won't come out until we're all gone, O my God . . . if only we were on our way!"

"Valeska, you go and talk to her," said Willi. "Damn it all, she and the children have got to come. We can't leave her here. And you, Rosa, go and tell Halina to burn all this." He pointed to the papers in the laundry basket. "One at a time in the kitchen stove. I'll go and see if Koziollek has found us a conveyance. Remember now, we want to be out of here by twelve . . . I don't want to be rounding you all up at the last moment." He threw on his coat and pulled his fur cap down low over his face. He was determined not to let anyone stop him.

First he went to the Hütten quarter. He'd get to Koziollek's in plenty of time; just now Koziollek was probably at Petersdorf, arranging for a wagon. Willi was surprised to see women in black on their way to mass, the same as on any other Sunday, and to find the streetcar still running. A no. 4 car stopped two steps away from him, so he hopped in and rode two stops to Hüttenstrasse. The only unusual thing about this car was that no fares were being collected. This seemed to amuse the conductor; at every stop he called out: "Free ride today. By order of our Führer! Compliments of the Greater German Reich."

Willi went to the front of the car and tried to question the motorman, who hadn't heard of any evacuation order. Maybe it hadn't got through. How about morale in the car barn? The man laughed mirthlessly. "The word is *gowno*. But a Prussian does his *powinność* to the end."

Neither Rosa nor Valeska knew that he had arranged for Gregor to stay in a monastery in the Hütten quarter. That was where he was going now. Prior Bonifazius was an old friend, dating back to his student days. Willi's brief flirtation with the Wittig brotherhood had not affected their friendship. After leaving the university, they had lost sight of each other, but when Bonifazius was appointed prior of the Franciscan monastery in Gleiwitz, they took to meeting from time to time and their old friendship revived. When it became necessary to find a safe retreat for young Grzegorz Bielski from Kattowitz, Willi had thought of the prior. Bonifazius had indeed taken the boy into the monastery and had even obtained new papers for him in the name of Gregor Biolek from Volhynia. Since then Willi had seen Gregor only three or four times and had stayed no more than half an hour—this on the advice of the prior, who thought it would be best for Gregor. Willi wanted to adopt the boy and take him home; this would be safe, he thought, now that Gregor had a new name. But Prior Bonifazius dissuaded him on the ground that the police would be sure to investigate the boy's genealogy and discover that his grandfather was Yizchak Weiss of Lwów. So Willi decided to wait. Once it occurred to him that the prior's reason for dissuading him was that he wished to take Gregor into the order as a novice. And that is just what he did when Gregor turned fifteen. Thus far Gregor had been well off with the Franciscans. But what would happen when the Russians occupied the city? The monks wouldn't leave the monastery, so wouldn't it be safer if Willi took the boy with him? He would find a place for him with the Franciscans in Görlitz or Dresden. He decided to talk it over with the prior and take his advice.

Wondrak rang the bell, then he kicked the wooden door, not because he was impatient, but because he remembered that there had been a power cut that morning which might still be going on.

A monk opened at once, but Willi had to identify himself before being admitted and taken to the prior.

Bonifazius thought it best that the boy should decide in their presence whether to stay in the monastery or to go with Dr. Wondrak and enter another monastery in the West.

Gregor was brought in. Surprised at finding himself face to face with Dr. Wondrak, he remained standing by the door, his dark habit silhouetted against the whitewashed wall.

15

She hadn't slipped on the ice, she had only turned her left ankle, and now she was hobbling home from church. Her left ankle was her weakness; this wasn't the first time. Why did it have to happen now, when she probably needed her feet more than ever before in her life. "Blessed Lord Jesus!" Anna bit her lips with pain.

Every step was agony, because the going was so bumpy. Snow had fallen during the night and the sidewalk hadn't been properly stamped down. She wouldn't mention it at home, why upset everybody? She would secretly rub her ankle with liniment and put on a tight bandage; then if she kept it warm it ought to get better in a few days. Anyway, what was a sprained ankle as long as she had her Franzek.

She was really lucky to have him at home. All the other husbands were in the war; you seldom saw a man between sixteen and sixty on the street. They would have taken her Franzek too, but he kept being deferred as indispensable to the war effort, and after all a locomotive engineer was practically a soldier, a home-front soldier, as Herr Thonk was always saying. Home front made a difference, though, you slept in a warm bed, while a soldier would be freezing in a cold dugout. Once Franz had volunteered for the front; blessed Lord Jesus, when she thought of all the excitement until they'd gotten him out of it. He didn't even have to join the Volkssturm, though they'd taken old man Berthold, the deaf and dumb glazier, and Hrabinsky in spite of his wooden leg.

Anna just couldn't imagine living without her Franzek, he had been there as long as she could remember. True, she never could have imagined living without her children either, and then they had left home one after another, and she went on living all the same. But maybe that was only because she recognized all her children in her husband; sometimes when her Franzek was excited, she would hear herself saying: "Just like little Paulek"; or when he was enthusiastic about something: "Just like Ulla"; or when he stood at the mirror combing his hair: "Just like Tonichek."

Now she was sorry she had gone out. But it was Sunday, and as far back as she could remember she had never failed to go to church of a Sunday. But everything was different now. She simply couldn't persuade herself that this Sunday had been like any other Sunday and this mass like any other mass, except that Father Jarosch had celebrated it and said the Agnus Dei with special fervor. There hadn't been any sermon, but then few of the faithful had showed up, and some of them had left after a single Our Father as though they had come only to see if mass was still being celebrated. She had seen no sign of her friends Frau Dolezich and Frau Wieczorek; and Frau Bortel, who had always waited outside the portal in the hope of a chat, had left right after the blessing.

While hobbling home, she thought of all the things that were different. The sound of the big guns, Kotik staying out all night, the Holy Communion which almost all those present had taken, the anthem *Behold a House of Glory*, only one stanza of which had been sung, the Jüngst villa on Friedrichstrasse where the windows had all been smashed, the overloaded farm wagons leaving town by way of Eichendorff-Allee—actually everything was different, and she wished she had somebody to talk it over with, someone who might have made all this seem a little less strange.

It was warm in the kitchen; before going out she had put plenty of coal on the fire. Thank the Lord, there was no need to scrimp on coal, because almost every day Franz brought her a briefcase full of briquettes from the depot. Kotik wasn't back yet. Maybe she should go to the schoolhouse where they met for the HY exercises, maybe someone would tell her which army post Kotik had gone to for his night problem. Heavens above, what did they want of these children, who were hardly big enough to hold a rifle?

While massaging her ankle, groaning all the while, she listened to "Treasure Chest" on the radio; she seldom missed it, it was as much a part of her Sundays as High Mass. She had read lots of novels in her life, but never any poetry, poetry was just too weird; but when Mathias Wiemann read poems, they became perfectly clear and simple, she understood every line, but once he had finished she forgot them. In between poems there was usually piano music; that was more in Ulla's line, it didn't mean much to Anna. Thank goodness, the pieces were always short, an allegro, an andante, a scherzo, or else a scherzando, an impromptu, a larghetto; little by little she became familiar with these terms, she had learned them for her daughter's sake. But now the piano had long been orphaned. That made Franz very sad; he was used to hearing Ulla practice and he couldn't do without it. Sometimes, when he thought no one was looking, he opened the lid, took the green felt mat off the keys, and touched them gently with his fingers; it always came as a surprise to him that those beautiful, resplendent, ivory-yellow keys consented to sound for so rough a hand. Ulla had come to stay at Christmas, though only for two days; both mornings she had practiced and no one was allowed to disturb her. Now she was a real pianist, though because of the total war she had to work as a nurse in Dresden and couldn't concertize. A real pianist, so she had said, has to practice several hours a day to keep her hands and fingers supple. After the war she would play in public again. She refused to accompany the carol singers on Christmas Eve, on the ground that a real pianist doesn't play such things, but she made up for it by improvising variations on the hymn *From Heaven High I come to you,* and Anna had liked that.

Anna was worried about little Kotik. He was the only son she had left, and at fifteen after all he was still a child. It was a terrible thing, their teaching these children how to fire bazookas, but luckily there weren't enough of these newfangled weapons, or they'd send the *hoppeks* into the trenches with them. Four of her sons were soldiers now, fighting all over the world, and Bruno lay buried in Africa. But Kotik wasn't a soldier yet, and she wouldn't let him go.

Some people claimed that Kotik was her favorite son; they said she spoiled him and let him get away with anything. This of course she denied, but to herself she admitted that she was fondest of her little one, because she could see that he took after her. Kotik alone had inherited something she detected in none of the others, the love of reading. In the beginning she had brought him books from the

Kaffanke lending library, but for years now *he* had been supplying *her* with reading matter, not only from Kaffanke's on Germaniaplatz, but also from the municipal library and from a shop in Hindenburg, which specialized in exotic adventure stories and English crime novels, the most exciting of course being a combination of the two, a crime novel that happened in India or among the tongs of Shanghai. They would read the books together and try to guess who the murderer was, and it was almost always Kotik who figured it out first. Lately, to be sure, he had been bringing home books she didn't understand. Stories about dikes and floods by Theodor Storm or *The Magic Mountain* by Thomas Mann, which she had dropped after the first five pages, it was so boring; the story just didn't get started. She'd let Kotik read it first and tell her about it. He had lately been bringing home books from somewhere; they already had two shelves full, there were piles of them on the chest of drawers and the piano, and Kotik had taken the old shoes out of the shoe chest and put in books instead.

Heavens above, what if she had to leave them all in case this evacuation thing actually happened. That was a word she'd never heard before, and now everybody was saying it. She had talked it over with Franzek, and they had both come to the conclusion that they just couldn't run off with a suitcase and a knapsack and drop everything. Their possessions didn't amount to much compared to those of Vally Piontek and some even richer people she could think of, but all the same Franz had worked all his life for them. And anyway they had no idea where to go, they had no one in the West who would take them in, except in Kreuzburg or Oppeln, and she had heard that the Russians were already there.

She decided to cook a real Sunday dinner. She would open a jar of potted meat, she'd have Polish dumplings with sauerkraut and cracklings, and for dessert there'd be pickled pumpkin. Forgetting her sprained ankle, she stood up to see what she had in the pantry, for her provisions were gradually running low. But when the pain reminded her of her ankle, she lay back down on the sofa and went on reading *The Dairywoman of Ottakring*.

"Blessed Lord Jesus!" said Anna. She had been so carried away by the story that she hadn't heard Franz come into the kitchen. He was glad to be home from work a little earlier than usual. He knelt down by the stove and put in a piece of wood. He liked the sound of the flames and the hum of the kettle. He missed little Kotik and wondered out loud whether the HY had any right to keep the boy out all night and day on some exercise. After all he was neither a soldier nor a Flak auxiliary.

"That's the way it is," Anna groaned. "I'm sure he'd rather be here, reading all these books; he has hardly had time to look at them."

"More books?" said Franz, motioning toward the pile on the piano. "There's looting all over town, sometimes in broad daylight." So he had heard people saying.

"What are you getting at?" Anna asked suspiciously.

"Just what I've heard. A lot of rich people have cleared out, leaving their houses and apartments empty. And gangs of kids are roaming around looting . . ."

"Go wash your hands," said Anna.

"I hear they've hanged a man for looting in front of the Main Post Office on Niederwallstrasse," said Franz. "Strung him up, just like that. An *ostarbeiter*. They say he took a silver pitcher out of an empty house . . . But they can't do that to a twelve- or thirteen-year-old, can they?"

Anna broke into a coughing fit.

"Take some hot water and sugar," said Franz. And then in a tone of deep concern, "Not getting sick, are you?"

"It's better now," she said, drawing a deep breath. "It's just on account of Kotik, I'm so worried. But have you heard anything about the evacuation?"

There were so many rumors going around, a new one every few minutes. Some said the Russians had taken Gross-Strehlitz and were heading for Gleiwitz, some said they'd been thrown back at Tarnowitz. Zielonka had come in with a report that the Russians had reached the Oder at Cosel and were encircling the industrial zone, the idea being to take it without damaging the munitions factories, which would go right on working . . . for the Russians. The workers had nothing to fear, only the Party big shots would get it in the neck. But most of them had already cleared out.

The trains that had gone west in the last few days hadn't come back, there were hardly any locomotives left. All day he and Zielonka had been working on a junked locomotive, trying to make it run. They could finish the job next day, but they could fiddle with it for another two or three days if they liked. "Anyway," Franz concluded, "I've thought up a plan."

"But what about the evacuation?" Anna persisted. That was what interested her the most.

"I don't know," said Franz. "We've been told to report for work tomorrow. That's all I know."

"But what about the gunfire out there?" Anna started peeling potatoes.

Franz shrugged. "You went to church all the same, didn't you?"

"Of course I went to church," said Anna. "There weren't many people, and mass was celebrated by Father Jarosch, the curate."

"What did he say?"

It was always best to be guided by the Church, Franz thought, especially in difficult situations.

"There wasn't any sermon. And I must admit we were all glad to get out of the bitter cold."

"But what did the people say?" Franz was helping her peel the potatoes.

"Oh, just rumors," said Anna. She liked to keep the conversation general. He preferred facts.

"They say the Archpriest has been arrested."

"Pattas?"

"Yes. They say he was arrested for saying the war was lost."

"Everybody thinks so," said Franz.

"Yes, thinks. But nobody says it out loud."

Franz walked back and forth in the kitchen. He couldn't possibly sit still with the thoughts that were prancing around in his head. He hadn't been so upset since the time a swarm of bees had flown away. But that was long ago. He hadn't kept bees for years. "I've got a plan," he repeated. "You and Kotik will come with me tomorrow.

We'll just take a suitcase and a carton, that won't attract too much attention. I'll hide you in my tender and take you to Heydebreck."

"But where can Kotik be?" Anna broke in.

"Do you understand what I'm saying? We'll beat it away from the Russians. I'll hide you in the tender. Zielonka is coming with us, he's taking his wife and two kids and his old mother. I'm not so keen on his old mother. If anything should happen on the way . . ."

"I don't understand," said Anna. She really didn't understand.

"I'm trying to tell you that I'll take you across the Oder with my locomotive. You'll be safe over there for the time being. Then I'll come back and attend to things here . . ."

Anna started grating potatoes for the dumplings. "So you think we should get out while all our neighbors stay here?"

Like most people Anna felt safer in a crowd.

"I don't know what the neighbors are planning, but everyone thinks of number one first, and the locomotive gives us a chance to get away . . ."

"You can't make me leave here without Kotik. So don't waste your breath."

Franz gazed spellbound at his wife's fingers that were moving a big yellow potato over the grater with amazing rapidity.

"No, of course not," said Franz. "But he's sure to be back before long."

"I certainly hope so. When we're having Polish dumplings! He's so fond of them. Let's talk it over with him when he gets here."

"Good idea," said Franz. And a moment later: "I'm going down to the cellar for the pickax."

"Pickax? What do you need the pickax for on Sunday? In the middle of winter?"

"To dig a hole in the garden. They're all doing it, to hide things."

"Yes, that's an idea," said Anna thoughtfully, wondering what they should hide. But she couldn't think of anything valuable enough to be worth burying in the garden. Now she was grating an onion; that's what gave the dumplings their flavor.

The doorbell rang.

"That must be Kotik," said Anna with a sigh of relief. "He has a key, but lately he's taken to ringing." She was so glad Kotik had come home that she burst into tears. Unless it was the onion.

Franz opened the door and stood there awhile talking with someone. Anna wiped her hands and hobbled out to them.

"Herr Mazura," Franz explained, "thinks we should take a rug and a mattress down to the air-raid shelter, because if the shelling comes any closer we'll probably be spending the next few days there."

"My advice," said Herr Mazura.

"Then you think . . . ?" Anna began anxiously.

"Definitely." He had heard that shells had already fallen on Petersdorf. And some of their neighbors had already moved to the air-raid shelter.

"Sacred heart of Jesus!" said Anna. "And our Kotik not home yet. What'll I do?" She let her arms droop and hobbled back to her bowl of potatoes.

"I don't think it's that bad yet," said Franz. "But it's true that things can move fast."

"Anyway," said Herr Mazura. "You better burn the stuff quick. You know . . ."

Franz Ossadnik didn't know what Herr Mazura was talking about.

"You want I should spell it out, Herr Neighbor?" Herr Mazura was losing patience. "All right, you gotta burn swastika flags and all Führer pictures, and every book with a Führer picture in it. When the Russians see them things in a house, they blow it up. And better burn your railroader uniform too. They might think it was something connected with the SS."

16

THE LUGGAGE WAS READY, all lined up in the entrance. Valeska had taken one more look through the house. In Josel's room she had found a peacock feather she thought she'd like to take along. Again she wound the clock that she had wound only the night before—as usual, while brushing her hair. Deep in thought she had picked up her books of music, and leafed through some of them. Oughtn't she, she reflected, to take *The Complete Waltzes of Chopin*? Or mightn't it be better to take Schumann's *Album for the Young*, or perhaps nothing at all. Then she remembered that she had already asked herself these same questions a dozen times. She paced the floor, stared at the myrtle in the window, at Millet's *Angelus* on the wall, at the lamp with the green silk shade, but without really seeing anything. She thought of going to Rosa's room to check her watch against Rosa's, or to Irma's to ask about little Roswitha's fever, but then she remembered she had done that twice that morning—and she had also compared watches with Rosa. She wasn't really there anymore, that's what made her so restless, and every time she fastened her eyes on some familiar sight, it made her heart bleed.

There were almost two hours left before Willi would come for them; that gave her time for a quick dash to church, though it was too late for High Mass. Then it came to her that she had promised Herr Apitt the day before to bid him good-bye when the time came—she hadn't suspected that it would be so soon.

Good, she'd go right away. For fear of being held up by questions, she called out to Rosa that she was going to pay a quick good-bye visit and would be back in plenty of time, not to worry.

Outside, the cold hit her in the face. The streets were full of people, mostly women hurrying to church. She headed in the opposite direction. She didn't know what she would say to Herr Apitt, she only knew that she had to see him and say good-bye. And she wanted to listen to him one more time. But would he even open to her today?

She should have arranged a signal with him. She was sure she wouldn't be so bold as to pound on his door and call his name as she had done the day before.

The outer door was open and she slipped in. She climbed the stairs quietly; outside Herr Apitt's door she loosened her head scarf, pushed it back, and rubbed her cheeks to warm them. Just as she was screwing up her courage to ring the bell, she heard a sound on the other side of the door, the security chain was removed, and there stood old Herr Apitt, bent slightly to one side. He was wearing the same dark glasses as the day before and a green cap that looked almost luminous in the daylight. Before she could open her mouth, Herr Apitt said in a soft, gentle voice: "Come right in, Frau Piontek. I've been expecting you for ages."

Valeska was speechless. She followed Herr Apitt through the entrance and kitchen to the living room. "Don't look," he said with a gesture indicating the disorder in the kitchen, "it's not very neat. I haven't had anyone to keep house for me in a long time."

Valeska couldn't remember passing through that room the day before. Or had it been so dark that she couldn't see it, but had only smelled it? She was glad when at last they reached the living room. It still seemed unnecessarily crowded with cupboards and chests and vitrines, but in the gray all-penetrating winter light all this furniture didn't seem as menacing as the day before. The immense cupboard, which had frightened her so in the darkness, was only a common rustic cupboard and the cabinet with its colored glass doors, one of which was broken, looked touchingly fragile. The tall tile stove, the footstool beside it, the phonograph in its old place, and the portrait on the wall—all these she found reassuring.

"I've come to say good-bye," said Valeska. "We're leaving in two hours. This morning an evacuation order came through, for all families with children." When Herr Apitt said nothing, she added with a sigh: "Who would have expected it to happen so quickly . . ."

She looked at her hand and at the crocheted cloth on the table. "There are no more trains. The western lines have all been cut. We're going by road in some sort of cart. Maybe it would have been better to stay here, come what may . . ." Valeska had asked herself the same question a hundred times in the last few days. And now it just came bursting out of her.

Herr Apitt had no comment to make. He had told Frau Piontek the day before that when the time came there could be no other decision for her. And now the time had come. For him, too, there was only one way, and his mind was made up. He sucked at his bad tooth, producing an audible squeak.

"I never thought a person could be driven out of the place where they'd grown up. Frankly, only two hours ago I was thinking I couldn't give up what my husband and I built up together. Because if we go away, we'll have nothing left. That's how it is in a war. My brother talked me into it. I mean, he convinced me that this is the right thing because of the children and grandchildren. We're heading for an uncertain future . . . I've thought about it. I envy you, Herr Apitt, for your certainty . . ."

Apitt raised his hand to stop her, but she went on: "No, no, don't interrupt me. I can't say you're making it too easy for yourself, no, because what you're doing is the hardest thing of all. Old man Willimczyk, the bookseller on Wilhelmstrasse, you know him, my brother married his daughter, he's seventy-two, he has been collecting sleeping pills. When the Russians break into his shop, they'll find only his corpse . . . Tomorrow shalt thou be with me in paradise . . . I can't do it. My religion forbids me . . ." Valeska's voice had risen to a scream.

Feeling utterly helpless, Apitt took refuge in phrases: "You mustn't say such things. A sincere Catholic like you. You must have hope, even when things look blackest . . ."

"Some things," said Valeska, absently tracing the pattern of the embroidered tablecloth with her forefinger, "are more than a human being can bear, they destroy us. God took our sufferings on himself and let himself be nailed to the cross. Our sins were to blame. Now we shall all have to die like Christ, each one of us nailed separately to the cross, without even the hope of salvation."

Breathing heavily, Apitt stood up and went over to the phonograph. Music alone could save him now. He sat down beside the bed, held a record in his hand, and stared at the black disk.

"I wish," said Valeska, "I could look just once through a window into the place we call the future; not everybody's, just my own; oh, if only for just a second, I could see myself as I'll look in a year or a month ... heavens above, I know such thoughts are sinful." Valeska's thoughts frightened her. She was too shaken to cross herself.

"No one who has looked through that window will ever return, Frau Valeska," said Apitt. He put a record on.

"I lost control," said Valeska. "God forgive me." She sat up straight in her chair. "These events are just too much for me. I believe in Jesus Christ, the son of God . . ."

Then the music began; the cavatina from Opus 130 reduced them both to silence, darkened the room, extinguished the fires of their yearnings and memories, transported them into a timeless time. Listening, they were carried away as by a dream, no, as by life.

They had no idea how much time had passed since the music stopped. Apitt said softly: "Think of it, Beethoven was stone deaf when he composed that quartet; he never heard it performed . . . I thought, I must listen to it over and over again and get to the bottom of its secret. But now I know, you can move closer to the secret, but you can never get to the bottom of it. You can come closer to God, but never penetrate His essence. Music is the highest of all things. Like the world itself, like ideas, whose multiple manifestation is the world of individual things, it is a reflection of the total will. That is why music affects us more powerfully and deeply than the other arts; for they speak only of the shadow, while music speaks of the substance. I have listened to Schubert so often that I sometimes thought his yearning would tear me apart, I have your beloved Chopin here, but listening to late Beethoven teaches me that perfect music is the world and that the world is embodied music. The intimate relationship between music and the essence of all things is brought home to us by the fact that the appropriate music seems to communicate the most secret essence of a scene, an event, an action, a place. This string quartet encompasses my life, the life of every man who knows how to listen to it . . . and it encompasses my death as well . . ."

It was time for Valeska to go. She stared at the portrait on the opposite wall, which had been troubling her for some time. "Tell me, who is that in the picture?"

"Schopenhauer," said old Herr Apitt. In that moment he looked very old.

17

THEY HAD BEEN riding for hours in an overcrowded train. It had stopped several times in the middle of nowhere and been shunted back and forth. The stations they passed were unlit; unable to read the signboards in the gloom, the travelers had no idea where they were. Once the booming of the guns had been fairly close; hearing machine-gun fire, they were beginning to think that the train was heading straight for the front. But then the battle sounds had receded and were drowned out by the regular clanking of the rails. The compartments were packed; children covered with blankets sprawled on the grown-ups' laps. People were sitting in the aisle amid suitcases and boxes; leaning on one another, they would doze off, only to wake up at every sudden jolt. When the train was running, it was so overheated that they were all in a sweat; impossible to turn the heat off or open a window. When the train stopped for any length of time, the compartments were quick to cool off, and the travelers wrapped themselves in coats and scarves.

When Traute Bombonnek woke up, the compartment was bathed in a dingy gray light that made faces look like pale masks. The sound of the wheels was sharp and hollow. She breathed on the frozen windowpane and rubbed away the ice; looking out through the hole, she saw a white surface, cloaked in a dreary light. An iron bridge pier passed; that must be the Oder. Fräulein Bombonnek furtively crossed herself.

The altered sound had awakened a few others. Those sitting by the windows breathed and rubbed and peered, trying to get a glimpse of the outside world. Frau Duda, who had arranged her seven children in the compartment in such a way that they were all somehow able to sleep, cried out with half-repressed triumph: "We've made it. We're crossing the Oder. Thanks be to the Blessed Virgin!"

Herr Thonk, who had fallen asleep on his suitcase, toppled forward and began to cough; he had coughed half the night and had stopped only when Frau Duda gave him some of the precious onion syrup she had brought along for her children. One of her seven children was always sick and she had a carryall full of medicine. When her two daughters sitting beside her woke up and rubbed their eyes, she joined them in murmuring a prayer—and the others gave them a grateful glance.

"The worst is behind us," said Herr Thonk, spitting into his handkerchief. "I was scared stiff during the night with all that backing and filling. I thought we'd never get through."

"It took us all night to cover a distance that normally takes an hour," said Fräulein Bombonnek matter-of-factly.

"As long as we were moving, I was easy in my mind," said another woman, whose face was ashen. "I wasn't scared until we stopped still. They say a train was captured by the Russians in East Prussia. They raped all the women and sent them back to the city on foot. In this cold!"

There was a long stop in Neisse. They were given hot soup and their names were put on lists. They were allowed to stretch their legs on the platform but forbidden to leave the station. The other tracks were full of trains overcrowded with refugees. Here the travelers learned that their train was one of the last to get through; a few hours later, the Russians had reached the line at Ehrenforst and blown up the tracks.

In Waldenburg there was a short stop. The travelers were given hot tea sweetened with saccharin. Here again they were counted and their names were entered on new lists. This procedure was repeated in Hirschberg, where an official at the head of a commission informed them that this was the last stop and they would be distributed among the surrounding villages.

Traute Bombonnek took her suitcase and looked about for a train going in the direction of Cologne or Dortmund. From there she'd manage to go on to Kamen. But the conductor informed her that no one would be allowed to buy tickets to destinations more than seventy-five kilometers from his place of work and residence; in other words, to any station beyond Waldenburg; for longer distances a special authorization was needed. Before she could ask where that was obtainable (in her eagerness to rejoin her Prohaska she was determined to leave no stone unturned), the commission came back and ordered the passengers to alight. The people in Fräulein Bombonnek's compartment were assigned to Agnetendorf: "Over there you'll find the bus that will take you there."

Again they were counted and again their names were entered on lists.

Fräulein Bombonnek left her suitcase and went up to the official. "Have I heard you right? Did you say Agnetendorf? Is it true that the people in this group will be taken to Agnetendorf?"

"Yes," said the official. "You will all stay in this district for the present. You're in luck. It's quiet here. Like peacetime."

Herr Thonk was taken with a coughing fit while looking desperately for his briefcase.

"This group to Hermsdorf, this group to Warmbrunn, this one to Agnetendorf," shouted the official, while showing the people their buses.

"I've always wanted to see the Riesengebirge," said Frau Duda. "But who can afford such things with seven children?"

Her two daughters were fighting. She pulled them over to her and wiped the smaller one's nose. She wanted so much to enjoy the houses she could see from the bus, white with black wooden roofs, and the snow-covered mountains that merged with the white winter sky . . . But when she thought that these two suitcases and the children's knapsacks contained all she had left in the world, she just wanted to cry.

"But Gerhart Hauptmann, the world-famous writer, lives in Agnetendorf," Fräulein Bombonnek suddenly remembered to her surprise.

"Yes'm," said the bus driver. "On the outskirts kind of, his place is called Wiesenstein, it's a regular castle."

She really hadn't expected anything like this, to end up in Agnetendorf after her agitated trip. One summer she had thought seriously of visiting Hauptmann; maybe he'd let her do a few sketches of him or even pose for a bust. She had written a letter, the summer was over by the time the answer came, and the answer hadn't been encouraging enough to warrant a definite plan for the following summer. It hadn't been a refusal, oh no, Frau Hauptmann had merely said she could come but her husband didn't have much time. That was the year when the newspapers were devoting long articles to his eightieth birthday, and she had modeled his head in clay after a photograph, but she hadn't been pleased with it and had destroyed it. Now she'd be able to make some sketches, she might even be able to do some work in clay, and once she was in Agnetendorf she'd surely be allowed to call on him. Then, one of these days, she would go to Hirschberg and take a look at the Kuh Bookshop, which had been famous for art books before the war. There was no hurry now. She could resume her journey to the Ruhr when the winter was over.

In a schoolroom in Agnetendorf the refugees were registered again and distributed among various families. The room was overheated and Fräulein Bombonnek began to perspire. Frau Duda's children lay down on the floor and fell asleep.

The man who assigned them their quarters was the local teacher. He was corpulent but astonishingly nimble, and he was wearing round glasses fastened on one side by a black shoelace instead of a bow. Fräulein Bombonnek was assigned to a Frau Haffner. But instead of going to her new lodgings, she sat down at one of the desks and waited until all the others had received their assignments and left the room.

The teacher was surprised to see her sitting there alone. "Have I forgotten you? What was your name?"

"No, no," she said, coming out from behind the desk. She had taken her coat off and draped her shawl over her shoulders to give it the effect of a stole. "I've stayed because I thought you might help me. You see, I'm a teacher myself, that is, I've been giving art and drawing lessons since the war started, but I'm really a painter and sculptress . . ." She paused a moment to lend emphasis to the an-nouncement that was to follow. "Two years ago I was awarded the City of Gleiwitz Art Prize. You must have read about it, my name is Traute Bombonnek."

The teacher, who had never heard the name, plucked at the shoelace that secured his glasses. "Why yes, of course I remember. Congratulations."

"I thought you might assign me to a tiny little room in Wiesenstein Castle . . ."

"Hmm, that's where I've put the Duda family. Seven children. I wouldn't know where else to put them."

Traute Bombonnek disliked having to speak so plainly, but obviously the man didn't see what she was getting at. "You can imagine why I'm asking you this. You see, I can't help thinking that fate had a purpose in bringing me here to Agnetendorf. Oh, if only I could observe Herr Hauptmann on his walks and do some sketches of him."

The teacher was relieved. "That's easily arranged," he said. "You mean you'd like to visit the Hauptmanns?"

"But," Fräulein Bombonnek persisted, "if I lived there it would be so much simpler and less obtrusive. He's an old gentleman after all, I'm sure he doesn't like being importuned. But late portraits of this kind are likely to be extremely valuable someday."

Through his round glasses the teacher watched Fräulein Bombonnek's narrow face and saw how much this meant to her. "Wait," he said. "Maybe something can be managed. I'll try."

He went to the adjoining room to telephone. Apparently it took him some time to get his connection. Then, if Fräulein Bombonnek wasn't mistaken, he was speaking to Frau Hauptmann, who was evidently furious at having a family with so many children foisted on her and certainly didn't want yet another person, especially not an artist. Traute Bombonnek swelled with pride at being referred to as an artist, and yet it embarrassed her in connection with the great man in Wiesenstein Castle. So now she was an artist; she must try to forget that she had started out as a handicrafts teacher at St. Mary's Convent School.

She could see that the teacher wanted very much to help her. "For the present," he said, "I'll take you to Frau Hafner's. You'll have a splendid room that she rents to vacationers in the summer. You'll have a fine view of the mountains with the Big Snow Bowl and the Little Snow Bowl and the Big Crested Helmet and the High Wheel, and in the foreground the Hemmhübel and Wiesenstein . . ." He stopped to consider. "And by the way, it's not far from the Hafners' to the schoolhouse. Maybe you could help me. I could use a drawing teacher . . ."

"Of course," said Fräulein Bombonnek delightedly. "Only I don't know how long we'll be here. It's not for me to decide."

"Only God can decide how long we shall have peace and quiet around here," said the teacher. "Until very recently we thought nothing could happen to us, and it's still hard for us to realize that people at the other end of the province have had to leave home . . ."

"We felt the same way," said Fräulein Bombonnek. "People from the Rhineland, who had been bombed out, came to us with a single suitcase and we treated them like tourists. And now it's us traveling with a single suitcase, and we don't even know when and where our journey will end. We don't really sympathize with other people's trouble until it hits us."

"Come," said the teacher. "I'll help you. You need a rest after your grueling trip. Once you've had a good sleep, the world will look more cheerful. And one of these days I'll take you to Wiesenstein. I often visit there. The old man likes teachers. He says that he thinks of himself as a teacher of the nation . . ." He plucked at the string on his glasses.

They were a strange pair as they walked side by side on the edge of the village street, she tall and thin, he short and stout, he hopping more than walking. The dusk rose up from the valley, sucking the whiteness out of the snow and bathing the landscape in gray fog.

When the teacher put the suitcase down in the entrance to Frau Hafner's house, Fräulein Bombonnek said: "If you have a moment, I'll tie up your glasses properly. I can't bear to see you plucking at your ear all the time."

Before going to bed, Traute Bombonnek listened to the news in Frau Hafner's kitchen. The Wehrmacht High Command reported heavy fighting in the Upper Silesian industrial zone, especially in the Oppeln-Gleiwitz area. Traute Bombonnek gave a start on hearing the name of her hometown. Then the Deutschland station was running *The Cousin from Squeedunk*, an operetta by Eduard Künnecke.

"I don't much listen to the radio, but I love operettas," said Frau Hafner, turning the volume up high.

Fräulein Bombonnek wasn't in the mood and retired to her room. It was simply furnished. The wallpaper featured boughs of Japanese cherry trees. There was a small wooden cross hanging on the wall. They're Protestants here, she thought. The window was not blacked out, only curtained. She had expressed surprise, but Frau Hafner had reassured her; not one foreign plane had come this far, and there had never been an air-raid alert, except for practice in the morning.

Traute Bombonnek massaged her hands with a cream she had brought with her in a small jar. Then she switched off the lamp and went to bed. The bed was high, she literally had to climb into it. In the winter these people slept with two featherbeds, one on top of them, the other underneath.

She heard the music through the wall and thought: He's fat but sprightly and graceful in his movements. He has quick, intelligent, mysterious eyes. Of course he's very different from Prohaska! He appealed to her in a very different way.

18

Ɪᴛ ʜᴀᴅ ᴀʟʟ ɢᴏɴᴇ so fast and it had all gone so slowly, they had made some progress but not enough, they had run behind the farm wagon, they had sweated and shivered, mostly shivered, and taken shelter from the icy wind behind the tarp when they could. But the worst was when the convoy stopped moving and there was no way of knowing when it would go on, because the road was crammed with fugitives as far as the eye could see and the snow was piled so high on both sides of the road that passing was out of the question. Any vehicle that attempted it got hopelessly bogged down after the first few yards. So they waited, jumping up and down, slapping their legs and shoulders. If the wait was too long, someone might make a fire in the middle of the road and people would flock to it from all sides to warm their hands and exchange new rumors and old fears. And when the convoy finally started moving again, the muffled figures cast a grateful glance at the gray, pitiless sky.

It had all gone so fast and it had all gone so slowly. Valeska Piontek was still confused when she thought back on the past hours. She had been last to leave the house on Strachwitzstrasse. Once again she had gone from room to room, looking for Halina to bid her an irrevocably last good-bye, but Halina was nowhere to be found. Perhaps she had hidden for fear of changing her mind at the last moment, for Valeska now realized that Halina's only reason for staying behind was fear that if an escapee from a concentration camp with close-cropped hair and no papers went along it would endanger the Piontek family. And her brother's immediate acceptance of Halina's decision suggested that he felt the same way. Valeska touched the little canvas bag that Halina had sewed for her that morning, into which Valeska had put a handful of earth, of Upper Silesian homeland, and a sprig of myrtle broken from the window myrtle with which she had decorated Irma's wedding table and the baptismal cushions of the three children, and a few sprigs of which she had laid on the eyelids of her dead husband. If she were to die anywhere outside Silesia, she wished to be buried with this little bag of home soil and the sprig of green myrtle.

Before leaving the music room, she gazed at the wall where Millet's *Angelus* hung between the piano and the clock. It was only a cheap reproduction, she would be able to buy another later on, but now she felt that she had to take the picture with her on her flight. She took it down off the wall, removed it from its frame, folded it several times until it was no larger than the palm of her hand, and slipped it into her coat pocket. A fragment of memory she could not live without. Then she went to the wall clock, opened the case, and stopped the pendulum. The time was exactly twelve seventeen. When suddenly the familiar ticking ceased, the house seemed so strange and bleak that without stopping to look around she left it with swift steps.

The others had gone ahead. Dragging the luggage on two sleds, they were fighting their way to the Ostertor, where Koziollek was waiting with the farm wagon. Valeska soon caught up with them and trudged along beside Rosa, who had not yet recovered from her shock at seeing her husband suddenly turn up with a Franciscan monk. Valeska herself was rather taken aback. The face under the hood seemed somehow familiar, could it be one of her former pupils? But then Willi told them in a whisper that it was young Gregor Bielski from Kattowitz, whom he had wished at one time to adopt and who was now on his way to another monastery in the Reich. Irma was surprised too, but Rosa was really flabbergasted. Where on earth could Willi have dug up this Gregor—wearing a monk's habit of all things? But this was hardly the time for questions, though Rosa had quite a few on the tip of her tongue, for apart from surprise, she was seized with fear and foreboding.

At the Ostertor, Lawyer Koziollek had had great difficulty in reserving space for his colleague Wondrak. Too few wagons had come from Petersdorf, and City Group Leader Sikorra, who had organized the convoy, had given orders that only women, children, and old people could ride in the wagons. The others would have to walk to Stroppendorf, the next village, or Kieferstädtel, where he would requisition further vehicles. For Irma and the children there was still room with Frau Koziollek, who was pregnant, and they managed to squeeze in most of the luggage. With only knapsacks to carry, the rest of them would easily make it to Kieferstädtel, or even to Rauden if need be.

The day before, the Petersdorf peasants who provided the wagons had been threatened with heavy penalties if they left their farms; that same morning, they had received the order to slaughter their animals and evacuate; and now they were threatened with dire punishment if they stayed. Every peasant was obliged to provide a horse- or ox-drawn wagon for the fugitives from the city. Group Leader Sikorra claimed that there had been ten or fifteen more wagons when they left Petersdorf, but that some of the peasants had slipped away at the first opportunity and returned home by the shortest route.

"Damn Polacks, you can't trust them, you shut your eyes and they're gone. Scum! No discipline! I wonder what they'll say when Ivan grabs their farms and turns them into kolkhozes!"

He had been cursing and grumbling the whole time, and Willi Wondrak knew why. The other city group leaders had left town during the night in Wehrmacht vehicles, and he was the only one left behind. Now he was acting as if he, as the only remaining Party official, had to shoulder responsibility for the whole of Gleiwitz. He created additional excitement by suddenly declaring that the evacuation order did not apply to factory workers and miners, who must remain in their places of work and wait for the order to destroy all machinery to keep it from falling into enemy hands. Accordingly, he insisted on checking the papers of all fugitives. He had no way of enforcing his orders, but the people were still afraid of him. Or perhaps they had merely become too lethargic to rebel.

Not wishing to risk delay, Willi submitted; he wanted to be on the open road with the wagons as soon as possible, because the gunfire sounded as if the suburbs were already being shelled. After the third wagon, Sikorra gave up checking papers; even for him this demonstration of his power had lost all meaning.

The head of the convoy started moving. It was some time before the Pionteks' turn came, but then they were relieved finally to be on their way. Their wagon was horse-drawn. Gregor had tied a blanket on the horse's back; both Koziollek and Wondrak were glad to have him along, because they themselves didn't even know how to handle the reins.

Willi wanted Valeska to ride in the wagon with Irma, there would be room enough for her in among the luggage, but Valeska insisted on walking; in such weather it was better to walk, it kept you warm.

Irma sat in the jolting wagon, looking forlornly ahead at the white plain. *Why do they want me to leave here? The truth is that I went a long time ago, I left everything behind, I left this country, these people, I can never go back. I've given up hope, given up happiness, happiness wasn't meant for me, and I wasn't meant for happiness. Anyone who stops hoping for happiness is dead. I know I'm dead. Some people stay young though their bodies grow old; with me it's the other way around, I'm a withered old soul in a young body. What life there is in me lives only for my children, and sometimes I think it's not enough life for them. But already they are leading their own lives, living in hopes of happiness. I've always wanted to get away from this country, but now I see that this country wants me, wants to possess me, won't let me go. O poor Fallada, hanging there! Yes, I belong to this earth, especially when it's being fought for, especially when it's suffering, when it's bleeding, when it's being tortured. I can't tear myself away from this earth; wherever I go, I shall drag this earth along with me.*

It all went so fast and it all went so slowly. They had been on the road for three hours, they hadn't gone far, the convoy was moving very slowly on the road to Rauden. Time and again they had had to stop. And then they learned to their dismay that they had converged with another convoy and that the road was clogged with refugees as far as Rauden and probably all the way to Ratibor.

They trudged along behind or beside the wagon, their faces so muffled in hats and scarves that no features were discernible, only eye slits. Some of the women had rubbed their children's faces with lard as protection from the cold.

Now and then a military vehicle overtook their wagon and pushed it to the side of the road, where the snow was still deep; then they all had to push to disengage the wheels. Sometimes the soldiers gave a woman with children a lift, but this happened so seldom as to seem a miracle, unlikely to be repeated. Willi signaled desperately to every Wehrmacht car that passed; he was worried about Irma's children —the youngest was less than a year old, and Roswitha had been running a fever for days. Here and there they passed abandoned cars that had broken down or run out of gas. Willi kept wondering how many of these people would make it to Ratibor, and whether at the present rate anyone would ever get through. Then finally his signaling brought results: the driver of an ambulance carrying wounded soldiers said he could take two women with small children. Irma resisted, she didn't want to be separated from the others, but she had to give in—if only because of little Roswitha's fever. Frau Koziollek, though in an advanced state of pregnancy, refused to leave her husband; as long as she could ride in the wagon, she said, she'd be all right. For a moment Valeska thought of going with Irma and the children, but the medics said the most they could take was one pregnant woman or one woman with a child, and at that very moment a woman from the next wagon came forward.

All day the sky had been gray; the visibility was poor. But now in the late afternoon, the grayness was so dense that the suddenly arriving planes could not be seen. First there was only a distant hum, then they came bursting out of the sky. The air seemed to vibrate, and a moment later the first bomb blasts were heard.

Willi and Gregor circled around the wagon like two sheep dogs, trying to keep their frightened flock together. The wagon couldn't get off the road. The fields to the right and left were flat and covered with snow, and there were no woods that might have offered shelter. Willi ordered the others to keep moving; if they stopped still or lay down in the snow, he said, they would provide even better targets.

The humming of motors did not go away. The bomb bursts came closer, then receded. The convoy moved on. There was no antiaircraft fire; the best you could do was accept the raid as a natural catastrophe and hope to come out alive. Gregor walked beside the horse, soothing it with soft words. Frau Koziollek had lent him a knife with which to cut the traces if the horse should bolt.

It had all gone so fast and it had all gone so slowly. Just then it

occurred to Valeska that she had forgotten her picture of Edwin
Fischer, the photograph he had signed for her at his last concert in
Kraków. It was crazy, she couldn't think of anything but that signed
photograph in the silver frame, resting on the black lacquer of the
piano. She held fast to the side of the wagon. She saw a bomb falling,
she saw a tree shooting upward, roots and all, she saw earth mixed
with snow whirling through the air, and she felt the blast lifting the
wagon. She clung to the side of the wagon with both hands for fear
of being pushed out of it. She saw low-flying planes coming toward
them; she saw people being flung into the air like dolls; she saw
wagons being overturned, saw the mangled bodies of horses and
great red stains in the snow; but all this seemed to be happening
behind a glass wall, strangely far from her. Since she no longer had
the old Upper Silesian soil beneath her feet, she felt, like the giant
Antaeus in Greek mythology, that all power and feeling had gone
out of her. A bomb exploded up ahead, and great clods of earth rose
into the air. She looked on with horror and a certain satisfaction.
This, she felt, was what had always been inflicted on the earth, and
here she was seeing it with her own eyes.

19

HEDEL'S FIRST IMPRESSION on waking was that the noise outside had grown louder. The muffled thunder seemed to have come closer, and the explosions in between were more clearly audible. A new day must have dawned, a pale, early light trickled through the windows. She was lying on a mattress; beside her she saw a man's head with short brown hair; the face was averted. Slowly her memory returned. She thought of her mother, her grandmother, the little kitchen at home, the drawer of the bedside table where she kept a few dried flowers along with her needlework and the old school copybooks. She knew she could get up, dress, and go home, and if the door downstairs was locked, she could climb through the ground-floor window through which she had come in. But she had lost all desire to leave. When Kotik's face emerged from the white pillow beside her and began to talk, she responded with a gentle caress. It almost seemed to her that something was breaking when she heard his voice saying: "The shots outside are getting louder. Do you hear?"

Kotik stood up. He was naked. She saw that he was really a child. He knelt beside the tile stove, opened the fire door, and blew. She saw him putting in crumpled newspaper and white kindling until a flame shot up and lit his face. He went to the window and raised the blackout shade. Then he leaned against the stove, which had retained a little warmth. It was all perfectly natural; only Kotik's nakedness troubled her a little.

Later they sat side by side at the table and looked at each other in silence, while drinking tea out of large cups. They still had no idea what had brought them together and what was keeping them here in the house. After awhile they searched the house from top to bottom, every cupboard and every drawer. Kotik wound the clocks in every room but left the hands just as they were; from then on the clocks ticked in all the rooms and struck at entirely different times, as if he had wanted to prove that for them time had ceased to exist. He dragged the phonograph out of the room with the dressmaker's dummies and brought it downstairs. The spring was broken and he set about repairing it.

At dusk they sat by the window, watching the street through the curtain. A muffled-up woman was pulling a sled loaded with suitcases and cartons, while another pushed it from behind. It took them a long time to reach the end of the street. These were the first people Kotik and Hedel had seen all day. Hedel stood up and looked after them until they disappeared from view.

Kotik went out to bury the dog in the garden. When he came back, Hedel was in the kitchen frying *platzeks* made of flour and water, by the light of a candle. *Platzeks* could be eaten with jam or with meat or pickled mushrooms.

Kotik was pale. "You smell of schnapps," said Hedel, not at all reproachfully, while turning a *platzek*.

"Yeah, I took a drink, I had to, on account of the dog. Do you know, it ripped my guts. I couldn't even bury him in the ground, it's frozen solid. Now he's deep under the snow, but next spring when the snow melts, he'll be lying there. You can see that I needed a drink."

"Yes, I can see," she said.

"Your hair smells good," said Kotik, closing his eyes.

"Yes, I found a little bottle of perfume upstairs and rubbed a few drops behind my ears." She was glad Kotik had noticed. She sat there wondering what she was doing in this strange house. She had wanted to leave as soon as it was morning. Now it was evening and she was still there. There was something about this boy.

Kotik laid his hand on hers. It was lovely, just touching her like this. "I love you," he said, "even if it makes you laugh."

But Hedel didn't laugh.

They sat there in silence, holding hands. "You don't know anything about me," she said out of a clear sky. "My mother has had a hard life. She was terribly humiliated, and to save me from that, she shuts me away from life. My father left her right after I was born. She never heard from him again. To support us, she went to work in a sugar factory, that's where she got her sciatica; she's been sitting in an armchair ever since, packed in hot-water bags that she fills every few hours. The only thing that makes her go on living is her hatred of men. If it hadn't been for the war, she'd never have let me out of the house. The first few weeks, while I was learning to be a salesgirl at Rebenstorf's department store, she got one of the neighbors to keep an eye on me. I was never allowed to go out on Saturday or Sunday. So after mass or the Marian Office I just stayed out, I simply had to talk to somebody else than my mother. But I paid for it. She beat me and cursed me when I got home, it was awful. If a letter ever came for me, she intercepted it, so I had to have them sent in care of a girl friend. And then I thought to myself, she'll hit me when I get home in any case, so I started going to the ice-cream parlor on Wilhelmstrasse and the Café Loske and to the park by the Wild Klodnitz, and I picked the soldiers I liked. I'm so afraid that when I really love a man, he'll leave me the way my father left my mother. That's the only reason I take up with a man, to give myself the feeling that I'll leave him, even if sometimes I don't want to."

"You'll never leave me, Hedel. Because I'm going to marry you."

"Stop it, Kotik, don't say such things, you'll make me cry."

The next string of explosions was louder than any that had gone before.

"They're getting nearer," said Kotik. "If it goes on like this, we'll probably have to spend the night in the cellar. It sounds like they're shelling the suburbs. I better go out and rustle up some cigarettes. At this time of day I'm sure to meet one of our *hoppeks*."

"Don't be too long," she pleaded. "I'll be scared all alone here."

Kotik didn't know how long he had been away. But the nearer he came to the house on Miethe-Allee, the uneasier he became. Despite the cold, he caught himself describing the interior of the house to his friends, as if they still needed persuading to come along. Actually they had been delighted to join him. Otherwise they'd still have been standing in a doorway with their bazooka, watching the river road, over which the Russians were expected to move in from Bischofstal. First Kotik had gone to his school, where they had last assembled for HY duty, but the building was dark except for the janitor's lodge in the basement. According to the janitor, all the *hoppeks* had cleared out; just a few, led by Dr. Röthel, the assistant principal, had gone to Schillerstrasse to guard the road. He had found Hannes Piechotta and Jochen Winter in a doorway not far from the Women's Clinic and told them about the villa on Miethe-Allee; "Yeah, I'm living there, with plenty of schnapsik and a woman." The *hoppeks*, who were frozen stiff, had been only too glad to leave their post. After ascertaining that each had at least half a pack of cigarettes, he had told them to come along.

Now they were sitting in the warm room, drinking hot grog. Hedel brought them food. They lit a cigarette and passed it around, and even Kotik, who didn't usually smoke, took a drag. Though the two guests had meant to stay only for a second, they just sat there. They had left a bazooka behind with a single projectile in it, with which they had planned to demolish the first Russian tank that came rolling into the city. Oh yes, their minds were made up. All the same, Hannes put a record on the phonograph. When Kotik told him it was out of order, he set about fixing it.

Kotik put on water for the next grog. They smoked and talked about their prospects under the Russians—not so good, they decided. But it didn't matter to Hannes, who was going to blow himself up with the first Russian tank. Jochen felt the same way, but he wanted a bit of music first, now that Hannes had got the phonograph working. Out of the loudspeaker poured the tinny sound of Heinrich Schlusnus singing: *"Oh, how fickle are the hearts of women!"*

"Play something we can dance to," Hannes shouted. He danced a few steps and his breath made a rattling sound.

Jochen put on another record. *"My sweetheart wants to take me sailing Sunday, Oh, how lovely that would be."*

"That's the stuff." Hannes rested a hand on Hedel's shoulder and spun around in a circle with her. Jochen danced by himself and joined in the song . . . *"After dinner the sunset beckons me to sail upon the sea."*

"Come on, join us," cried Hannes, grabbing hold of Kotik. Hedel took him around the waist, and the three of them whirled around, all completely out of time, but that didn't matter now. Kotik spun around, he had one arm around Hedel, and he felt Hedel's arm around him. Hedel danced faster and faster, goading the two boys on with piercing little cries. Kotik bent back from the waist; he felt as though he were gliding; the light and the walls and Hedel's hair spun around him in an endless whirl.

20

Halina had spent the whole day in the attic, afraid to go downstairs until it was so dark that she couldn't distinguish the white wall from the black roof beams. The attic was warm because the chimney flue ran through it; she was sitting on a mattress with her back to the chimney. The place smelled of glue and charred wood. Once she had fallen asleep and dreamed she was escaping, running across a snow-covered field. Far and wide there wasn't a house or the least clump of trees to hide in. A man was running after her, coming closer and closer, no need to look around, she could hear his panting and see his shadow getting bigger and bigger. She prayed to the Blessed Virgin, and suddenly, before the shadow hand could reach out for her, she herself turned into snow, the man burrowed in the snow with both hands, he dug deeper and deeper until his hands were coated with ice, his movements became more and more sluggish, and in the end he turned to ice. She woke up and it was some time before she knew where she was.

She had shut herself up in the attic that morning, because she couldn't bear to look at the Pani and her grief-stricken eyes anymore and she was afraid Lawyer Wondrak would insist at the last minute on her coming along. She was glad the Pani had finally agreed to leave her behind, because who else would keep an eye on the house and furniture and especially the piano. She wasn't afraid of Russian soldiers; what she feared were the men in green uniforms who had arrested her here and dragged her out of the house, and who had taken her Kolya away from her. She had had no news of him. His real name was Arkadi Shevchuk, but he wanted her to call him Kolya. She'd never forget him. If the war ever stopped, she'd go and see him in the village on the Dnieper where he lived.

She hadn't been able to lock the door, because the key to the attic had been lost years ago and no one had bothered to look for it, because the door was always left open. She had taken a chair from

Josel's room and wedged it under the door handle, so it couldn't be opened from outside.

Now she went through the whole house, from room to room. She opened the doors and lighted her way with a candle, as though to make sure that no enchanted king or *utopletz* was hiding anywhere. After that she felt safer, though she was still afraid to switch on the light. She lit a candle in the kitchen, made herself something to eat, and moved into the music room, where she put the candle down on the mahogany table. For a while she sat in the armchair that was Pan Dr. Wondrak's usual place. Peering into the half-darkness, she distinguished the outlines of the piano, the vitrine, and the little cabinet. She saw the room inhabited as it had been, she heard sounds and voices, heard a melody, which became clearer and louder until it drowned out every other sound; there sat the Pani at the piano playing a mazurka, a polonaise, a waltz. The music sounded in Halina's ears as it had never sounded before, because in those days she had usually been in the kitchen and heard it through a wall and two doors. But now the room was empty and still again, the candle flickered and cast shadowy shapes on the wall. From time to time she stood up and put more briquettes in the stove. That was the only sound, the sound of the fire in the cast-iron stove, for she had ceased to hear the muffled sound of the explosions outside.

go down to the old brickworks the door is open

I won't let you out of my sight

go down there and wait for me walk naturally if you go too fast and look around too often it will arouse suspicion

but I'm afraid you won't follow me

go down to the old brickworks

that night brought the first frost the meadows were white and in the morning the grass crunched under one's shoes the fog hung on the trees

if you look closely the old elm tree with its gnarled branches is writing a letter on the sky in a language that anyone can read you just have to look closely with your eyes and your heart what can you read tell me what can you read

run run, but you won't overtake the wind in the fields

in our country the snow sets in at this time of year water freezes
in the meadows it sparkles like glass and makes cheerful sounds when
you walk across the meadows at this time of year

go down to the old brickworks I'll follow you

do you see that tree over there with its withered black branches
it's writing a letter on the clouds come I'll teach you to read the
letters the trees write

you can't hitch happiness to your wagon like a horse

I'll follow you wherever you go

you're looking at me oh don't look at me that way Kolya no man
ever looked at me that way the grass melts under my feet when you
look at me that way

and the way you took hold of me

the way you pressed your lips against my lips I know that no one
ever looked at me like that before I got these new teeth yes I want
you to know that I've got brand-new teeth

it was October there was frost at night and already the country
was cloaked in fog but about noon when the sun forced its way
through it could get pretty warm you taught me to read the secret
writing of the trees I need only look out the window

the bare branches in every part of the white sky are love letters
for me Kolya Kolya Kolya

21

THE BOMBARDMENT BEGAN at about five in the morning. The whole house came awake. The tenants ran frantically up and down the stairs, whispering and shouting. Frau Aubitzky's youngest child screamed. Herr Mazura went from door to door telling the people to keep calm, take a few indispensable belongings, and go slowly down to the air-raid shelter.

Anna Ossadnik jumped up, forgetting her sprained ankle. She winced with pain. Oh, where could Kotik be? Her worry about him had kept her awake all night—she could swear to that. And it was true that she had twice got up, looked out the kitchen window, which was on the street side, and called his name. Because he wouldn't have been able to get in, because Herr Mazura had barricaded the door against the *ostarbeiter*, who had been roaming the streets and looting right and left. These days no one dared to stop them and the police had disappeared. Even so, Franz looked into Kotik's room, in the hope that the boy had somehow managed to creep in; boys of that age developed aptitudes that their mothers couldn't begin to suspect. But he found the bed untouched.

"Of course he's not there," said Anna. "I knew it all along. A mother can hear it when her own child comes home. And if she doesn't hear it, she senses it."

"They must have kept him at the Volkssturm," said Franz, tying a length of clothesline around the cardboard suitcase with the lock that kept coming open.

"At the Volkssturm! A child of fifteen!" she cried, as though anything could be too irrational at such a time.

Franz Ossadnik was still thinking about his plan. But at six, when he and Zielonka should have gone on shift, the bombardment was still going on. Franz conferred secretly with Zielonka, who had already given up all thought of leaving. His old mother was determined to stay whatever happened, she had grown up here and she wanted to be buried here. So he too would stay, he wouldn't dream of leaving his old mother behind. So they decided not to go on shift, and backed each other up in their decision even when the shelling died down, leaving only the muffled rumbling to which they had become accustomed.

No one dared go back to his apartment. The shelling could start up again any minute. The shelter was overheated, the coal stove in the middle was red hot. On the stone floor the occupants had spread carpets taken from all the apartments, including the Pieczyks'. Pieczyk was the block warden. When none of the Pieczyks turned up in the shelter and there was no answer to repeated ringing and knocking at their door, it occurred to the janitor, Herr Mazura, that they might have killed themselves, there had been lots of suicides lately. Mazura had decided to go and see, but he insisted on Franz Ossadnik going with him. "You gotta come," he had said, "I need a witness." Showing surprising dexterity, he had picked the lock with a safety pin and entered cautiously, sniffing as if his nose were running. As Franz soon realized, he was afraid Pieczyk had turned on the gas. But then they saw that the family had fled in haste. The floor was littered with articles of clothing, and a half-packed suitcase had been abandoned in the hallway. The Pieczyks had fine, expensive carpets and Mazura decided to take them down to the shelter. Since the apartment was on the top floor, they would be destroyed if a shell hit the house. His real reason, Franz suspected, was that he hoped, at some future date, to claim the carpets as his own. The two men had searched the apartment for official documents, anything with the eagle-and-swastika stamp; these as well as the block warden's Party uniform they took downstairs and burned.

Anna removed the braid and the shoulder patches from her husband's Reichsbahn uniform, making it look like an an ordinary dark blue suit. She would do the same with his coat; such material was not to be had anymore.

With Pieczyk gone, Herr Mazura was boss. He gave orders, which the others obeyed willingly, because deep down they were glad it was Mazura instead of the block warden, and after all somebody had to give orders, didn't they. Some of the tenants seemed to remember that Mazura had once been a Communist Party member, that might be useful, they thought. Others remembered seeing him not so long ago selling one-dish meal coupons and taking collections for Winter Aid. Probably both were right.

The women decided to pool their provisions and cook one-pot meals for all as long as they had to stay in the shelter. The children fought, played checkers or mill or halma, and fought some more. The little Grochowiak boy challenged one after another to a game of jackstraws; he regularly beat the grown-ups, who with their work-worn hands were no match for him. Zielonka told a long story, to which no one really listened, about the battle of the Somme in which he claimed to have taken part. His old mother sat sweating by the stove.

In a whisper she said all the mysteries of the rosary, the joyful, the sorrowful, the glorious, and finally the comforting, and when at last she had finished, she burst into tears. Frau Smolka's father, old man Bednarz, chewed on a plug of dried oak leaves and pontificated about the ravages of scurvy, illustrating his lecture by fingering each one of his wobbly teeth, which fortunately couldn't be seen very clearly in the candlelight, though the decay could be smelled. Frau Smolka made herself useful, helping Frau Zielonka melt down candle ends and pour new candles. To take her mind off Kotik, Anna tried to go on reading *The Dairywoman of Ottakring*, but soon gave up because it made her eyes smart.

At about twelve noon a sudden silence fell. There was something eerie about it. And the quiet went on for quite some time, as though in preparation for some stupendous event. What could it mean? No one dared ask. Mazura watched the street through the area window, but there was nothing to see. He explained to Franz Ossadnik that one of the women had made two white flags out of a bedsheet and that he was going to hang them out of the windows if the Russians came.

"Why not do it now?" Franz suggested. "Then whichever side comes along will see that we're peaceful folk."

"You're crazy," said Mazura. "The German soldiers wouldn't give a damn, but now the SS has taken over, a white flag would make 'em so mad they'd blow the house up. It's all in the timing." And he concluded solemnly: "Timing is the biggest thing in life."

Next he suggested a scouting party; he and Ossadnik should go out and look around, they might even go into town to see what was going on. But Franz had something else in mind and asked his friend Zielonka to come along. He wanted to go looking for Kotik.

"A kid can't just vanish into thin air," he said. "He's got to be some place."

Anna wanted to go along; after all, she knew more about her son's habits and hangouts. But Franz said no, it was too dangerous, the shelling could start up again at any moment. Anna should just make him a white arm band, of course he'd keep it in his pocket and put it on only at the right moment.

At this point Frau Grochowiak intervened: "Where are you going to look for him? You ought to have more sense. Are you going to ask for him at every street corner? If you do that, you'll never come back."

Frau Grochowiak had two children. The younger was just three. Her husband was socially superior to the other men in this railroad workers' house. He had his middle diploma and had just obtained a post in the railroad administration when he was drafted. She would have been entitled to an apartment on Raudenerstrasse where the administrative staff was housed, but she hadn't wanted to move away from here. Before her marriage, she had been a nurse, she knew all about diseases and medicines—anyway a lot more than Frau Ossadnik, who had formerly kept house for a Dr. Bermann.

"He went out Saturday afternoon and hasn't been home since," said Franz Ossadnik in despair.

They all knew that, his wife had been talking about it for hours.

"But your wife said he'd gone to the Volkssturm," said Frau Grochowiak. "He must be out somewhere defending the suburbs."

"No, he's not with the Volkssturm. He went to an HY meeting. Sometimes they have bazooka practice."

"Just wait for him," said Frau Grochowiak. "It's safer. He knows where you live, and you haven't the faintest idea where he might be."

"I'll go to the school and ask," said Franz Ossadnik resolutely. He felt he'd be abandoning his son if he didn't try something.

"There's nobody at the school. Christmas vacation has been extended to January 28 on account of the coal shortage," said little Grochowiak, who was well placed to know.

"Exactly," said Anna. "That's why the HY kids go there for their exercises."

"I'll go with you," said the boy. "I know the way."

"You just pipe down," said his mother.

The men agreed on a signal, three long and two short knocks when they came back. The women shouldn't open unless they heard that signal.

"Holy Jesus!" cried Anna when she saw the three men bundling up. "Are you really going just like that?"

Up until then it hadn't occurred to her that the only man left in the house would be old man Bednarz, Frau Smolka's father, who was almost stone-deaf and just sat there quietly slobbering.

"I'm afraid too," said Frau Jacob, who looked as if she never stopped quaking with terror.

So Herr Mazura decided to stay with the women in the shelter. He'd only go as far as Hauptstrasse, no further, just to see if he could pick up a bit of news.

And true enough, he was back in a few minutes. "Three Volkssturms on the corner," he reported, breathless from running. He'd even spoken to them, they were terrified and frozen stiff, and he had the impression that they stuck it out only because of the armored reconnaissance car that came by every few minutes. When the Russian tanks appeared, they wouldn't shoot, they'd throw away their bazookas, tear off their arm bands, and hide in some cellar. At least Herr Mazura hoped so. Because if the Russians ran into resistance, they'd shoot up the whole neighborhood.

"The road to Kieferstädtel is supposed to be open, they say convoys are leaving from Peter-Paul-Platz, but only for women and children under twelve."

Frau Grochowiak pricked up her ears. "Convoys, you say? Yes-

terday they said we'd have to walk to Ratibor with our sleds. In this
cold with little Ingelore? Nothing doing. She'd freeze to death. It's
more than thirty kilometers."

She turned to the other mothers, Frau Smolka with her two daughters, Frau Aubitzky with her three sons, and Frau Jacob with two
children, a boy and a girl. "What do you think?" she asked.

"I won't go," Frau Jacob whispered. "I *must* stay here." She stressed
the *must* so heavily that the others made no attempt to argue.

"If there's a bus or a truck I'll go," said Frau Aubitzky resolutely.
At first she hadn't wanted to leave. But the closer the firing came,
the more she believed the atrocity stories spread by refugees who
were passing through. "I can't make the children walk to Ratibor,"
she said. "But if there's a truck, I'll go."

"Let's go and ask Father Pattas," Anna suggested. "He's sure to
know something. Just me and Frau Grochowiak. We'll come back
and tell you."

All nodded assent.

As the two women hurried through the snow-covered streets, they
felt that they had returned to the world. Living in the cramped, dark,
overheated, airless shelter was like being buried. Now the gray sky
arched over them, the muted January light cloaked them, and the
snow muffled their footfalls. It was very cold, but they were glad to
fill their lungs with the fresh air.

On the way, they passed other women who hurried by without
a word. Only one of them, Frau Kowallek, stopped for a moment:
"Don't go to the Butter Market," she said. "They've hanged three
Hitler Youths, with signs around their necks saying: I was too cow-
ardly to defend the fatherland. Monsters, those Party bosses, that's
what they are. And now they've all cleared out."

Anna had to clutch Frau Grochowiak's arm to keep from falling.

"Why is it suddenly so quiet?" she asked Frau Grochowiak. "Have
you any idea?"

"They say the Russians are going to storm the city tomorrow. I
hear they're already in the suburbs of Ratibor."

"Holy Jesus!" cried Anna. Her face was convulsed with pain.

"Are you leaving?" Frau Grochowiak asked Frau Kowallek.

"Where to? It's hell wherever you go. Maybe we'll envy the dead before long."

"I want to go to the Butter Market," said Anna.

"The Butter Market? Where they hanged those young fellows?" said Frau Grochowiak. "We can get along without seeing that."

"Maybe . . . Maybe my Kotik is one of them," cried Anna, the tears welling from her eyes.

"Frau Ossadnik!" Frau Grochowiak shook her. "Have you taken leave of your senses? You're coming with me to see Father Pattas. Why should one of them be your son? How can you think such a thing? Your son has never been a coward. When he has to fight, he fights. But he's too young . . ."

Frau Grochowiak pulled Anna along. Under no circumstances would she let her go to the Butter Market. She didn't believe for one moment that little Kotik could be one of the hanged boys, but she was determined to spare her neighbor the gruesome sight.

From a distance they saw a cluster of people on Peter-Paul-Platz, crowding together as though to warm one another, hundreds of women with their children; they had knapsacks on their backs, the rest of their baggage—suitcases, cartons, featherbeds—was piled up on sleds. Just a few old men among them. They had all been driven here by fear, they wanted to get away from the Russians, no matter where to, as long as it was westward. They had been here the day before, they had waited; at nightfall they had been sent away and told to come back tomorrow, there'd be trucks to take them away. So they had spent the night at home but gone down to the shelters when the Katyushas began sweeping over the city, and about noon, when the shelling stopped, they had come back to the assembly point. Now they were waiting again, mute, frozen, apathetic.

The two women stopped in the lee of a house, at some distance from the crowd, and watched them. "How long have they been waiting here?" Anna asked.

"Good God, they look half frozen," said Frau Grochowiak. She didn't dare go any further.

A convoy of six or seven horse-drawn wagons emerged from

Schröterstrasse. Anna couldn't count them because women with children took the wagons by storm. Screaming, they threw featherbeds, sacks of potatoes, pieces of baggage out of the wagons, and put their children in instead. Then they themselves climbed in. Meanwhile, far from stopping, the drivers lashed their horses on. One woman tied her sled with her belongings and two children on it to an oxcart and ran after it.

The whole incident had lasted no more than five minutes, then the wagons were gone. Those who had been left behind regrouped, resumed their wait for the promised trucks, and went on exchanging rumors in which they had ceased to believe, repeating them over and over because they had nothing else to say.

In the crowd Anna suddenly spied Frau Aubitzky with her three little boys. Had she set out because she and Frau Grochowiak hadn't come back soon enough?

Frau Grochowiak poked her. "Look, over there, your Pattas!"

Anna looked. True enough, there was the Archpriest, crossing the snow-covered square. He had on a long black coat and a black broad-brimmed hat. He was holding his hands over his ears, as though he had been walking a long way in the cold. After him came Father Jarosch, the curate. They headed straight for the waiting crowd. A few women rushed toward them, others followed and formed a circle. The Archpriest towered over the crowd, he must have climbed up on a suitcase or a sled.

The two women rushed forward, eager to hear what the Archpriest had to say and unwilling to miss a single word.

His voice was not very loud, but it was firm and incisive; it cut through the clear, dry air like a knife: ". . . and let our faith in God make us strong . . . let us all be brothers and sisters in love . . . one family; for where else shall we find the strength to endure what awaits us now? Let us trust in God and implore Him to deliver us from evil. And if hardship comes to us, let us bear it, just as the Son of God bore the cross.

"Dearly beloved, go home; it is too late for flight. I have just found out that the Russians have occupied the Rauden highway, the last road to Ratibor across the Oder. The Party has fled; so has the civil administration, they have deserted us. The law is gone, and we don't know how long this lawless period will last. But we bear within us the highest law, the Christian law of charity. Keep order, respect the property of your neighbors, including those who have fled, and if any of you think the time has come to take revenge for injustices you have suffered, abstain from doing so. Observe with humility God's law that is within you. Heed the voice of the Church; it will help you wherever possible, as it has always done in your hour of need. Dearly beloved, I see among you Christians who are not of our congregation. I beseech you, accept them in your midst, shelter them, and let them not hunger or thirst. And if any be homeless, let them come to the presbytery, we shall help them."

The Archpriest paused and looked around. "You may wonder why I have waited until today before coming to you, and why you have not seen me in the last few days. Dear ones: some of you already know. I was obliged to go into hiding; I had received orders from the Party to leave the city and go to Görlitz; the same order was sent to all the Polish-speaking priests in Gleiwitz; the Party wanted to separate us from our congregations—but can a shepherd leave his flock in time of trouble? We therefore decided to hide until the Party's power lapsed. That has now happened, and I am with you again. You must trust me. I have served you for twenty years, and I will not forsake you in the future. No secular authority has the right to separate me from you. I belong to you, and I shall stay with you, now and in your hour of need."

There were some among the listeners who wiped away the tears with great crude handkerchiefs.

The priest himself kept his feelings under control. He went among the people and looked into their faces. There was compassion in his eyes, but his voice was free from pathos when he said: "Make sure there are no arms in your houses, no pictures of Hitler and no swastika flags. If the Russians find such things, you can expect them to set fire to your house. Don't loot. Keep calm. Hide your valuables. The women among you should wear old clothes, have your hair cut short, and wear a scarf over it. If Russians come to your house, let those of you who know some Polish speak to them. Keep the schnapps away from them. Destroy what liquor you have in the house. If no one prevents us, we shall celebrate Mass next Sunday. Before we part, let us say a short prayer together, the Ave Maria."

The Archpriest said the prayer quickly. He was cold, and he could see that his listeners were cold too. He blessed them and bade them go in peace.

22

F RAU WIECZOREK RARELY left her apartment since her two sons had been drafted as Flak auxiliaries. Her only human contact was with her old friends Verena Schimitschek and Erna Dolezich, whom she met in church once or twice a week, on Friday or Saturday afternoon and of course at High Mass on Sunday, when Father Pattas preached. It seemed to her that the Archpriest had aged in the last few years, his hair had gone gray and thin, and his sermons had lost their old fire. She too had grown older; she had only to look in the mirror as she combed her hair—it was hard to hide the gray strands under her brown curls. In wartime, as Frau Wewerka had always said, the years count double; she might just as well have said triple, Frau Wieczorek thought, especially since the day when word came that her husband had been killed in the Crimea. How could she ever forget the years when she had had her husband and five children in her little apartment, when she had been kept busy all day providing her "menfolk" (as she had always called them) with ample food, clean shirts, darned stockings, and soled shoes. Her husband did not make much at the Gleiwitz colliery, and many a time she had had to call for him at the pithead on Saturday afternoon to stop him from going straight to the nearest bar and coming home drunk with a half-empty pay envelope. And then, one by one, her men had been taken from her, until no one was left but herself. Everything around her reminded her of her *goroliks*, every reglued chair, every cup without a handle, every pair of shoes with those characteristic bumps and knobs. Sometimes she stood there holding a bent fork, remembering those lost voices and longing to have them back again. Accustomed to working all day for others, she suddenly had nothing to do; used to having others to talk to, she was suddenly condemned to silence. Sometimes, in her thoughts, she talked to her dead husband, asking him what he thought about some event or other, and when a letter came from one of her sons, she read it aloud for her husband's benefit.

For a while she had washed and ironed her sons' shirts every few weeks and put them back in the cupboard. But more recently she had contented herself with opening the cupboard, to make sure that everything was in its place, and checking the provisions in the pantry, the peas and beans and lentils, the dried fruit, the potted meat, the can of coffee beans, the small bag of powdered milk—not very much, but at least there'd be something in the house in case her sons should pay her a surprise visit.

In the end her two friends Schimitschek and Dolezich were her only connection with the outside world. She would have liked best to give them up if she hadn't been afraid they would come looking for her, so she preferred to meet them in church, since she felt that her apartment was unfit to be seen. They at least kept her informed of what was going on in the world and in the next street, and though such things didn't mean much to her, she was grateful, for she had no radio and she had canceled the newspaper when her two *goroliks* went off to the barracks. She hadn't even heard that the other tenants had fitted out the air-raid shelter with carpets and chairs and installed a stove in the middle.

Jutta Wieczorek had waited for the first shell to strike home. She took that as a signal. When it happened, she put on warm clothes and left her apartment. On the stairway she passed a neighbor, who took such fright at the sight of her that she dropped the featherbed she was carrying and scurried down to the shelter. A moment later others came up from the shelter and crowded around her. All talking at once, they overwhelmed her with questions. She didn't know what to say, and it was some time before she grasped the situation. Frau Stoklassa, who sang soprano in the St. Cecilia choir, claimed to have seen her in a convoy heading for Ratibor, and now they all wanted to know how she could be here all of a sudden and what had happened on her journey.

"What do you want of me?" said Frau Wieczorek. "I haven't set foot outside my apartment for days, except to go to church. Didn't I tell you ages ago that nothing would make me leave here, I've got to wait for my sons. And now let me go, I have to visit a friend on Lohmeyerstrasse to see if she's still there."

The women exchanged glances. Was she a madwoman or a witch, wanting to go out in the street with shells falling all around! The elderly house warden took her by the hand and spoke gently to her as one might speak to a backward child. If she ever wanted to see her sons again, she should pack her emergency suitcase and get down to the shelter as fast as she could, because the Russians were expected to storm the city within the next few hours.

Jutta Wieczorek looked at the house warden. Then she went upstairs with him. He carried her suitcase, while she quickly packed her thirty-six-piece gold-rimmed dinner service into two cartons and took them down with her.

The air-raid shelter, an ordinary cellar that had merely been reinforced on the outside with a few sandbags, was lit by a single candle, around which the children sat playing. The grown-ups just sat there listening to the gunfire. If any of them said anything, it was only to tell the children to make less noise. Frau Wieczorek waited for a favorable moment, when it would be possible to leave the house and go to Lohmeyerstrasse. In the meantime she kept busy with her prayer book, but she didn't read very much. Either the children interrupted her or her eyes filled with tears in the dim light. But the silence in the shelter was more than she could bear, and she began to sing a hymn, or at least the first verse, which she knew by heart. *Beloved Jesus, what law hast thou broken, that such a cruel judgment should be spoken? What has brought thee among the evildoers?* She didn't know the words of the other verses, she just hummed the tune— there must have been a good many verses, for her humming went on and on. Frau Stoklassa whispered to her husband, who had nodded off while wondering who would pay out his next month's pension: "Haven't I always said Frau Wieczorek was kind of *chaychay?*"

By midday, Frau Wieczorek had managed to persuade the house warden and the others that they couldn't just sit there waiting forever and that someone should try to find out what was going on. That was her only hope of escaping from the cellar, because the outside door was locked and barred. And so, taking advantage of a prolonged lull in the firing, she went out with the house warden. Three Volkssturm youngsters were still guarding the street corner with a single bazooka. The house warden tried in vain to convince them that it might be better to guard a different street corner. And then, as she had often done in her thoughts, Frau Wieczorek started her trek to Lohmeyerstrasse. She passed children pulling sleds so heavily laden that another child had to push from behind. It occurred to her that she should have brought a sled. For what she had in mind a sled and a large sack would have come in handy.

At No. 23 Lohmeyerstrasse she found that the door of her friend Frau Schimitschek's apartment had been forced. For a moment she stood paralyzed by fright. The lock was still dangling from the door, the wood around it had been smashed. Cautiously she pushed the door; it moved slowly on its hinges. She peered into the hallway. On the floor lay a coffee mill, a top hat, a washboard, an iron, a gutted sack of flour, a rumpled black blouse, an open book, a lady's shoe.

Frau Wieczorek leaned against the wall and burst into tears. When she had more or less recovered her composure, she went slowly in, careful not to step on any of the scattered objects. Others had come here before her and desecrated the apartment, torn open cupboards and drawers, overturned furniture, rolled up carpets, pulled down curtains, smashed dishes.

At length she gathered together a few articles of clothing and threw them over her arm. She pulled a tablecloth out from under an overturned table; it was soiled, but she couldn't fail to see the fine open-work embroidery. She picked up a pillow that felt like eiderdown. And just as she was about to go, she spied on one of the walls a fussily realistic painting of a horse's head in a gilded oval frame. The mark on the wallpaper beside it told her that another, similar artwork must have hung there. She took the picture down and examined it closely; yes, it would look nice in her living room between the window and the wall clock.

She was on the point of leaving her friend's apartment when Erna Dolezich stepped through the shattered door.

"Goodness gracious!" cried Frau Wieczorek, and dropped the picture.

A cold wind blew in. Only then did she discover that a windowpane had been smashed. Moving a chair into position with one foot, she sat down with her loot on her lap.

"My goodness! You still here? You were in such a hurry to get away from the Russians." In one hand, Frau Wieczorek held the embroidered tablecloth, in the other a couple of clothes hangers.

"Oh my God, Frau Wieczorek!" Erna Dolezich muttered. This was the last person she expect to see. She had to say something to help her over her embarrassment. *"The harpie cries, 'Tis time, 'tis time."*

Frau Wieczorek was baffled. "What did you say?"

"Round about the cauldron go, in the poisoned entrails throw." Someone else seemed to be speaking from inside her. But then she said politely, "What a surprise to see you here!"

"I just dropped in to see if everything was all right . . . And look what I find! Isn't it terrible?" She cast a despairing look around. Partly because she didn't want to look Frau Dolezich in the face.

"And the Russians aren't even here yet." Erna Dolezich was more surprised than horrified by what she saw. "Does the whole apartment look like this?" She didn't go in any further.

"It's the same all over," said Frau Wieczorek.

Frau Dolezich looked around. Her own apartment, she thought, would look like this in a day or two. "Heaven help us," she sighed. Then, feeling that she had no right to embarrass Frau Wieczorek, she started talking. "We took the road to Ratibor, the only one that was still open. But when we got to Kieferstädtel, we couldn't go on, the street was clogged with refugees and soldiers, the Russians had cut the road to Rauden. So we came back."

"In this cold," Frau Wieczorek groaned, clinging to her loot. "What's become of your white chinchilla?"

"Hidden," said Frau Dolezich with a sly look. "With all these *ostarbeiter* looting right and left. Tearing the fur coats off our backs."

"Verena's coat really looked good on you, I can say that without envy," said Frau Wieczorek.

"Oh yes, Verena had nice things, it's a fact, she knew the right people."

"Well anyway, we're too late," said Frau Wieczorek, summing up the situation. "They've cleaned the place out."

What she needed now was not so much a friend as an accomplice. Most of all she wanted to get out of here. She'd leave the picture of the horse's head. But she'd take the clothes and the fine tablecloth. But how was she to explain this to her friend? "Holy Saint Anthony, protector of the poor!" she muttered under her breath. What must Erna Dolezich think of her! Then she wasn't a friend. But *she* hadn't smashed Verena's door. She felt the blood rising to her head. She'd only wanted to protect Verena's property. The best things were gone anyway. And now anyone could come in and help themselves. All right, she herself didn't need these dresses. They were too tight anyway, and it wouldn't help to let them out at the sides.

But she couldn't say all this to Frau Dolezich. One look at her told the whole story: obviously she had come only to grab her old friend's belongings, the chinchilla wasn't enough for her, you could tell by those shifty, greedy eyes that she'd come only to rob her friend. That was her all over. Oh, you couldn't rely on anyone nowadays, no, not even on a good friend.

Frau Wieczorek arose to go.

The two women stood face to face, each discovering herself in the other. In that moment they realized how bitterly they hated each other.

23

AFTER LIVING THROUGH moments that lasted for years, Valeska had lost all feeling for time. She had ceased to believe that she would once again arrive at a destination, for on this road the idea of a destination had lost all meaning for her. If someone had asked her why she was trudging down ice-covered roads with a convoy of horse-drawn wagons and oxcarts, she wouldn't have known what to say. At some time or other, long long ago, she had started out; she had left her house and half her life behind her and started out, without knowing whether the road led to life or to death. At a certain moment she had ceased to be Valeska Piontek, the piano teacher, sister of the lawyer Willi Wondrak, mother of Irma, grandmother of Irma's little daughters, sister-in-law of Rosa, and become a bundled-up old woman, trudging along behind a wagon with a tarp over it.

Night was falling, the planes had turned away, the convoy had moved on. They had considered spending the night in some peasant's barn, but then, fearing that the planes would be back again the next day to bomb and strafe them, they had kept going. They had kept on all night in the hope that dawn would find them safely across the Oder in Ratibor.

The convoy ahead of them had been hit; they passed shattered, overturned wagons and the tattered, bloody carcasses of horses. The wounded were picked up by the wagons that followed, the dead wrapped in blankets, loaded onto sleds, and tied fast. And then the convoy moved on.

An old woman was lying in the snow by the side of the road. All Willi could get out of her was that her children had left her behind or lost her, he was unable to discover which. In any case, she wanted to be left lying in the snow. Willi and Gregor had to pick her up by force and load her into the wagon with the pregnant Frau Koziollek. She'd find her children in Ratibor, they assured her.

If only they could get to the Oder without another air raid. In

Ratibor, they had been told, all possible preparations had been made for the reception of the refugees; schools and barracks had been made ready, and there would be trains to carry them westward. All hopes were focused on the one word Ratibor, which up until then had meant little to most of the fugitives.

Later, Herr Hupfeld was taken aboard. A bomb splinter had hit him in the thigh. Blood had soaked through his trousers and frozen. Rosa recognized the city editor of the *Traveler* instantly. Only the day before, at the newspaper office, she had been furious with him for denouncing a young apprentice to the authorities as a "deserter" because he had been absent without an excuse. But that didn't matter now, the man needed help or he would bleed to death. Valeska, too, remembered Herr Hupfeld. Long ago, he had published her husband's articles on the castles of Upper Silesia, illustrated with his own photographs. Leo Maria had spoken of him occasionally, and wasn't it this same Herr Hupfeld who had written a favorable review of Ulla Ossadnik's debut, in which he had even mentioned the name of her teacher?

The convoy had kept on all night. In the morning they reached Budzin, where women came out to meet them with tea and the frozen travelers had warmed their hands on the hot pitchers and mugs. In the suburbs of Ratibor the road from Rybnik joined theirs, and on the new Oder bridge the Gleiwitz convoy merged with another of equal length, coming from the direction of Nikolai, Kattowitz, Königshütte, Sohrau, and Pless. There were ambulances full of wounded, trucks loaded with children from a boarding school, all wearing the same blue coats, and a long column of concentration camp inmates in striped clothing.

And then came an eerie, fantastic sight, a long column of Vlasov's troops: first officers on horseback, then orthodox priests with church banners and banners of the Blessed Virgin, and lastly soldiers in German uniforms with wild faces and great handlebar mustaches. Valeska was so enthralled by this vision that she almost forgot her own plight. But the convoy moved on. Determined despite their exhaustion to cross the Oder to safety, the marchers proceeded as mechanically as the legs of a centipede.

When Valeska woke up, she saw a naked light bulb hanging over her head. She sat up and looked around in the dingy light. People lay sleeping on the floor, the room smelled of urine and damp blankets. Leaning against the wall, she reached for her knapsack, and cautiously, for fear of waking anyone, took out a notebook and pencil. Just as District Judge Montag had kept a journal for his daughter, she would record the events she was living through for her son Josel. Propping the notebook on her knees, she wrote on the first page: "Ratibor, January 23, 1945."

Suddenly voices and steps were heard, the door was flung open. Some of the sleepers started up. Valeska shut her notebook and hid it under her coat. Two soldiers were standing in the doorway. One turned the light switch, but no additional light came on because there were no bulbs in the lamps. He shouted: "Attention, everybody! Any members of the Wehrmacht separated from their units? Report at once!"

Wondrak disentangled himself from the coat he had rolled up in and blinked at the dim light.

"Members of the Volkssturm or Flak units? Report at once! All men will show identity cards."

Though himself still befuddled, Willi shook Gregor awake.

"Those are Schörner's bloodhounds," said Rosa in a hoarse whisper.

One of the military policemen stood by the door, the other passed through the room, looking with narrowed eyes at the people lying on the floor. He took Willi's papers. Born in 1894. Men of that age were of little interest for his purposes. In returning Willi's papers, he said: "You're liable for Volkssturm duty. Report to the District Defense Command in your new place of residence. Where are you going?"

"Dresden," said Willi, with a glance at his sister.

Next the MP took the monk's' papers from his hand. Valeska watched closely as he looked suspiciously at the boy's face.

"What's the idea of the caftan?" he asked, pointing to the monk's robe. "How come you're not in the army?"

"I'm . . . I'm a novice with the Franciscans, I'm on my way . . ."

". . . to Dresden" Willi completed. "He's going into another monastery there."

The MP roared at Willi. "Shut your trap. Nobody asked you."

"Born in '29. That makes you about sixteen. No military training?" Gregor shook his head.

"Never called up?"

Again he shook his head.

"Good health?"

No answer.

"I asked you a question."

"Y-yes," Gregor stammered.

"Where are your buddies-in-Christ."

"They've stayed at the monastery in Gleiwitz," Willi answered for him.

Again the MP bellowed at him.

"Look here," said Willi. "What are you shouting for in the middle of the night? You have no right. I'm an attorney. I'll—"

"You keep your trap shut, you shitty attorney. We're in charge here, see!" He motioned to the other soldier to come over. "We're taking the kid. Thinks he can keep out of the army with a cross on his chest and a Jesuit's caftan."

Gregor looked at Willi, but Willi didn't raise his eyes.

"Let's go. Take your stuff and get moving." The MP put the monk's identity card in his pocket.

Gregor left without a word. He merely moved his right hand as if to bless them all in parting.

Willi put his shoes on. "I'm going too," he said tonelessly. "I've got to see where they're taking him."

The women didn't want to let him go. "Don't worry," he said. "I only want to find out where they're taking him. Tomorrow I'll find out more. Did you hear what he called me, a shitty attorney, that's what he said. I'm not taking that lying down . . ."

Rosa wanted to go along too; it was all Valeska could do to hold her back. Some of the other people approached and formed a semicircle around them. They'd been curious all along about the boy in the monk's habit, but they had been too tired to ask questions; now neither shame nor exhaustion deterred them.

"My son wasn't even sixteen and they drafted him as a Flak auxiliary before Christmas. Why should this little monk get away with it . . ."

"But he's only a child," said an old woman.

"A human life," said another, lying down again in the straw. "What's a human life worth these days . . . nothing, not a thing . . ."

24

WHEN HALINA WOKE UP, the wall clock had stopped. The silence in the room was almost palpable. That may have been what woke her. She got up, raised the blackout shades, and made a fire in the stove. She filled the kettle and put it on. She rummaged in Frau Piontek's clothes cupboard, picked a warm coat at random, and put it on. She did all this mechanically, with indifference; there seemed to be no connection between one movement and another. She pushed the pendulum of the clock, but after a few swings it stopped again. She looked for the key to wind the clock. She looked on top of the chiffonier, she looked in the drawers, on the little table beside the sofa, in the vitrine, on the windowsill between the potted plants, on the shelf in among the books of music. She racked her brains: where could it be? She searched frantically; after a while she may have forgotten what she was looking for. In a drawer she found some crocheted hats of various colors; she selected a pale blue one and put it on. It was somewhat too big, so she cleverly sewed a few stitches together until it fitted. She pulled the cap down low over her forehead and tied her head scarf over it; now no one would notice that her hair had been shorn. Then she went out and wandered aimlessly around the town. She avoided the main streets and crossed the Butter Market. She tried the doors of All Saints' Church but they were all locked. The telegraph office was dark. A streetcar turned screeching into Niederwallstrasse.

A group of men and women poured out of a shop, the door and windows of which had been smashed. Their coat pockets were bulging; the women had taken off their head scarves and filled them with miscellaneous articles. The men's caps were like the one Kolya was wearing when she had seen him for the first time.

Halina spoke to them in Polish. She had to repeat what she had said before they understood. "Come with me," she said. "My masters have run away. I'm alone in the house. There's plenty to eat and drink, it's warm, and no one will look for you there. You can stay until the Russians get here."

They listened, hesitated, and whispered distrustfully among themselves. Suddenly Halina blurted out: "Just look at me. Because I loved an *ostarbeiter* like you, they shut me up in a camp." She took off her head scarf and the blue hat. When they saw Halina's shorn head, they went with her.

Back at the house on Strachwitzstrasse, Halina led her guests to the music room and lit the lamp with the green shade. The guests looked around. "Are we really alone here?" asked one of the men. His cap was full of bouillon cubes, which he now emptied out on the table.

"Yes, we're all alone. You can look all over. But don't walk off with anything." Then Halina gave crisp instructions: who should set the table, who should bring up coal from the cellar, who should help her in the kitchen.

While peeling potatoes, a woman named Lydia asked her: "Why are you doing this? Why did you bring us in from the street?"

Halina said nothing.

"We hate the Germans. We hate the Poles too. They haven't treated us any better."

Halina pointed at the potatoes they had peeled together. "Will this be enough for all of you? How many are we? Three men, four women. With me that makes eight. The men must be hungry."

While the potatoes were boiling in the kitchen, Halina went into the music room and spread a white tablecloth on the large dining table. She saw the women rummaging in the drawers of the chiffonier and in the clothes cupboard, taking out dresses and trying them on. Lydia put on a white hat with a bunch of cherries on it, admired herself in the mirror, and laughed. A man brought the big wall mirror in from the entrance and placed it in such a way that the women could look at themselves in the light of the green lamp. The women exchanged their old clothes for new. Their faces glowed with excitement and greed. They kept jumping up, standing at the mirror, and sitting down again, as though forgetting what they had put on and having to reassure themselves. One of the men asked if there was any vodka in the house, or at least a few bottles of beer.

Halina dished out the mashed potatoes; in each helping she made a hole and filled it with goulash; then she folded her hands, looked at her guests, and said aloud:

> Boże, dzięki Ci składamy
> za to, co pozyvać namy;
> Ty nas żywić nie przestajesz,
> pobłogosław, co nam dajesz. Amen.

The woman called Lydia crossed herself very quickly from right to left, as though ashamed to let the others see her.

"Your name is Kolya, isn't it?" said Halina to one of the men. "I know another Kolya. His real name is Arkadi Shevchuk. He's from a small town on the Dnieper, where it loops around. I've forgotten the name of the place."

The others laughed and ate.

"Kolya worked near here. We met in town every Sunday. But somebody must have watched us. One day two years ago, it was Maundy Thursday, the police came and dragged me away. They arrested Kolya the same day and nobody knows where they took him. I've asked all over. But I'll find him someday. And then we'll get married."

The others ate and laughed.

"If you don't even know the name of the town your Kolya comes from, how can you expect to find him? Half the people in the Ukraine are called Shevchuk, and the Dnieper is a long river with a loop every few miles."

"Can anybody play the piano?" Yuri wanted to know. "A march! The fascists are kaputt! Now it's our turn! Our people have won the war!"

"Vodka!" cried Volodya. "Isn't there anything to drink?" He went into the kitchen and sniffed at the empty bottles.

"I want a fur coat," one of the women shouted. "Where have the fucking Germans hidden their fur coats?"

"We gotta go to houses with owners that haven't cleared out. We gotta take the fur coats off the German whores," screamed Lydia who was eating too fast and spilling gravy on her dress.

Yuri went to the piano and opened it. "If nobody wants to play, I'll give it a try. But I don't play so good." He ran his hand over the keys and played a few chords. Then he sat down and hammered out a Ukrainian folksong, *Oy ty misyatsu, miy misyachenku*. It was a simple rhythm, repeated over and over, and with each repetition Yuri's playing became more assured. Kolya hummed the tune.

Volodya found two bottles of schnapps in the cellar, though one was only half full. He brought glasses from the kitchen, and then he too joined in the singing.

"*Oy ty misyatsu, miy mizyachenku.*"

"Not so loud," said Halina. "You're making more noise than the guns out there."

Nobody listened. Halina got up and went out into the entrance. Pushing the blackout shade aside, she looked out the window. It was dark now. The explosions seemed to have grown louder. From time to time a red-hot projectile flew hissing over the house.

She came back to the others, who were happily clinking glasses. "The Russians are attacking the city," she said. "I think we better go down to the cellar."

"The cellar? Any vodka down there?"

"No, no vodka. But we'll be safer. Take your glasses with you."

"Change your dress," said one of the women to Halina. "Why should you run around like a scarecrow? We're the top people now. Come on, take this one. God knows how long we'll be able to keep these things . . ."

"No, no," Halina resisted. "That's my Pani's dress. Never." But then it occurred to her: "One of Frau Wondrak's dresses, why not? That wouldn't be a sin."

The dress she put on was light blue taffeta, with an enormous artificial rose on the bodice. It made her feel good and she stood for a while posturing at the mirror. It was a little too wide in the hips, a tuck would be needed. The silk was cold, so she put on a knitted jacket Irma had given her over the dress. If she left the collar open, the rose could still be seen to good advantage. A string with a piece of amber on it hung from her neck.

> *"Viyut vitry, vivut buyni,*
> *az dereva gnu-utsya,*
> *oy, yak bolit moye sertse,*
> *a slyezy ne lyutsya . . ."*

sang the women, and Yuri did his best to accompany them on the piano. Halina sat listening. This was the first song she had really liked. She would try to learn it, and one day she would sing it with Kolya. The tune was new to her, and she had difficulty in humming it, but after each verse it sounded more familiar, and in the end it seemed to her that she had known the song all her life.

in the camp I was in I asked the women if they knew a man named Arkadi Shevchuk from a small town on the Dnieper where it loops around I've forgotten the name of the place they all said they knew an Arkadi Shevchuk but when I described you with your eyes and your nose and your funny cap that was a little too big for you and when I told them you wrote me love letters in the sky with the trees every day a new one they all said they didn't know that kind of Arkadi Shevchuk.

"Does anybody know how to wind that clock?" Halina asked. "I've lost the key. Does anybody know how to wind that clock?"

No one was paying attention. They all sang and clapped their hands and began turning slowly in a circle. They were dancing a gopak.

25

"WE GOTTA GO NOW," said Jochen.

"Wait a minute," said Piechotta. "Hedel is making me a hot drink to clear my bronchial tubes. If I go out in the cold like this, I'll catch my death."

He didn't really want to go. But there was that bazooka in the doorway on Schillerstrasse, he'd love to fire it at a tank; this was his chance and he didn't want to miss it.

"There's only one bazooka for the two of us," said Jochen, "and we still haven't decided who's going to fire it."

"I've told you a dozen times," said Piechotta. "When the time comes we'll draw lots."

"Is that one of the new miracle weapons?" Hedel asked innocently while pouring hot water into the strainer. She spilled some of it and burned her fingers. "*Pyerunnye,*" was all she said.

"It won't make a dent in their new tank, the T-34."

"Oh yes it will. You just have to get a little closer. At forty yards it won't stand a chance."

"It's very hot," said Hedel, pushing the cup over to Piechotta. "Take care not to burn your lips."

"Fine," he said. "This'll clean the muck out of my bronchial tubes."

"The trouble is you'll never get as close as forty yards," said Jochen. "They'll shoot you full of holes first."

"The best way is to let them pass, and then fire it from the window." Piechotta took a sip of his hot drink, tea with a shot of schnapps in it. "And then get out of there on the double, because the next thing you know there won't be anything left of that house."

"In other words," said Jochen dryly, "a suicide job."

"We'd better go," said Piechotta, rising to his feet. "If a patrol comes along and we're not there, we'll be in trouble."

"We've never taken the oath," said Jochen. "We might just as well

stay here. Nobody knows where we are. Kotik Ossadnik never came
to get us."

"But we've taken an oath," said Piechotta. "What about our HY
oath?"

"It makes no difference," said Kotik. "If you stay here, nobody'll
ever find you, that's for sure. But you better make up your mind
soon. It sounds like they're shelling the city."

"Quiet," said Jochen. "Stop slurping for a second."

They all listened.

"They're shelling the city," said Hedel. "Wouldn't you rather stay
here? There's a glow in the west, like something's burning. How do
we know if any of your bunch is still there?"

"If I know my *hoppeks*," said Kotik, "they cleared out long ago."

"The grown-ups beat it," said Hedel, "and kids like you are supposed to stop the Russian tanks. It's crazy." She had given them
food and drink, she had talked and even danced with them. So now
she felt responsible for them in a way, though she was only a few
years older than they were.

The two boys couldn't make up their minds. They avoided looking
at each other. They hoped for something to happen that would force
a decision. But nothing happened. Except that Kotik brought out
his *Zarathustra*, leafed through it, and began to read: "Here. Listen
to this. On Voluntary Death. *Many die too late and some die too soon.
It sounds strange to say: Die at the right time—But that is Zarathustra's
teaching: Die at the right time. Yet, how can those who have never lived
at the right time die at the right time? Better if they had never been
born. That is what I have to say to the superfluous. But even the superfluous
make a great to-do about their dying and even the hollowest nut wants
to be cracked. All make a big thing of dying. But death is not a
festival—*"

"*Pyerunnye!*" Piechotta broke in. "I'm going now. I'll fire my
bazooka and make myself scarce. You can't lose a bad penny. Can
somebody show me how to get out of here?"

"Sure," said Kotik absently. "I'll let you out." He led Piechotta
to the window and helped him to climb out. When he came back,

Hedel was putting on her heavy *galoty*. Kotik stopped in the doorway and stared at her as if she were a stranger.

"I'm going too, Kotik," she said. She tried to put a little tenderness into her voice; she herself was surprised at how cold it sounded. "I've got to go home. My God, what have I done, leaving my mother alone, how could I do such a thing? No, Kotik. Don't say anything. I have to go. We'll see each other again. God willing."

Kotik couldn't see her face. The candlelight was too faint and he was too far away from her. "I'll take you home," he said softly.

"No, don't. I know my way. And there are shells bursting out there."

"I know. That's why I'm going, I won't let you go alone. And I'll take two jars of preserves for your mother, one of meat and the other of *reines-claudes*. You told me you liked the name, didn't you? *Reine-claude*."

26

IN THE EVENING red-hot projectiles came whistling across the black sky and landed in the outskirts. Young Grochowiak and Frau Aubitzky's two eldest sons had just come home with a heavily loaded sled. Herr Mazura welcomed them at the door and the women came up from the cellar to help them unload.

"A whole sack of corn! And milk powder! And cornstarch pudding. And soup powder! A whole carton. A pail of synthetic honey! And Dextromalt, a whole carton of Dextromalt. And grape sugar, food for the nerves. And egg powder!" The women sang out the name of each item as they caught sight of it.

"Where are such things still to be found?" Anna Ossadnik had to touch every single article to convince herself that it was real.

Frau Aubitzky was horrified. "What if you'd been caught!" she cried. But she was proud of her sons. One was ten, the other twelve. She had kept a tight hold on the youngest to keep him from going along.

"Grape sugar!" Old man Bednarz tore open a package, stuck his finger in, and licked it.

Only Frau Jacob stayed in her corner with her two children, because it was all she could do to keep hold of them.

Herr Mazura was awestruck. "Where can it all come from?" he wondered. It was he who had sent the two boys out, while solemnly adjuring them not to tell a soul. He had seen sacks being hauled out of the house next door and heard that Schnapka's Bakery had been broken into and that flour and sugar had been carried away. The houses and shops of people who had fled were being pillaged, and what you didn't take would be taken by someone else. Friends advised him to send children to Schnapka's on Wilhelmstrasse as soon as possible, before the whole place was cleaned out, but not to let any grown-ups go with them, because there were still patrols going around; true, they were only looking for deserters and they had their hands full with that, but you never could tell when they might take it into their heads to set an example by shooting a looter, as they had threatened to do in the last number of the *Traveler*.

"We found the stuff at Schachtner's Grocery Store," said Thomas Grochowiak proudly.

"Delicatessen," Tobias corrected him.

"Actually we were too late," said Klaus, still flushed with excitement. "The best stuff was gone. Chocolate, cigarettes, schnapps, and so on . . ."

Some twenty children from all over town had been there; they had hauled crates and cartons out of Herr Schachtner's private apartment. The store had already been cleaned out, the plate-glass window had been smashed, the floor was littered with broken glass, cornstarch, canned goods, dehydrated potatoes, sugar—they'd had to wade through all that to reach the apartment in back. And everything had gone so fast, by the time they had taken a carton off the shelf and carried it down to their sled, other kids had stripped the whole shelf. And the few cans of airman's chocolate—well, they'd had to swipe those from another gang. It wasn't fair for one gang to monopolize all that chocolate.

"So there was nothing doing at Schnapka's Bakery?" Mazura asked. "Flour and sugar and powdered milk would come in handy . . ."

"All looted before we got there."

"Hush!" The women didn't like to hear that word.

"But Schachtner's shelves were full. I've always said that what that man hoards in his cellar is nobody's business," said Frau Grochowiak triumphantly.

Anna Ossadnik hid a can of chocolate under her coat for Kotik. The poor boy, he'd even forgotten what chocolate tasted like.

"None of that!" said Mazura, who was keeping a close watch. "It's for everybody." He proceeded to collect everything the women had secretly put aside. "And now we'll divide it fair and square."

The boys put on their caps, prepared to go out again.

"We gotta hurry," said Thomas, "if we want to get anything. Some of the kids have gone ahead to loo—"

"Hush!" said the women.

". . . to see that they can find at Defaka's."

But the women wouldn't let them go. Not in the darkness and not with the city under fire.

Next day the mothers went with their children. That way, they thought, they could keep an eye on them. And they appeased their consciences by telling themselves that they would take only ownerless property; there couldn't be any harm in that. Anna went along and inquired about Kotik wherever possible. In the soap factory on Lohmeyerstrasse they filled sacks and towels with soap powder. Somewhere they heard about enormous stocks of wheat flour at the Danziger Mill, so they went to the mill, dumped out the soap powder, and filled their sacks with flour. In a shed near the rifle club they found new automobile tires, and in a factory on Damaschkerstrasse there were thousands of leather soles tied up in bundles according to size, enough to mend the shoes of all Gleiwitz, though for years it had been impossible to have a pair of shoes soled. So they loaded tires and soles onto their sleds, and when they got home they didn't know what to do with them. Someone came and said there were dried vegetables stored in the old radio station, so they all went running and filled their sacks with lentils and split peas. Someone else reported potted meat at the railroad workers' canteen, so they all went there.

After a while Anna gave up and went home, mainly because on Preussenplatz she had seen a soldier hanging from a tree. His head was bare, the epaulets had been torn off his uniform, and a cardboard sign had been hung around his neck. Anna had no desire to read it. It was just as well, she thought, that she hadn't gone to the Butter Market with Frau Grochowiak. It seemed that the priest of Holy Cross Church had cut down and removed the three hanged Hitler Youths to spare the faithful of his congregation the gruesome sight.

Anna had told her husband about it. Time and again she looked up, hoping and expecting to see Kotik standing in the doorway just as he had gone out, wearing his woolen cap and thick earmuffs and the long winter coat she had bought for Bruno, which Andreas had worn later on, and which, if the truth be known, was most becoming to Kotik. If Kotik had been drafted like the others, she would have reconciled herself. But going out to an exercise and not coming back, that was a matter for the police.

Franz only laughed bitterly. There wasn't a single policeman left in town. The criminals had let themselves out of their jail cells and now they'd be all over town looting.

Yes, the Archpriest had spoken of a lawless period. But she hadn't expected it to be like this.

Thomas Grochowiak and Frau Aubitzky's eldest came back after dark. There were no more food stocks to be had; they brought a pile of towels, a laundry basket full of dishes, and an Underwood typewriter.

"You look frozen," said Frau Aubitzky, mustering the cheap hotel china with distaste. "Oh well, you can't always be as lucky as yesterday. That grocery store was worthwhile."

27

"HANNAH, THE FLAG!" Herr Mazura shouted, and his wife, who was generally thought to be deaf and dumb because she never opened her mouth, came up from the cellar with two flags, which she clumsily unrolled.

"Now is the right time to hang out the white flag," he said. "Then they won't blow us up."

He decided to hang one flag from Frau Grochowiak's apartment on the top floor. They went upstairs together. The toilet window seemed best, the Russians would see it as soon as they turned the corner from Hauptstrasse.

Mazura wedged the flag into the window frame. That meant leaving the window open a crack, and Frau Grochowiak protested vehemently. She was afraid the water pipes would freeze. But Mazura couldn't worry about a little thing like that, not in this situation. He was visibly relieved once the flag was in place. He hung the second flag from the Pieczyks' kitchen window; the Pieczyks couldn't protest because they weren't there. Now a white flag could be seen from either direction.

"I been thinking a long time about a white flag, but it's a funny thing, you know, you hang 'em out too soon a soldier patrol come by and string you up for a coward. It's the timing that counts. Timing's the biggest thing in life."

Once in his life he had got his timing wrong; in January 1932 he had joined the Communist Party. That hadn't done him any good at all. He had been worried about timing ever since.

"Look," said Frau Grochowiak. "Those people over there have hung out a bed sheet on a broomstick."

Mazura leaned out the window. "But we was first," he said proudly.

Just then they heard a violent pounding on the front door. Followed by something that sounded like windowpanes being smashed.

"*Bozhe kokhany*, here they are," said grandmother Zielonka, holding out her knotted, rosary-entwined old hands to someone whom in her semiblindness she assumed to be a Russian. But it was only Franz Ossadnik looking for his wife.

With one finger Frau Aubitzky scraped soot from the stovepipe and smeared it on her face. She sat her smallest child on her lap and told the other two to sit beside her. Frau Grochowiak turned pale. She picked up little Ingelore in one arm and imprisoned little Thomas with the other. She would never let them go. Anna sat on a kitchen chair at the back and pulled a black cloth over her face. Her husband threw an old gray blanket over her. Frau Smolka's teeth chattered audibly and she covered her mouth with her apron. She pushed her old father forward and hid her two daughters behind his back. Frau Zielonka put on a pair of child's glasses and tried to comfort her old mother-in-law.

Mazura kept mumbling something. *"Da zdrastvuytye tovarishchi. Ya tozhe tovarishch."* An *ostarbeiter* had written that down for him a while ago and he had learned it by heart. Greetings, comrades. I too am a comrade.

When the Russians came, he would shout that through the door at them. And now, here they were. His chin trembled with excitement.

"I think we'd better open," said Franz Ossadnik when the pounding grew louder. "If we don't, they'll throw a hand grenade at the door, and that'll be the end of us."

Shouts and screams were heard and sounds of shattering glass as if the upstairs windows were being smashed one after another.

Mazura, Ossadnik, and Zielonka ran to the door. Shouting *"Ya tozhe tovarishch,"* Mazura knocked the chock out from under the door handle and opened.

Outside there were several people, it was hard to get a good look at them. One was holding an iron bar, another an ax, one was carrying a suitcase on his shoulder. There were five or six of them, all in civilian clothes. The man with the suitcase was ludicrously bundled up. Over his heavy sweater he was wearing two jackets, and over the two jackets an overcoat that was bursting at the seams.

"Ya tozhe tovarishch," said Mazura, but with less assurance than

before. Intimidated by the iron bar, he held his hands up. Ossadnik did likewise.

For a moment they all, newcomers and defenders alike, froze stock-still. Then the man thrust the iron bar against Mazura's chest. "You Gitler!" he said. "Gitler kaputt!"

His companions laughed.

There's no red star on their foreheads, Ossadnik thought.

One of them spoke a little German. He was holding a carbide lamp of the kind used in coal mines. He shined it into the shelter, but as he was standing by the door it didn't show him much. He therefore ordered the people in the shelter to leave their belongings and come out. He spoke extremely rapid broken German, but repeated his few sentences so often that in the end everyone understood.

When Mazura tried to say something in Polish, the man with the iron bar poked him in the chest and told him to shut up. "Yesterday Gitler, today tovarishch, *nix, malchik*. All fascist. *Davai, davai!*"

One by one they climbed slowly out of the cellar. The man with the iron bar hurried them with loud unintelligible threats. Frau Aubitzky put on her fur coat as inconspicuously as possible. Old Frau Zielonka prayed aloud and rattled her rosary. Old man Bednarz slipped his package of grape sugar into his trouser pocket. Frau Grochowiak fished her Dresden Savings Bank deposit books and a couple of papers out of her suitcase and stuffed them into her underpants. Frau Smolka was so terrified that her false teeth fell out and she was afraid to bend down and pick them up.

Anna Ossadnik and Frau Jacob with her two children were the last to leave the shelter. One of the invaders reached under Anna's head scarf and pulled her ears. Then he made her show her hands. "*Psiakrev!*" he cursed. "You give gold or me smash whole business!"

But Anna had hidden her jewelry under a loose brick. She showed her hands and said: "*Nix* gold! We poor people!"

They were driven into the stairwell and made to sit down on the cold steps with their hands over their heads. The man with the iron bar held them at bay. The other marauders went down into the shelter and from there sounds were heard that made the victims fear the worst. Frau Smolka wept and wailed. From under her dress she drew a pouch and handed it over. But she implored the invaders not to smash her sewing machine. She believed that as long as she had her sewing machine she and her two daughters and her old father wouldn't starve, because there's always sewing to be done, even the Russians need to have things sewed. Talking without her teeth, she couldn't really make herself understood, least of all by the Russian. He opened the pouch, found a pair of earrings and a few coins, and seemed satisfied. But the others kept on with their work of devastation in the shelter, and Frau Smolka wept inconsolably.

It was not until much later that Anna remembered what had happened. Cradling her head in her hands, she sat with the others in the stairwell. Her arms were numb, she was not afraid, her only feeling was one of emptiness, the soul had gone out of her, leaving only an empty shell.

When the Russians were gone, Franz bent over her and slapped her cheeks. "Anna," he said. "Wake up. Anna, can you see me? Can you hear me? Anna, Anna." She seemed to come back from far far away; it was a long while before the whitewashed wall turned into Franz's pale face, as though she had to learn to see. She and Franz were the last to return to the shelter, where the other women were looking for their belongings by candlelight. Anna saw feathers floating through the air, getting into people's eyes, sticking to their lips and, attracted by the heat of the candles, catching fire and burning with a soft hissing sound.

Before leaving, the invaders must have gutted the featherbeds and tossed them into the air.

Only now did it dawn on Mazura that the vandals had been *ostarbeiter*. "They ain't allowed to loot," he said.

"We should have resisted," said Zielonka.

But no one had resisted; they wouldn't have known how to resist.

"A week ago," said Ossadnik, "they stepped off the sidewalk to let us pass. Now they walk over us."

"It's their revenge," said Frau Grochowiak calmly, as though she thought it only natural. Anyway, she had saved her safe-deposit books.

"They were Ukrainians," Frau Smolka insisted. Holding a lighted candle, she was looking frantically for her lost teeth.

"So what?" said Frau Aubitzky. It was all one to her whether they were *ostarbeiter*, Italians, Ukrainians, or Russians. Her wedding ring was gone. She hadn't wanted to give it to them, but the man with the ax had threatened to chop off her finger. Such brutality! She wouldn't have thought it possible. But she consoled herself with the thought that they weren't really human. "Subhuman!" she hissed. "Subhuman!" And she swallowed a quarter of a sleeping pill to quiet her nerves.

Frau Smolka was having another crying jag. But now she was crying for joy; she had found her teeth, and her sewing machine lay unharmed beside the stove.

"How can people do such things?" lamented Anna Ossadnik, who was looking for her husband's blue railroad worker's coat. "*O Bozhe*, where can it be?" she sighed. "Oh, Franzek, it's the only warm coat you've got."

"So we been looted," said Mazura. He sounded almost relieved. Deep down, they had all expected as much. In a way they had paid tribute to the victor. But what made Mazura go purple with rage was that it was *ostarbeiter* and not Russian soldiers. And one of them had said to him: "Du Gitler!" That was more than he could stomach.

"Those lovely white flags that we hung out the window!" said Frau Grochowiak. "It just wasn't any use."

28

"THE FIREWHEEL SPINS in the snow." Gerhart Hauptmann sat motionless in his armchair at the window, his beige cashmere blanket drawn up almost to his shoulders, his head inclined slightly to one side.

As usual, he had taken his afternoon nap in the tower room. From there Annie had led him to the library, where tea was served in winter, and he had asked her to move his chair close to the window, beside the big Silesian oak table. Snow was falling, and he wanted to watch the whirling flakes, while pondering what he would dictate to Annie after tea. In the failing light, the fir trees outside the window lost their green and became black silhouettes against a white, snowy backdrop. He followed a large snowflake with his eyes, watched it dance, leap, flutter closer, cling to the windowpane, and melt away; he often lost himself in such games.

Voices and sounds rose from the entrance hall. Hauptmann passed his hand over his face. He had seen the firewheel spinning in the snow, flaring up and fading away.

Frau Hauptmann came in, followed by Annie carrying the tea tray and, behind her, the secretary. Frau Hauptmann went straight to the table lamp and switched it on. Instantly, the snowflakes outside the window vanished in the darkness. The yellow artificial light enlarged the room, accentuated the heavy cupboards and bookshelves, and made the white markings on the walls revert to what they had always been, death masks, while at the same time the Charioteer—who in the dusk had returned once again, greeted by the jubilation of the crowd, to Delphi, proud, unapproachable, triumphant in the awareness of his perfect beauty which had transformed his robe into an Ionic column—became once more a copy of a museum piece.

"How are we today?" Frau Hauptmann asked with her familiar voice, leading her husband to the upholstered bench, above which hung a lithograph of the temple at Paestum.

Hauptmann opened his mouth and made a sound. Hard to say whether he was sighing or yawning. Annie put down the tray. His wife distributed the cups and looked among the books for a place in which to put the majolica dish with the tea cakes on it. She preferred to do this herself as it enabled her to determine the seating order of the guests. But today they would be alone, just the four of them. She always placed herself diagonally across from her husband, who sat in the shadow. That way she could keep an eye on him and help him when necessary.

She wore a simple black dress, a black silk stole, and a double string of white pearls. She always wore her white hair short and parted on the left, as she had worn it even before it had become fashionable in the twenties, and she continued to do so long after everyone but a few shopgirls had given it up. Her face could still be called beautiful, though it now seemed burned out from having passed through many fires. It had a cold, marmoreal quality, and when she just sat there listening it resembled one of the many death masks on the wall.

The secretary was as usual correctly dressed, in a three-piece suit with a silk handkerchief in his breast pocket and a pearl in his tie. The severity of his features and bearing was tempered by his large, round tortoiseshell glasses, which contributed a note of gentleness and indulgence. As usual, he was holding a folder and a book. It was the old man's habit to dictate after tea, but he had been feeling tired of late, especially since his fall in the park a few days after his birthday. Today he would decide during the tea ceremony whether to dictate afterward or have something read to him. He had not worked for several days; he complained of fatigue and a lingering catarrh, which was hardly noticeable but which had undoubtedly weakened him.

Frau Hauptmann passed the cups, first to Annie, who withdrew with hers to a place near the lectern and away from the lamplight, where she was almost out of sight but ready to take dictation if necessary. The secretary took the next cup and seated himself at the little table. Frau Hauptmann poured tea for herself and then it was her husband's turn; for him she poured coffee from an English silver coffeepot. In the afternoon he always took coffee, as a rule with cognac. Today the bottle was absent from the tray; this he had been the first to notice, but he had said nothing. His wife put two spoonfuls of sugar in his coffee and stirred it. She then put the spoon down on her own saucer—he had dropped so many spoons—and silently handed him the cup. His hands trembled, but only as long as she had her hand on the saucer.

The procedure was the same as every other day. Frau Hauptmann said something important or irrelevant, and the old man said something irrelevant or important in reply.

Until he spoke of the firewheel.

"Beg your pardon?" said Frau Hauptmann, pouring herself a second cup.

"Firewheel," said the old man. "I saw a firewheel in the snow."

"Firewheel?" his wife repeated, dragging out the strange, unusual word.

"It happens now and then before a snowfall. The clouds open and for a matter of seconds a strangely vibrant light shines through."

"Foul weather we're having," said Frau Hauptmann matter-of-factly. "We haven't had so much snow for years. It's really a good thing that we're going to Dresden."

She passed her husband the majolica dish and watched to make sure that he dipped his cinnamon cookie in his coffee before biting into it.

The idea of going to Dresden for the cure had first come to her when it became apparent that the old man was not throwing off his catarrh and was having a recurrent fever. They must really get away from the cold east winds and snowstorms, which had been especially violent up here in the mountains this winter. Besides, she could have her gallbladder looked at, for she was not at all pleased with the results of her recent treatment in Warmbrunn and was again having pain at night. Hauptmann had soon come around to her plan; he had brought it up time and again, and soon the projected trip had become associated in his mind with the hope of being able to start writing again.

Frau Hauptmann had made a number of phone calls; the sanatoria

were all crowded with wounded soldiers, but in the end she had
luck; the Weidners in Oberloschwitz were able to promise them a
garden house where the great man would be undisturbed.

"Ah, Dresden," Hauptmann murmured. "Dresden . . ." After a
short silence he asked, "When will the car be here?"

He knew it couldn't be there before Saturday or Sunday; they
had talked about it a number of times. He had been having moments
of anxiety lately. Brought on perhaps by his poor health or possibly
by the thought that his archives were due to be moved to the West
and that he didn't want to be present when the movers came for
them. Plans had already been made. Voigt wanted to entrust them
to the care of a Herr Ebermayer at the Kaibitz estate; Herr Ebermayer
had called on Hauptmann several times and hadn't been at all to his
liking: a vain, pretentious nonentity. Still, that secluded spot in Fran-
conia might actually be the safest place. If only he had his son
Benvenuto to advise him. He hoped to see him in Dresden, at least
for a few days. And oh yes, all those things that Voigt had unearthed
from time to time in the archives; he himself had been surprised,
things begun years and years ago . . . he had forgotten most of
them—there were some that he might finish now. He could get back
to Winckelmann, for instance. All his life he had been impressed by
Winckelmann, the son of a Silesian shoemaker born in Brieg, who
had made the sun of Hellenic beauty rise over Europe . . . yes, he
might do some more work on that.

The secretary took his tea with very little sugar, though he liked
it distinctly sweet. After all, he had tea with them every day; he had
offered the lady of the house his sugar coupons, but she had declined
them. She still had her "sources," there was always cake and cookies
in the house, and the table was always amply supplied. He himself
had once heard her complain to the Gauleiter's office in Breslau that
she hadn't enough coal for so large a house, and a week later more
fuel had been delivered.

Frau Hauptmann played with her necklace. She looked at the
grand old man's face, at his hands, at the book that lay open, spine
upward, on the table: Hafiz, *Poems*. So he was still working on the
cycle. According to Annie, he hadn't dictated anything in the last

few days but had only had her read to him. That was alarming. Because his new *Poems from the Tavern*, which he had dictated at Christmastime, seemed to have poured from him in one continuous stream. She had especially liked the one that began: *"Sleepily I make my way to the tavern,"* though Annie had read it abominably. Out of consideration for her delicate health he wouldn't let his wife read to him, though she read his poems better than anyone else. No, it didn't tire her in the least, and she would resume her cherished habit of reading to him in Dresden, when she was better. She would play the fiddle again too, because she knew that would make him happy and banish all gloom from his thoughts. She mustn't forget the precious Stradivarius that he had given her after the success of *The Sunken Bell*.

"How long shall we stay in Dresden?" he asked.

"Until . . . hmm, I wonder. Until March? Or April? What do you think? I'd like to stay until the crocuses bloom. And the daffodils and the forsythia. And the almond trees . . ."

"Yes," said Hauptmann. "Spring comes a lot sooner there . . ."

"It's hard for me to leave all this here," said his wife, "even if it's only for a few weeks . . ."

"We won't be gone for long," he said. "And it's not far. We shall still be on the right bank of the Elbe. The Silesian bank."

He would always keep faith with his Silesian destiny. If this was the end, he wanted to be in Silesia. It was here he belonged, here he wanted to die. But buried? It was from here that he had drawn his power and his poetry; as a child he had come alive to the miracle of Silesia, since then it had been his life. "Silesia's narrowness," he had always felt, "has become my breadth." He had grown up in the mountains, in the Riesengebirge, and Rübezahl had become as familiar a figure to him as the Man on the White Horse to Theodor Storm. He longed to rest by the sea. In Hiddensee? Or in Rapallo?

"Ah, the Silesians," he said. "Fate has not always dealt kindly with them. Far from it. It's no accident if the Silesian doesn't yodel or dance the schuhplattler. He is more inclined to contemplation and piety. He has worked hard and suffered enormously. The Silesian songbook is heartbreaking. But suffering finds many ways of achieving greatness. Consider, for instance, Angelus Silesius and the shoemaker Jakob Boehme . . ."

The secretary opened his folder unobtrusively and made a note. Frau Hauptmann collected the cups. "You know, my dear, Herr Pohl is coming this evening with the village teacher, who is bringing a sculptress, who wants to sketch you . . . She's a refugee from Upper Silesia, she arrived only a few days ago . . ."

If it were up to her, she thought, she would stop having people in. But the old man liked to have company in the evening.

"Let them come," he said. "Crazy Ferdinand always has the latest political news. Let them come. And you," he added, turning to the secretary, "be sure to place this sculptress in such a way that she can sketch me to her heart's content. But the sketches stay here. Don't forget that. I'm counting on you."

Frau Hauptmann left the room. She had pushed the tray to the back of the table, where it wouldn't be in the way. The maid could take it away later on.

The secretary tried to remember where they had left off in their last conversation. They had talked about Electra's hatred of her mother, which had been her dominant passion, because when she was a child her mother had treated her like a Cinderella. For are not all the great passions of drama rooted in the slights and grievances of childhood?

"Read to me," said the old man to the secretary. "But not Hafiz; something from that old manuscript Voigt discovered. The Wild Ride."

He sat there and listened. After quite some time he cleared his throat, motioned to the secretary to come closer, grasped his hand and held it for a moment. "Did I write that?" he asked thoughtfully. "Really? It's beautiful . . ."

The guests did not stay late that evening. The old man's catarrh made itself felt; at times he was too stuffed up to speak. "Crazy Ferdinand" told the old stories that they all knew, but this evening they sounded a litte sadder than usual. The teacher with the tiny glasses that kept sliding off his nose spoke interminably of the new

Atlantis that would emerge after the war. The sculptress sketched,
but she wasn't satisfied with her work and she wouldn't let anyone
look at her pad.

Before the guests came, Frau Hauptmann had combed the old
man's hair and sprinkled it lightly with blue powder, which made
his head larger and more sculptural.

"I have delivered two important speeches in favor of a German
Upper Silesia," said Hauptmann. "Don't you remember?"

Traute Bombonnek looked up when the poet addressed her. She
nodded, but she did not remember.

Hauptmann asked the secretary to bring him the *For Nation and
Spirit* volume of his speeches. They must be in that one, he thought.
He had delivered one in Hirschberg, the other in the overcrowded
Berlin Philharmonie.

The secretary brought in the resplendent blue-linen volume published by S. Fischer in 1932. Yes, there were the two speeches along with
memorials to Leistikow, Otto Brahm, Paul Schlenther, Richard Deh-
mel, Walther Rathenau—"None of all that could be published today." Wearily he shut the book. Why lose himself in his memories?

He turned to the sketching Fräulein Bombonnek. "I hear you're
from Gleiwitz," he said. "I've visited the industrial zone quite a few
times. After *The Weavers* I was going to write a play about the misery
of the Silesian miners . . . the poor devils . . . Someone actually did
write the play but not until much later . . ."

"*Underground Front* by Wiessala," Herr Pohl volunteered. But the
old man's thoughts had hurried ahead.

"I have always felt a kinship with the Silesian farm country. That's
where I'm from. I know the polarities between Upper and Lower
Silesia. The one industrial, the other agricultural, the one Catholic,
the other Protestant. But they are identical in their naive piety, their
unquestioning faith, their mysticism. Here a bit sunnier, there a bit
darker, gloomier. The farther I've gone from Silesia, the more keenly
I've felt that the two belong together."

This Herr Pohl felt able to corroborate. He had visited the miners'
housing complexes in Gleiwitz before the war. "They were still living
like the weavers of Langenbielau a hundred years ago."

But the old man hardly listened. He was tired and wanted to go to bed. It was time for the guests to leave. Frau Hauptmann led the old man upstairs to his bedroom. In the Paradise Room, with his back to the Avenarius murals, the secretary bade the guests good-bye.

Fräulein Bombonnek feasted her eyes. How glad she would be to come back and see all this at leisure in the daylight. And the imposing bust of the grand old man on the gallery. "Whom is it by?"

"Oh," said the secretary, "that's Goethe by d'Angers."

"Really?" said Fräulein Bombonnek apologetically. She was disappointed.

Frau Hauptmann plumped up the old man's pillows and helped him to put on the hairnet he wore at night. She laid the book of Hafiz's poems on his bedside table, as he wished to read a while before going to sleep. When she had gone, the old man read a few poems, then closed the book and took his diary out of the drawer. He held it for a time and stared at the flowers on the binding. Without having opened it he put it back on the table.

29

THE SUN, which had long been absent, reappeared on the milky horizon. It came almost as a surprise to Valeska that here in a strange city the sun should still be a great golden ball, balancing on rooftops, making the snow sparkle, giving the air a new transparency, and glittering on windowpanes. She had the impression that the people in the street walked differently, as though expecting a certain consolation from its kindly beams.

The town was crowded with refugees. It was all Valeska and Rosa could do to find shelter in a girls' high school not far from the town hall. As there were not enough mattresses to go around, straw had been strewn on some of the classroom floors. A flood of refugees was still pouring across the Oder. When she and Rosa went to the bridge, they still saw an almost unbroken stream of horse-drawn wagons, sleds, and heavily bundled figures. How, they wondered, could room possibly be found for so many people? The crowding was made worse by the few trains that had got through from Ratiborhammer, but then the line skirting the Oder had been cut. Gleiwitz and Rauden had been either captured or encircled, the flood of fugitives from there had been stopped, and only a few isolated peasants from the surrounding villages were still getting away over back roads. The only road from the industrial zone to remain open was the one from Rybnik, and it was from there that the bulk of the refugees were now coming. It was rumored that Gauleiter Bracht of Kattowitz, known to be terminally ill, and his entire staff had crossed the Oder bridge in a long convoy. Conditions on the road seemed to have become even more appalling than when Valeska and her family had come.

The armed forces had received orders to withdraw to the Moravian front. As Valeska heard from an exhausted woman, the refugees had been obliged to wait for hours, with the roaring of the Russian guns growing louder and louder, to let Wehrmacht convoys through.

There had been clashes between soldiers and refugees; the refugees had thrown up barricades to stop the soldiers—they wanted the army to defend them instead of running off to the Reich. But the soldiers were unable to fight. For fear of being cut off, they had had to abandon their heavy matériel, and in any case the order to retreat had come too late. The evacuation had been a race with death for all concerned, and the woman found it hard to believe that she and her family had actually come through.

All day long, from dawn to dusk, Valeska and Rosa had made inquiries. They had rushed from the Red Cross to the hospital, from the district military command to the Party offices, from the Bar Association to the district courthouse, from army posts to the schoolhouses serving as refugee barracks, trying to find a trace of Irma and the children or of Willi Wondrak. From time to time they would stop on the Oder bridge and look on as fresh waves of refugees passed. Now and then they would ask some of them where they had come from and how long they had been on the road, just as others had asked them when they first arrived.

On the third day, by which time they should properly have left the city, they found Irma in a children's hostel attached to a Franciscan convent. Little Roswitha's fever was being treated there.

The Wehrmacht car had brought them as far as Ratibor. They had spent the first night in the municipal hospital. Irma had refused to leave the hospital until her sick daughter was examined; a doctor appeared but a few comforting words and a few pills were the best he could do for her. She was then attached to a group scheduled to take the train to Dresden. But Irma insisted on waiting until Roswitha recovered from her fever. Besides, she thought she would be most likely to find her mother here in Ratibor. A nun took her under her wing and arranged to have her lodged at the Franciscan convent. Luckily this was the first convent Valeska and Rosa went to.

In search of Willi, they then went to two monasteries, but at neither was anything known of a monk by the name of Gregor remotely corresponding to their description. There was nothing more they could do. Nevertheless, wishing to continue their journey with Irma and the children, they applied for authorization to spend three

more days in the city, which was granted because they moved in
with Irma at the convent, thus making room for others in the school-
house. Because of supply problems, refugees were allowed to spend
only three days in the city. It came as a surprise to Valeska that
wherever they went with their inquiries they were greeted with a
"Heil Hitler." In Gleiwitz this had long ceased to be the case except
in Party offices. Here she even came across women who were still
talking about final victory and the miracle weapon that would suddenly change everything. She could only shake her head, quite forgetting that up until recently she had talked in exactly the same way.

"It's just that they haven't been through anything," she said.

In general, there were now two classes of people, those who had
"been through it" and those who hadn't "been through anything
yet," the "yet" implying that their turn would come. In these days
Valeska thought about her house, her garden, the hiding place under
the gooseberry bushes, the piano, the wall clock, and Halina. She
thought about Leo Maria's grave in the cemetery on Coselerstrasse,
and the marble tombstone on which room had been left for her
name. It all seemed so far away, a beautiful memory already fading,
though it was only a week since she had left Gleiwitz.

"Maybe Willi and Gregor are still on the other side of the Oder,"
said Valeska.

"But only soldiers are left there," said Rosa.

"Exactly," said Valeska. "They'll make soldiers of them."

"In that case, I'll try to cross over tomorrow," said Rosa, who
had already lain down on her mattress. The mattress was thin and
horse hair was sticking out at the sides.

"They won't let you through," said Valeska. "I hear the east bank
is mined and the bridges are fitted with explosive charges."

"Didn't you give Willi an address of some sort when he left us?"

Valeska looked at her hands. They had swollen during the night
on the road and there were cracks in the skin. Now they were slowly
healing. "I only said something about Dresden and Oberloschwitz,
where Ulla Ossadnik is. Josel wrote me that he has been corresponding with her. So that's the only address in the West that we both
know about."

"I know an address in Freiburg," said Rosa. "The Albert Book-store, where I once worked. I'm sure they'd remember me."

"Freiburg?" said Valeska. "But the Americans will be moving in any minute."

"Better the Americans than the Russians," said Rosa.

For a time nothing was said. Then Rosa asked: "Do you think Willi was in love with that monk?"

"What gave you that idea?" Valeska affected surprise, though she had been thinking of nothing else for days.

"They didn't take him away, he could have stayed with us," said Rosa. There was no reproach in her tone.

"He felt responsible for the boy. You know my brother," said Valeska, pretending to take it lightly. She didn't want to think about it.

But Rosa didn't see it that way. "He sacrificed himself for Gregor."

Irma came in, putting an end to the unpleasant exchange. "I hear you're thinking of going to Dresden. Maybe we shouldn't go so far. If we stay near here and the Russians are beaten back, we'll be home in no time. What do you think?"

30

I T W O U L D H A V E been better if Kotik hadn't taken Hedel home, but he insisted. He was bent on showing her mother that he, Kotik Ossadnik from Teuchertstrasse, had protected her daughter and brought her safely home. *Frau Zock takes pleasure in announcing the engagement of her daughter* . . . But far from being glad to find her missing daughter in good health and the best of spirits, Frau Zock flew into a rage and threw hot-water bags at her. Even so, they were lucky it was a *hoppek* who had brought her home and not a soldier, because then she would have murdered them both.

Kotik took two jars from his knapsack, one of potted meat, the other of stewed fruit, and put them on the table in the hope of mollifying Hedel's mother, but the effect was quite the opposite. Hedel's grandmother, however, grabbed both jars and took them to her private cache behind the stove.

Kotik stood awkwardly by the door. The room was overheated and he was bathed in sweat. So this was where Hedel lived. With these two old women. No wonder she took off whenever she had a chance.

Hedel didn't say a word. After calmly removing her coat and shoes, she picked up the hot-water bags and refilled them from the steaming kettle. She was so used to her mother's vituperation that she hardly heard it. The only thing she minded was the presence of a witness. She gave Kotik a glance and a gesture meaning that he'd better go. But he stood rooted to the spot. "I'm getting you out of here," he said. "This is no place for you."

But his words were drowned out by Hedel's mother's flow of invective. "The shameless slut! They'd all like to know, and so would I, where the shameless slut spends her nights, when she's not home under the care and protection of her ailing mother who's worried sick. Does she ever stop to think of that, the slut, holy St. Barbara of the coal miners, you've seen where she spends her nights, so tell me, by the Turin Shroud, I really want to know. And what's this kid doing here, come here, you *dyobok*, what have you been doing to my daughter, the daughter of a sick, respectable old woman, have you been touching her, tell me that, where have you been touching her with your greedy filthy rotten fingers . . . ?"

Tears of rage came to Kotik's eyes. He'd have liked to leap at the creature in the armchair and choke her with his filthy rotten fingers. Christ, what a life! He decided to take Hedel right home, there'd be plenty of room now that Ulla and his brothers were gone.

"You better go, Kotik," said Hedel. "It'll pass. Mother screeches at me because she has no one else to talk to. Grandmother's deaf. She'll lay off as soon as you're gone." She took him by the arm and pushed him gently out the door.

From there it wasn't far to Teuchertstrasse. But he went out of his way. He wanted to see what was going on at the villa on Miethe-Allee. The house was dark. The only sign of life was a wisp of white smoke rising from the chimney. Jochen would be listening to music down in the cellar, reaching now and then for the schnapps bottle while waiting for Kotik's return. But Kotik wanted to go home first. He'd come and see Jochen tomorrow and of course he'd drop in on Hedel even at the risk of starting her mother off again. *Herr and Frau Ossadnik are pleased to announce the engagement of their son to Fräulein Hedel* . . .

He pushed his thick earmuffs aside. The shells, he figured, must be coming down in Petersdorf or the suburbs of Ratibor. None were reaching Gleiwitz so far. There were still people in the streets, though not many. Then suddenly he saw a muffled figure running around the corner, as though in a hurry to take refuge in some shelter.

Kotik knocked on the front door. He was surprised to find that Mazura's downstairs windows had been smashed. He knocked harder, he pounded. There must be somebody home, there was smoke coming out of the chimney. Then he heard voices from inside. "Open up, Mamochka. It's me, Kotik."

Anna hugged her son, held him tight, kissed his hair and forehead. The tears welled from her eyes, but she laughed; then she pushed him away to get a better look at his face, hugged him again and pushed him away again, as though to make sure that it was really Kotik, safe and sound.

The way she treats me, thought Kotik, trying in vain to break loose. I'm not a kid anymore.

"I always said Kotik would make it," said Mazura, who had been standing at the door the whole time.

"But now come upstairs, Kotik, you'll wash and change your clothes. Franzek will make a little fire in the stove, you'll be nice and warm. You see, we've all been living in the air-raid shelter, because shells are falling in the street. Have you seen any explosions? And what have you been doing all this time?"

Anna was so glad to have her son back. She wanted to hug him again but he wriggled loose.

Franz patted his son on the head. That was all. They understood each other without any words.

"You must be hungry," said Anna. "I'll make you some broth with bouillon cubes. Nice hot broth with a few noodles. And then you'll tell us what you've been doing."

But Kotik couldn't tell them what he had been doing; they wouldn't believe him anyway, even if he showed them the soap and the book. Knowing they would ask him lots of questions that he wouldn't want to answer, he made up a story, a simple one, which like many made-up stories sounded more plausible than the truth. It popped straight into his mind because at one point he had expected something of the sort to happen. He and his friends had been sent to the suburbs with a bazooka and a few hand grenades to wait for the enemy; they hadn't been able to leave their posts long enough to send a message home; in the end they had found out that they were the only defenders left, at least in that sector, so they had made tracks. There had been plenty to eat and drink, the owner of the house had split; he had even found time to read a book—to prove it he pulled *Zarathustra* out of his knapsack.

Parts of the story were true.

Anna wanted to see the book, but Kotik only showed her the jacket. "I don't think it would interest you," he said. "It's philosophy."

This was the first time he had declined to give his mother a book.

Franz took a shirt out of the cupboard. "Here," he said. "Put this on. A man has to change his shirt once in a while."

Though mended in several places, the shirt was clean.

Anna poured hot water into the little tub and put it down at Kotik's feet. Then she crumbled a Maggi cube into a cup for his broth.

"Franz, you must tell Kotik now."

Franz ambled in with a towel.

"Well, what is it?" Kotik asked suspiciously. "Has something happened? Well, come on. What's up?"

"The Russians came and looted us," said Anna with a sigh. She bent down and massaged her ankle. Kotik leapt to his feet. "It's not so bad," she hastened to reassure him. "They didn't come up here, they were only interested in the valuables we had in the shelter. We can't be sure exactly what they took, they opened all the suitcases and threw everything around . . ."

After Herr Mazura had called out two warnings, the Ossadniks went down to the shelter. Kotik took his book along in preparation for a long stay. The neighbors were glad to see Kotik; now at least they wouldn't have to listen to his mother's moans and groans. And they hoped he had brought some news, if only rumors. But Kotik had little to report. In the villa on Miethe-Allee he had been even more cut off from the world than they were here, and if Piechotta and Jochen hadn't turned up he wouldn't have known anything at all. According to him, the situation was confused. It seemed likely that the Russians were already fighting in the city streets; there couldn't be much resistance from the Volkssturm, which had nothing to fight with, but there was talk of an armored column being brought in from Hungary to defend the industrial zone, so it was only a question of who got there first.

The others listened but were too deep in their own preoccupations to respond.

Anna made room for Kotik on the mattress. But Kotik wanted to read his book for a while. He liked to read before going to sleep;

then in the dark he would spin out the thoughts provoked by his reading.

Anna looked at her son with a sad but delighted smile. Now that her Kotik was back, she wasn't tired anymore. Her ankle had stopped hurting and she had completely forgotten her goiter. Herr Mazura edged over to her and began to whisper.

"We got a new man here," he said, turning his head toward the corner where Frau Jacob was lying with her two terrified children. "He came when you were upstairs; I been wanting to tell you; he escaped, see? If the Germans find him here, he's a dead man. We'll be cooked too."

"Oh, a deserter!" Anna whispered excitedly.

"Psst!" Now Mazura's voice was scarcely audible. "Not exactly. He was in a concentration camp; when the camp broke up, he beat it and somehow found his way home."

"Good for him," said Franz.

"But why here?" Anna asked.

"Well, you see, he's Frau Jacob's husband."

"Frau Jacob's husband?" Anna repeated incredulously. "What was he doing in a camp?"

That came as a complete surprise. How was it possible that nobody knew? Frau Jacob had been living on the ground floor for years. Come to think of it, Anna knew hardly anything about her. But then she wasn't as curious as the other women in the house.

"I better tell you about it. Herr Ossadnik should know too, because we're all in this together. Frau Jacob's husband is sick, we can't send him away like this. Besides, he's a Jew . . ."

"But I see Frau Jacob in church every Sunday . . ."

"Psst!" Anna had spoken too loudly. "Didn't you know? It was a mixed marriage, the wife was Catholic and the kids were brought up Catholic, so he had to go and work in a sewage plant."

"I thought he was in the railroad administration," said Franz guilelessly.

Kotik's curiosity was aroused. He came closer with his candle and his book.

"That's right, but for the last few years he was in a sewage plant.

And in the end they sent him to a concentration camp, because he always hid his yellow star behind his briefcase. And now he's escaped."

So that's Herr Jacob, thought Anna, looking into the flickering candlelight. "I never knew . . ."

"As usual," Mazura went on, "it's all in the timing. If the Germans come and find him, heaven help us; if it's the Russians, we got somebody who'll protect us. If Herr Jacob had been here before, them *ostarbeiter* would've left us alone."

"To think that we've been living in the same house for years and we hardly knew anything about each other. How were we to know that Herr Jacob was a Jew when we kept seeing his wife and children in church? If at least their name had been Scheingesicht like Frau Kulicke's neighbors, then we'd have known what was what, or the Fensterkreuzes on Niederwallstrasse, who were resettled in the East, or Frau Lustig, who went to South America years ago, where I hear she's doing all right. But Jacob? That's a name like any other."

"How do you suppose we could help Herr Jacob?" Franz whispered. "There must be something we can do."

Kotik, who had heard most of this conversation, stood up. He had made all the decisions in the villa on Miethe-Allee, and now was the time to show his parents that he wasn't a kid anymore.

"Of course," Kotik said energetically. "From now on the Jacob family is under our protection. They're our collective responsibility."

He went to the corner where the Jacobs were lying. "Do you need a doctor?" he asked.

"No, no," said Frau Jacob softly. "He's just a little weak. But thank you, child."

Kotik had spoken rather loudly. The others pricked up their ears. Old man Bednarz shuffled over in his undershirt and suspenders. "I've got a little grape sugar left . . . pure food for the nerves," he said, scraping a bit of white powder from his trouser pocket.

"I could try and get through to Oberwallstrasse and call a doctor. Or to the hospital on Friedrichstrasse. If anyone's still there, I'm sure they'd come in a case like this."

"No doctor will go out with all these shells coming down," said Franz.

"I still have a few pills," said Frau Aubitzky.

"I'm already feeling a lot better," said Herr Jacob. "Who is the nice boy?"

"Oh, that's Kotik, the littlest of the Ossadniks," Frau Jacob explained.

"The youngest," Kotik corrected. "If Herr Jacob isn't better tomorrow, I'll get a doctor."

"I'm just weak. I've been on the road for three days. But I'll be up tomorrow," said Herr Jacob, surprised to find everyone so friendly.

31

THE NEXT MORNING Kotik set out for the Municipal Hospital on Friedrichstrasse. He had cut a strip from a bed sheet and painted a big cross on it with red ink. His mother watched him in silence. When he fastened his arm band to his coat sleeve with a safety pin, she only sighed and finally let him go with a scarcely audible prayer to the Virgin Mary. Herr Jacob had a high fever. Kotik figured that if the doctor wouldn't come out in the bombardment he would at least send some medicine; Frau Aubitzky's pills could hardly be the right thing.

All life had gone out of the streets. At the corner of Roonstrasse two houses had been destroyed. On Friedrichstrasse a house was on fire, smoke and flames were pouring out of the upper windows; the lower floors were still intact except for the windowpanes that had been shattered by blast or heat. Kotik looked through a half-open curtain and saw a potted plant, a cupboard, and a tall grandfather clock, its pendulum still swinging. There was no one in evidence, trying to put out the fire or even to save something. The fire was making crackling sounds. The door had been broken open and the entrance was strewn with broken china. Smoke was pouring down the stairwell. Kotik went in, but only far enough to pick up a demitasse with a black-and-gold checkerboard pattern, which had remained miraculously unharmed. He looked for the saucer but found only shards. Oh well, he'd have to make do with the cup. He went back out to the street. The sounds of explosions were coming from the station now, or from still farther north, from the wire works.

He clung to the walls of the houses and looked around at every intersection for fear of running into Russian troops. If Dr. Thönsberg hadn't beat it, he'd be at the hospital and would surely give him some medicine for Herr Jacob. He hoped the doctor would remember him, he had taken out Kotik's appendix two years ago.

Not far from the hospital a German army car sped by, stopped abruptly with a screeching of brakes, and backed up to Kotik so fast that he barely had time to jump out of the way. A soldier with a tommy gun slung from his neck jumped out and pushed Kotik against the house wall, as though afraid he would run away. "Which way to Beuthen?" he demanded. Kotik was terrified. "W-Wilhelm-strasse," he stuttered, "then f-follow the car tracks." And he threw out both arms to indicate the direction.

"Damn!" said the soldier. "We've spotted Ivan that way. We gotta circle around." He lifted Kotik bodily into the cab. The soldier at the wheel was scraping the ice off his window. "You'll show us the quickest way," he said.

"But I'm getting a doctor," Kotik protested, pointing at his home-made Red Cross arm band. "We've got a sick person in our air-raid shelter."

The soldiers reassured him. As soon as they were out of town and on the straight road to Beuthen they'd let him off, but now they were in a hurry. Kotik guided them down Breslauerstrasse and Hindenburgstrasse, across the big bridge to Bergwerkstrasse. On the way, the soldiers told him the Russians had entered the city from the north and northwest, meeting with next to no resistance; but that there was fighting in the south and southwest because the Wehrmacht wanted to hold the road to Ratibor, which was clogged with refugees and retreating troops. All other troops had received orders—much too late—to escape encirclement by withdrawing via Beuthen and Kattowitz to the Carpathians. While one soldier drove like a lunatic, the other pointed his tommy gun out the open window. Russian tanks, they said, had reached the Oder, but in between there were German troops trying to slip past, and they, too, the devil help us, hoped to get through.

Kotik thought God's help might prove more useful, but it was none of his business; all he cared about was getting back to town. They reached the Hindenburg Bridge without incident. From there, Kotik explained, they had only to go straight ahead and follow the car tracks. The soldiers stopped and let him out.

"Wait a second," said the driver, pulling a bottle from under the seat, "you need a drink, kid. You're as white as a sheet." Kotik took a long pull. They even gave him a can of sardines and a chunk of army bread. Kotik stuffed the bread and sardines into his knapsack. For a moment he considered driving on with the soldiers and escaping from the Russians, but then he thought of Hedel; he couldn't desert Hedel, could he? *"Pyerunnye!"* he said. "I hope you make it."

"Pyerunnye in Gleiwitz!" The soldiers laughed. "That ought to bring us luck."

Crossing the Hindenburg Bridge on his way back, he saw hundreds of people in the railroad yard below, looting a freight train. He stood there awhile, watching them from above. The looters looked like black driftwood in a river. He went to the end of the bridge, scrambled down the embankment, climbed over a fence, and joined them. It was a food train; the car that had just been broken open was full of semolina. Too bad he didn't have a sled. In times like this it was no good running around with nothing but a knapsack. With a sled he could easily have taken two sacks, one for Mamochka and the other for Hedel, that would shut her mother up. But he couldn't very well carry a hundred-pound sack on his shoulders.

The looters were fighting over the semolina, pushing and shoving and tearing sacks out of each other's hands, though there was plenty for everybody. No one looked at anyone else, no one spoke; only an occasional scream or curse.

Kotik plunged his hands into an open sack and filled his knapsack. He wondered for a moment what these people would do if he were to sing out: "The Russians are coming." But then, seeing their look of fanatical concentration, he knew they would batter him with iron bars and kill him if they found out that he was only trying to frighten them.

When he got home, he emptied a chunk of army bread, a can of sardines, and a black-and-gold checkered demitasse out of his knapsack along with the semolina. He explained why he hadn't gone to the hospital. When they heard about the freight train under the Hindenburg Bridge, Frau Aubitzky's two eldest boys wanted to go there without delay, but their mother said it was too dangerous, they should just stay home. On the other hand, food couldn't be sneezed at, and no one knew when there would be anything in the stores. "A man gotta eat," said Herr Mazura, "to keep body and soul together." And undoubtedly he was right.

The upshot was that Frau Aubitzky went along with her eldest sons; as for the youngest, she got a quarter of a sleeping pill down his throat with the help of some sugar water and left him with Frau Smolka. Taking her Thomas by the hand, Frau Grochowiak joined them. When Kotik insisted on going back with the sled, Frau Ossadnik, in spite of her still painful ankle, was unwilling to stay behind. On the way, they would see about a doctor for Herr Jacob.

When they reached the freight yard under the bridge, the train had been stripped bare. Only the soiled, trampled snow and a few torn sacks bore witness to the recent turmoil. But only a few hundred yards farther on—Kotik was the first to discover it—a human anthill was at work. Kotik ran toward it and the others followed. As he approached, he heard the roaring of cattle. The looters didn't seem to hear it, they were too busy carrying full sacks out of the cars and loading them onto sleds. The bellowing grew so loud that Kotik began to feel afraid.

"There are animals in there," he called out to a man who was running past him, the only man he had seen thus far; all the rest of the looters were women and children. "It sounds like cattle are dying in there . . ."

The man looked at Kotik incredulously and without saying a word grabbed a sack out of the car.

The bellowing of the cattle didn't stop the looters for a moment. They just went on loading their sleds with beans and lentils. Frau Aubitzky urged her group to go home, and Anna Ossadnik agreed. They were just looking for young Grochowiak, who had disappeared.

Kotik ran from car to car, trying to get someone to help him open the door of one of the cattle cars. The only response was vacant stares. One man pulled down his muffler and said: "So what? We can't slaughter them, can we?"

Finally Kotik found the young fellow who had broken the locks on the cars with hammer and chisel. He agreed to smash the locks of the cattle cars. The lock was beyond his reach, but Kotik picked him up on his shoulders. That done, the two of them pushed the door open. At first Kotik saw only the heads of the beasts, brown with flashing, light-colored horns, a billowing sea of heads. Then a bullock rushed from the car. Its forelegs buckled under it and it tumbled roaring into the snow; another followed; it too fell, tried in vain to get up, and rolled over on its side. Then more and more stampeded into the snow, impossible to tell whether in response to their own terror or whether forced out by the beasts behind them. A horrible bellowing, screaming, rattling, moaning filled the air, and the mound of animal bodies grew higher.

Kotik moved back a few steps. Horrified at what he and the other boy had done, he was powerless to move. A man with an iron bar came running and struck one of the beasts that had been trying in vain to rise on its forelegs. He struck between the eyes, blood spurted; women came and attacked the hide with pickaxes, tore it open, chopped great chunks of meat from the steaming body. One woman plunged her hands into the bleeding mass, pulled out the heart, cut it loose with a spade, and carried it to her sled.

Kotik was in a daze. He didn't come to until his mother poked him. "Come on," she said. "They've all gone."

Kotik took the sled and pulled it across the tracks. The bellowing of the cattle pursued him long after they were out of earshot. He didn't once look around until they got to Teuchertstrasse. Though last to leave the railroad yard, they were the first home. Kotik had run so hard that he was bathed in sweat. He took off his coat and inspected every square centimeter of it for blood. When he found none, he tested his coat by sniffing. He still had the bellowing of the cattle in his ears.

By then Herr Jacob was feeling a little better. His wife said his fever had gone down. She and the children prayed to Jesus Christ, as they had always done.

"The Russians are in the city, aren't they, Mama?" Thomas asked.

Frau Grochowiak nodded. She was still in a state of shock and couldn't talk.

"We saw them on Bahnhofstrasse," said the boy.

"What do the Russian soldiers look like? Tell us about them," urged Frau Zielonka, who was stirring semolina into some soup.

"They were in wooden wagons, pulled by horses," said Thomas. "Little ponies like."

"But what about their tanks, those big T-34s? Ain't ya seen any of them?" Mazura asked excitedly.

"No, no tanks. Only horse cárts, and a few beat-up cars. Kalmuks were riding in them with their balalaikas."

"Their what?" Franz Ossadnik asked.

"Balalaikas. That's what they call their tommy guns. Szymanski told me that, and he knows practically everything. Doesn't he, Kotik?"

"Oh yes," said Kotik knowingly, though he had never heard the word before. He had something entirely different on his mind.

"I'm going to run over to the hospital quick," he explained. "The Russians won't bother me with my Red Cross arm band."

But his mother absolutely refused to let him go. Not now, not with the Russians fighting in the city.

"There's nothing to worry about," said Kotik. "We're occupied, the fighting's over. No more war for us. And I've promised to go see my girl. I can't leave her alone the whole time."

"Oh, my blessed Lord Jesus," Anna groaned. "Did you say girl? Now, who may that be?"

"All right, it's Hedel Zock. And as soon as things get back to normal, we're going to get engaged."

Anna crossed herself only once. From right to left as she had taught herself to do in the last few days. "*Muy Bozhe.*"

32

THE CITY WAS on fire.

Gleiwitz was burning under the snow. The smoke over the inner city could be seen from where the Ossadniks lived. It was a cold, clear winter day, the cold kept the smoke low, and made it form black columns in the air. Young Grochowiak had been the first to discover this phenomenon, he had told the others about it, and now they were all running upstairs to look out the top-floor windows.

Machine-gun fire could be heard from all directions and no one dared go out in the street. Herr Zielonka, who had fought against the French in the First World War, thought the Russians would bomb the city house after house; that, he said, was what the Germans had done in France.

Mazura had worked out a plan, and he wanted to give it a trial run for fear that things would go wrong as when the *ostarbeiter* had broken in. The idea was that as soon as the Russians knocked on the door he and Herr Jacob would come out with the white flag. Herr Jacob would tell them his story and he, Mazura, would help with a bit of Polish. Too bad Herr Jacob hadn't escaped in his camp uniform, that would tell his story better than any prepared speech. By that time the women had made white arm bands for everyone, and even Kotik Ossadnik was wearing one in place of his Red Cross arm band. Now they were all waiting for a knock at the door.

Then they smelled the fire. An acrid smell of resin and charred wood seeped into every house, clung to wallpaper and clothing. For days people smelled it in their hair. At night the sky was aglow and the horizon in flames. Kotik developed a complicated system for deducing the location and intensity of the fire from the color of the smoke, the quality of the smell, and the degree of darkening. He was so eager to check the accuracy of his calculations on the spot that his parents couldn't let him out of their sight. Frau Aubitzky consoled her children with halma and quarters of sleeping tablets dissolved in sugar water for not being allowed to go out and watch the big fire.

From a neighbor, who had tried to reach his sister in the Stadt-wald area but had got only as far as the Klodnitz, they learned that the houses on the Ring and on the western end of Wilhelmstrasse were on fire, as was the Upper Silesia House. They all stared at the smoke in the sky. This, they felt, was a catastrophe that threatened them all.

Then at last Russian soldiers appeared. They shined their flash-lights into the face of every single occupant, while Herr Jacob, trem-bling like a leaf and holding out some sort of paper that they scarcely looked at, told his story. The tenants were made to stand in line, the women on one side, the men on the other. They were counted, the number was marked on a wooden board. One of the soldiers informed them in broken but intelligible German that no one must leave the house until further notice and that no one must be let in from outside. And by noon the next day the *starik,* the eldest—here he pointed at Herr Jacob, who was far from being the oldest inhabitant—should draw up a list of all the occupants with their names and dates of birth. It all went fairly quickly, but it was some time before the tenants realized that the Russians had gone. Anna Ossadnik's relief expressed itself in tears. She held Franz and Kotik tight. The soldiers had taken neither her husband nor her last son; for that she would have to light a candle to St. Barbara if the Peter and Paul Church hadn't been turned into a gasoline depot. This evening, in any case, she would pray the joyful mysteries of the rosary. Frau Aubitzky hugged and kissed her three sons, and Frau Gro-chowiak rubbed the soot off their cheeks with saliva. Herr Mazura praised Herr Jacob and himself and his mute wife and himself again to the skies for the impression they had made on the Russian soldiers, who had been too frightened to steal so much as a handkerchief. Old man Bednarz took package after package of Dextromalt from various hiding places that had escaped the Russians. What a miracle that nothing had been looted. Several explanations were offered, each one more fanciful than the last.

Nightfall brought silence, broken from time to time by distant cannonading and machine-gun fire nearby. A time for reflection and fear. All sorts of rumors were going around and no one knew who was spreading them; it was as though hope and fear and despair had crystallized into words. All men between sixteen and sixty would be treated as prisoners of war and dragged off to Russia; babies would be snatched out of their mother's arms and sent to state orphanages; V-2 rockets launched in the Jüterbog area were devastating Moscow; infuriated by the quantities of swastika flags and pictures of Hitler they had found in the Upper Silesia House, the Russians had set fire to the building; a group of Party members had tried to destroy the membership files; Göring was negotiating a separate peace with the Americans, after which the Americans and Germans would join forces against the godless Bolsheviks.

Anna didn't really want to listen to all this talk, but you can't get away from rumors. After almost a week in the air-raid shelter, the tenants had become one big family. Before the *ostarbeiter* made off with everything worth taking, there had been certain differences between them. But indigence makes for solidarity. And since there was no way of knowing how long they would be able to keep what little they had, they had even begun to leave the apartment doors unlocked.

Kotik went on reading his *Zarathustra*, and when he had finished he started all over again. Forgotten the stuffy cellar; now he was living in rugged, windswept, mountainous country. An old man in a long hairshirt went down into the valley. As the air grew milder, more and more people came to him. Struck by the light that emanated from him, they gathered around him and listened in devout fervor to his words. Thus spake Zarathustra.

"*When he came to the forest he suddenly came face to face with an old man who had left his hut to gather roots in the woods. And the old man spake thus to Zarathustra: This wanderer is no stranger to me. He passed by here some years ago. Zarathustra was his name. But he has changed. Then you were taking your ashes to the mountains; are you now taking your fire to the valleys? Do you not fear the punishment of the incendiary? Yes, I recognize Zarathustra. Pure is his eye, and in his mouth there is no foulness. Does he not walk like a dancer? Zarathustra has been trans-*

formed; Zarathustra has become a child; Zarathustra has awakened:
what then are you seeking among the sleepers? You lived in solitude as
in the sea, and the sea sustained you. Woe! Are you going onto the land?
Woe! Are you going to carry your own body? Zarathustra replied: I love
mankind. Why, said the saint, did I take to the forest and the desert?
Was it not because I loved mankind too much? Now I love God; I do not
love mankind. Man, to my mind, has become too imperfect. Love of
mankind would kill me."

"What's that book you're reading?" Herr Jacob asked.

Kotik didn't want to tell him. He had bound the book in wrapping
paper to hide the title. "Oh, just a novel," he said. "It takes place in
wild country. A knight is fighting for the truth . . ."

"For what?" Herr Jacob asked.

"He's fighting against evil," said Kotik.

Herr Jacob nodded. Maybe children are better than their parents,
he thought.

"How about letting us sleep?" came Mazura's voice from his corner.

Kotik put out his candle and stared into the darkness. He thought
of Zarathustra, whose disciple he felt himself to be. Now, I love
God, Kotik thought, but I do not love mankind. Man is too imperfect. Love of man would kill me. But who is God? And what
does he look like? Obviously he would have to look entirely different
from the man his mother took down off the walls and hid in the
coal cellar. But different in what way?

He thought of Hedel Zock, who was slowly becoming estranged
from him. He could not have said why, but when he tried to visualize
her, her features were more and more blurred. He often thought of
her, but not as often as he meant to. What had happened in the villa
on Miethe-Allee now seemed far away. As though it had happened
in a different life. He had gone to see Hedel, but she had been
different, he had hardly known her. Or was it he who had changed
so? When he ran his hands over his body, he had the impression
that it no longer belonged to him.

"Are you asleep, Franz?" Anna's voice groped in the darkness.

"No . . . I've been thinking. Wondering if the war is over for us, or if it's just beginning." Franz was only too wide awake.

"I'm going to ask Frau Jacob if she can get her husband to vouch for you," Anna whispered.

"You think they'll come for me?" asked Franz, who had been thinking of nothing else.

"Herr Mazura says they're starting in. For a few days the jail was empty. Now the cells are crowded. They say that in Gross-Strehlitz the Russians have got hold of the whole Party membership file; all in one night they arrested every last one of them, the big ones and the little ones without distinction. *Muy Bozhe.*"

"The big ones cleared out in plenty of time," said Franz bitterly.

"People are running to the nearest Russian sentry and denouncing their neighbors. I'd never have expected that."

The thought of such human baseness brought a tremor to Anna's voice. Well she remembered how terrified she had been when her Franzek had volunteered for the army because he couldn't bear to go on driving trains to Auschwitz, and all the trouble she had had prying him loose with the help of lawyer Wondrak.

Franz thought about the millions of people in the Party; the Russians couldn't lock them all up, not the little fellows like him, could they? He hadn't even owned a Party uniform, because when he joined they had run out of clothing coupons. He had signed up only because of Anna's prodding; she had always wanted him to get promoted, and if he hadn't been a Party member he'd never have become a senior locomotive engineer. At heart he had always been against.

Anna listened with only half an ear. Why Franz had joined the Party was of no importance; what mattered was that his name was in the card file. And even if, as she hoped, the card file had gone up in smoke with the Upper Silesia House, there was still Herr Mazura, who would be sure to denounce her Franz just to put himself in the clear. That's how it had always been. You accused other people to keep from being accused yourself. Something would have to be done. Undoubtedly Frau Jacob knew who had been in the Party and who hadn't. She could offer her some of the money she had put aside for Ulla's music lessons; they hadn't spent it all because Ulla had soon started making money with her concerts. The only question was whether she would still be able to get at her savings.

"Maybe you should hide with Aunt Angela for a few days," she suggested. "Nobody knows you there."

"Don't make me laugh," said Franz. "Even in peacetime Aunt Angela was so scared she put double locks on all her doors and a big fence around the garden. If you ask me, she won't even let me into the house. And anyway, I can't leave here now. We've been registered, and if one leaves it will make trouble for everybody."

"Yes, you're right," said Anna. "But if they take you away, I'll go with you."

"So will I," said Kotik unexpectedly. "They'll have to shoot me before I'd leave you, Papochka!"

"My God, Kotik, I thought you were asleep," said Anna, fighting down her sobs.

33

T HE CAR HADN'T come yet. They had been waiting since twelve
noon; the luggage was already at the porter's lodge, ready for loading.
As the sky began to darken, Frau Hauptmann had put in a long-
distance call to the Weidner Sanatorium in Dresden. After waiting
three hours for the connection, she found out that the car's gasogene
engine had had to be changed, but that the driver would set out
bright and early the next day and could be expected at Wiesenstein
about midday. By then it was time for dinner. The atmosphere at
table was subdued. The radio reported that the Russians had crossed
the Oder at Steinau and were approaching Grottkau in the south; a
pincers movement threatened to cut off Breslau, and Gauleiter Hanke
proclaimed it a fortress. At dinner the old man hardly opened his
mouth. He even left his red wine untouched. The secretary said
something about the need for a psychological change of air.

"In Dresden your catarrh will clear up," said Frau Hauptmann.
"You'll see."

Hauptmann seemed grateful for the secretary's words. "That's it,"
he said. "A psychological change." Everything oppressed him. Even
the mountains, the Silesian mountains that he loved, weighed on
his soul.

After dinner they moved to the hall and sat by the fireplace.
Though the room was pleasantly warm, the lady threw the cashmere
blanket over the old man's shoulders. He liked to sit by the fire after
dinner and watch the flickering bluish flames. At his bidding, the
maid brought cognac and seltzer, and he mixed himself a *pyolter*.
Frau Hauptmann saw that he took more cognac than usual, but said
nothing.

The secretary was prepared to read Leskov's novella *The Sealed
Angel* aloud. He had begun a few days before; Hauptmann had been
visibly delighted and had commented with enthusiasm on certain
passages. The secretary was sorry he hadn't recorded certain remarks

that showed a profound understanding of Russian legends. He remembered, though, that after listening to a passage relating how the
Raskolniki, or Old Believers, derived peace of mind from the contemplation of angels' wings, the old man had looked upward almost
nostalgically and said: "Yes, in the present situation, I am beginning
for the first time to understand the profound magic of icons. Great
works of religious art have always given me such peace of mind. But
I must make it clear that great religious art is the opposite of mawkish
religious art, which I have always despised." He had gone on to talk
about the air raids that had destroyed Nuremberg. He had known
Nuremberg well; whenever he had business in the region, he had
gone to see Peter Vischer's masterwork, the Shrine of St. Sebald.
He had known and admired it all his life and had once thought of
writing a book about it.

The secretary hoped that his reading would distract the old man
from his gloomy thoughts.

"*I have no wish,*" he began, "*to bore you with the details of the inquiries,
in which my companion and I literally passed through the eyes of needles
to elicit information. Instead, I shall speak of our grief at discovering that
the icons had been moved to the basement of the Consistory, where they
lay entombed—*"

The old man interrupted him. "History has blundered," he said
suddenly in a tone suggesting that prolonged thought had led him
to that conclusion. The others looked at him in silence. The firelight
cast its glow on his serene, still majestic face. The secretary wondered
whether to go on reading. He looked at Frau Hauptmann in the
hope of receiving encouragement. But she sat impassive, staring at
the fire.

"There are cultural monuments," said the old man, "that it is not
permissible to destroy. Not even in war. It is a crime, yes, a crime.
Because culture transcends man and wars and time. I have stood
before the Shrine of St. Sebald, as other pious men stand before a
church altar; to gaze at it was for me an act of worship, which moved
me deeply. That work of art has given me my happiest and most
solemn hours."

The secretary shut the book, Frau Hauptmann leaned back in her chair. Herr Hauptmann went on so softly as to be scarcely audible:

"The great importance of that work is known to art historians. But it has not penetrated the consciousness of the people. This, as a German, I cannot help deploring. *Faust*, too, is unpopular, an unpopular book. Just as the Shrine of St. Sebald is an unpopular artwork. Thus they can plausibly be compared. They are both soul crystals. Goethe's soul attained its most universal expression in *Faust*, Peter Vischer's in the Shrine of St. Sebald. These are also the most German of their works. And they are the most German of artists. I can't avoid using that word: German. And why should I? Because the word has been profaned, profaned by people who . . ." He raised his voice, but the words that followed were not quite intelligible. "And with those people I have nothing in common. Because my language is German, because I am German by birth and nationality, I can only be a German artist . . ."

He stood up and put a log on the fire. Frau Hauptmann arose and stood beside him as though expecting something different. Something she didn't want to think about but had recently been driven to think about by the increasing weariness and resignation she saw in his lusterless eyes, and still strong, beautiful face. For fifty years she had looked upon that face with its imposing forehead. She had watched it day after day, and in it she had seen fire and lightning, shadow and ashes.

His Germany of the arts, the old man went on, had no Chinese Wall around it; it was open on all sides. All birds of passage were welcome, all songbirds, falcons as well as storks, all manner of game shuttled back and forth across its borders, all strangers met with hospitality—but he was of the sedentary species. "True, sedentary folk aren't what they used to be. They too travel nowadays. But from all their wanderings they return home after storing up riches on foreign pathways; and perhaps those prevented from returning home are all the more full of their country . . ."

His voice remained suspended. He was no longer looking in the fire; his eyes were focused on the stairway at the end of the room, with an intensity that seemed to pierce the walls.

He gets that look now and then, his wife thought.

"Do I get another *pyolter*?" he suddenly cried out in a very different voice, raising his empty glass.

"Of course," said Frau Hauptmann and rang for the maid. She stirred up the fire and put on two fresh logs. "Is it warm enough for you, my love?" she asked with feeling. She straightened the flowing cloth that he wore instead of a tie and stroked back his white, blue-tinged, still abundant hair. That was something she never forgot.

The old man's words about German art had undoubtedly been inspired. His wife hoped the secretary had written them down; that was his job, after all. He wasn't really a secretary; the secretary was Annie, good old reliable Annie, who had been her lady's maid for years. He had been sent by the publisher, and he wasn't a man to miss an opportunity to play Eckermann. She was glad to have him there; in Dresden, he'd be busy with the archives, and there wouldn't be anyone but Annie. Maybe she herself should take down some of the great man's sayings. He probably wouldn't let her, but what a shame if words like those he had just spoken were lost to posterity.

"A *pyolter*, if you please," she said aloud when the maid came. "And you may as well leave the seltzer here."

"The cognac too," the old man added. Then, seeming to remember that he had interrupted the secretary's reading, he said in an affable, almost familiar tone: "You might read a bit more—what do you think, Grete?" And before she could answer: "Did you like it?"

She didn't know if he was referring to the reading or to his speech about the Shrine of St. Sebald. "Oh yes," she said, "it was beautiful." To her it was inconceivable that she might never come back to Wiesenstein. But to be prepared for every eventuality, she decided to pack the little Buddha he loved so, there would be room in the car. It couldn't be very valuable, but he had had it on his desk for years and would be sure to miss it if it were not on his table at the Weidners'.

The old man downed his half-full glass at one swallow. "I'm really thirsty," he said by way of an excuse.

"Do you feel feverish?" his wife asked anxiously. "Have you been coughing?"

Actually, the catarrh was almost gone. She laid her hand reassuringly on the hand with which he had been clutching the knob of his armrest.

"I'll throw it off in Dresden," he said. And he glanced at the secretary, who as usual was making himself inconspicuous.

"My friend the scribe here hasn't got anything to drink. I'm not blind, you know. Hey, there," he called out to the maid. "Bestir yourself. Kindly bring us a bottle of the red Bordeaux that we had for dinner. There must be a few bottles left in the pantry," he said with a mildly theatrical gesture.

When the maid brought the bottle, he insisted on feeling it to check the temperature. "It's fit to drink," he announced genially.

He looked at the secretary as though expecting some word of praise. "What about you, Grete? Will you have some? A sip?"

The secretary raised his glass. He looked across at the old man, whose features seemed firmer than before. The old vitality was gone, but in his words and gestures there still remained something of the spirit he had observed and admired on so many evenings.

"Good," said Hauptmann. "Go ahead and read." He drew the cashmere blanket over his shoulders.

"From the legend? From Leskov?" the secretary asked. The old man nodded. The secretary picked up the book and looked for the place, but was slow in finding it.

"Go ahead and read. No, don't read. Just talk. Tell me about your life in Berlin. What do I know about you? Not a thing. Isn't that so, Grete, what do we know about the scribe here? Weren't you at one time director of the Prussian Trash and Smut Bureau or whatever they called it, before the brownshirts took over? You were too liberal for them, I suppose . . ."

"Yes, that's it. The Trash and Smut Bureau," said the secretary softly. So much interest in his person made him uncomfortable. "It does sound rather foolish. Still, it served a purpose. Before it was set up, every bigoted, narrow-minded politician with any influence could suppress whatever he pleased. That was no longer possible, once a special government bureau took the matter in hand. And believe me, we were serious about our work. We wouldn't have suppressed *The Weavers*, for instance."

He stopped suddenly. Was he reviving bitter memories? He knew the old man was afraid of his memories; probably because so many of his old friends had left him forever. But what was he, the secretary, to say about himself? He had come here to listen to Gerhart Hauptmann, to write down his sayings, to dig up forgotten old jottings that lay buried in the archives.

"My work is a beacon of the past," said the old man abruptly. And after a pause: "The world is truly mad and disorder reigns supreme. Isn't it time for me to take leave of it?" His voice was firm and imperious.

"Tell me, my friend. Should I have left the country? Back when the brown barons came to power? Have I ceased to belong here? I have always felt myself to be first a German, then a European, then a citizen of the world, in that order. My roots are here in Germany, in the language, in the people, in their souls, in the air that they and I breathe. I've been abroad a good deal, my plays have been produced all over the world, I have taken pride in hearing the Silesian dialect spoken in Vienna, in the world-famous Burgtheater of the Habsburgs by the greatest actors in Europe. And strangely enough: even in translation, my plays, conceived in elemental Silesian dialect, in the German language, have made their way through all the languages and countries of the world. And all foreign art, when I consider it as an artist, does only one thing for me, it makes me aware of myself as a German. Goethe started out as a German and ended up as a German. Never before him and never since has an artist embodied so universally German a consciousness, none has been so thoroughly at home in Germany, none has known it as well, none has made such full use of his powers or extended his frontiers as widely. And let me add: None has loved Germany as he did. But what of the present time? Is anyone more German than I? Has anyone suffered more at the hands of this new Germany? It has rebuffed me, battered me, suppressed my work, held me up to ridicule. My beginnings were harder than those of many who have risen to the top today. Should I have gone away when the brown devils conquered the

Reich? You don't answer? You have nothing to say? When my Jewish friends went away, when they scattered to all the winds, would I have had a place among them? Would they have accepted me? Wasn't I different from them? Didn't they sense the difference? That Jewish critic Alfred Kerr poured barrels of filth on me from abroad. At a time when hatred was being stirred up against me at home. When my world-famous name was withdrawn from that school in Breslau. When the people of Bunzlau were forbidden to name a street after me. That Oedipus in Berlin expunged my name from the readers, suppressed my writings. But am I not so much a part of this people that for better or worse I had no right to leave it? Would a Goethe have emigrated? He carped at his Germans, but he loved them. I, too, have always wanted to be with the German people, in good times and bad. No, I will not sidestep the destiny of the Germans . . ."

Frau Hauptmann and the secretary sat silent, their gaze turned inward. Time passed and the fire burned down.

"I'm tired," said Frau Hauptmann. "This has been a hard day for me and tomorrow will be even harder. But I'm looking forward to seeing the children, Benvenuto and Ecke, and perhaps it won't be so cold in Dresden."

The old man asked the secretary to lead him up to the tower room. There he read the poems of Hafiz for a while. Then he took his diary from the drawer and wrote in ink:

> *Nowhere, thought sorrow, is it more*
> *desolate than in my innermost being.*
> Hafiz Vol II p 183

> *Swift riders give no thought*
> *to those who creep heavy laden*
> Haf V II p 275

At about three o'clock the next day the car arrived from Dresden. By then, the old man had taken a short nap. They helped him into his sable coat, and his wife selected a soft hat for him. He would have liked to go through the house once again and take his leave of all the rooms. No, said his wife, it was late, and they were due to spend the night at Schluckenau in the Sudetenland. And after all, they would be back. The secretary held the old man's arm. As they passed through the Paradise Room, the old man stopped to look at the vitrine where his Nobel Prize citation, his medals, decorations, and various prizes were kept, including a fountain pen and a seared reed. He stood there for a long while. "All those things can stay here," he said to the secretary. "Just this reed. Wrap it carefully. Annie will bring it to me. It's a souvenir of Shakespeare's birthplace. I got my feet good and wet more than thirty years ago, wading out into the River Avon to break it off. Little things like that, you know, can mean either nothing to us—or everything."

At the door Gerhart Hauptmann turned his head and looked up at the windows. The three of them took the familiar path through the snow-covered park to the porter's lodge. The Duda children were inside, pressing their faces to the windowpanes. The lady had relegated these refugees from Upper Silesia to the porter's lodge. The sky was overcast. One couldn't see far into the mountains. Out there, in the direction of the Great Helmet, was where he had recently seen the firewheel whirling in the snow. It had flared up for a few seconds and quickly died away.

His wife bundled him into the car that was already packed full of suitcases and bags, and sat down beside him. She wrapped his legs in a fur robe and put his hands into a coonskin muff. The sound of the engine was so loud that no one could make himself understood. The others stood at the gate and waved. The old man did not look around. Nor could he have, wedged in as he was. In the hurry and confusion he had forgotten to say good-bye to the secretary. Now it was too late.

34

THE SOUND OF GUNFIRE had receded and could be heard only occasionally when the wind blew from the southwest. There was talk of heavy fighting in the Ratibor region and along the Oder. It seemed that the Russian offensive had been stopped and some spoke of a counteroffensive, in preparation for which the Gross-Deutschland Division and other elite units were taking up positions on the Oder. People were moving from the shelters back to their apartments, some of which, to their amazement, had not been broken into. Since there was no water or electricity, the women melted snow and rendered tallow to make candles. The stores had been ransacked, but a few bakeries were working again, the slaughterhouse had reopened, but all the bread and meat went to the Russian military.

Then someone hit on the idea of opening a water hydrant on the street, at least for a few hours a day. The women stood in line with their pitchers and buckets, glad of an excuse for escaping from their cramped lodgings and exchanging gossip. Since more had happened in the last few days than ordinarily in a whole year, there was plenty to talk about. Some of the women would run home, empty their pitchers, and come right back, eager to go on with their tales of woe.

"Frau Kandziora from Raudenerstrasse—oh, you didn't know her? The one with the wart on her chin?—they banged her one after the other, her husband tried to interfere and they shot him dead on the spot . . ."

"Remember those concentration camp prisoners, that were being marched to the Reich from Auschwitz, a lot of them died on the road, well, I was told that dozens of corpses were found in the snow near Alt-Gleiwitz, shot by the SS, the Russians took revenge by shooting ten hostages, ten perfectly innocent men, and now their children are fatherless, oh my God!"

"What, you didn't know about the fire on the Ring? The Russians went into one house and shot the men and raped all the women, they kept it up for two days, and when they were through they set fire to the house, the fire spread to other houses, and in the end half the Ring was in flames, yes, that's the way it was."

"And they shot Hannes Breitenbach, the sculptor, in his studio, when everybody knows he wasn't a Nazi, his wife was, but he wasn't."

"At 17 Niederwallstrasse, across from the synagogue, some looters broke through a partition and found the ritual objects of the Jewish congregation, documents and books, scrolls of the Torah and a solid gold menorah. The last Jews must have hidden them there before they were taken away. I wonder how many Jews will come back. Herr Jacob—have you heard?—is here already. We'd better get on his good side . . ."

"The whole Sobisiak family, they lived on Miethe-Allee, Herr Sobisiak was the manager of the iron foundry, he was in the Party, pretty big wheel in fact, but no fanatic, he'd go and talk with the workers in the plant, he wasn't too proud, well, the whole family have killed themselves, five children, all as pretty as pictures, their mother gave them poison mixed with cough medicine. What? You say Christians aren't allowed to . . . ? Of course not, but they left the Church long before the war."

"Not far from here, on Strachwitzstrasse, at the Piontek villa, you know Frau Piontek, the piano teacher . . . it happened the very first night . . . the Russians shot some *ostarbeiter* who had been hiding in the house, it seems they were afraid of the Russians because they'd been working in the German munitions factories, they'd been forced to, but that wouldn't cut any ice. Well, the Pionteks' maid, who was there, went out of her mind, stark raving mad, that's right, really *chaychay* . . ."

"*Muy Bozhe,* what's that you're saying? You mean Frau Piontek, the piano teacher?" Anna went hot and cold and hot again. "That's not possible," she said. "It's not possible." She said it over and over because she didn't want it to be true.

"Well, it's what I heard," said Frau Sibarski, who had the most news because, speaking Polish fluently, she thought it safe to venture into other neighborhoods. She took the innumerable oh's and ah's and ohmyGod's provoked by her tales as well-deserved applause; still, her main reason for passing on horror stories was to persuade herself as well as other women that they hadn't come off too badly.

Anna wanted to go straight to Strachwitzstrasse, but she was afraid to go alone, and none of the other women was willing to accompany her. Then she thought of asking Father Pattas to go with her. If this maid—Anna wondered who she might be, because Halina had been away for over a year—was really out of her mind, as Frau Sibarski claimed, only a priest would know what to do.

Notices had been posted on the house fronts. The women read them in silence. Then they went home and told the men, who were afraid to go out, because any man who still had two legs, two arms, and a head was as likely as not to be picked up and held as a "prisoner of war."

> *Order No. 1 of the Military Commandant of the City of Gleiwitz: The population is ordered to:*
>
> 1. *Surrender arms, ammunition, and weapons of every kind.*
> 2. *Surrender all radios, typewriters, telephones, microphones, photographic equipment, etc.*
> 3. *All adult members of the German civilian population must wear white arm bands on their left arms.*
> 4. *All motor vehicles must be delivered immediately to the Kommandantur.*
> 5. *All looting must stop immediately.*
> 6. *Members of the population are permitted to leave their houses between 7 A.M. and 6 P.M. After 6 P.M. a special permit is required.*
> 7. *Blackout regulations must be strictly observed. It is forbidden to light fires on the streets and squares.*
>
> *Failure to comply with this order will be severely punished.*
>
> *Gleiwitz, January 29, 1945.*
> *Colonel Grigorenko, The Military Commandant*

White flags were still hanging from the windows, and Herr Mazura was in favor of leaving them there for a while. It was all in the timing. Kotik unscrewed the tubes from the radio and hid them in the cellar. He then smashed the Bakelite casing with an ax and buried the wreckage in the snow.

"Wouldn't it have been better," Franz Ossadnik asked, "to take the radio to the collection point? If they come and ask for it, what can we say? They'll think we've hidden it."

Franz would have liked best to turn the radio in himself. But Anna insisted on his staying in bed with the kidney trouble she and Kotik had told everyone about.

"How do we know?" said Kotik. "Maybe they'd keep us there along with the radio. It's safer to keep away. Don't attract attention, that's my policy."

That had been his policy for a long time, and thus far it had kept him out of trouble.

"Kotik is right," said Anna. "What you haven't got you can't turn in."

Kotik insisted, however, on going to Frau Piontek's house with Mamochka to see if the maid had really gone mad. First they went to the presbytery of the Peter and Paul Church, where they had to wait a little while, because the Archpriest had just got back from blessing graves. There had been no regular funerals for some time; the dead were taken to the cemetery and buried without coffins; sometimes names were written on a wooden slab, but sometimes only the date and the number of persons buried. Once a day the priest went and blessed the fresh graves and said a prayer for the dead.

It took them some time to get to the Pionteks' house. Father Pattas was wearing his cassock and biretta, and the women they met on the way would not let him pass without engaging him in conversation or at least getting a blessing out of him.

Kotik wanted to ask him on the way whether Zarathustra should be regarded as a wise man or a saint, but he couldn't get a word in edgewise, because Mamochka wanted to know about plans for a "cave church" and Father Pattas kept, despite countless interruptions, trying to convince her that her fears were unwarranted, because he had seen the military commandant, who assured him that religious freedom would be respected, though the churches were closed for the present because all assembly was prohibited throughout the occupied territory, a measure which the Archpriest did not find too unreasonable. He went on to speak of hard times and hard trials which God had sent them and which must be borne with patience. Frau Ossadnik nodded. She was not finding it easy, with her bad ankle, to keep pace with the swiftly striding priest.

The Pionteks' house was closed. They knocked at the door, then at the windows. Finally a neighbor woman appeared, burst into tears at the sight of the Archpriest, and haltingly told him what had happened. "Halina, that's the maid, was arrested by the Gestapo for keeping company with an *ostarbeiter*. Maybe you'd heard." Of course they had heard, the whole town had heard. "Anyway, she came back. But nobody knows whether the Pionteks were still there, probably they had already left, because otherwise they'd have taken Halina with them, she seems to be some kind of distant relative. Anyway, Halina must have hidden some *ostarbeiter* in the house, and they had a party, a regular orgy, so I've heard. So then"—here she burst into sobs—"some Russian soldiers broke in and shot the Ukrainians— for collaborating, is what they said later on—and raped the women. It was two days before we dared to go in, and do you know what we found . . . ? Four or five corpses on the music room floor, and the maid was sitting on a footstool with an *ostarbeiter* on her lap, you could still see the OST patch on his jacket, and she was cradling the dead body in her arms. Believe me, Father, it looked like a . . . like a Pietà . . ."

"Then what?" said the priest. "And where is this Halina?"

The woman shuddered. "Some men came and took the bodies away, but Halina hasn't stirred out of the house, she talks a lot of crazy stuff, she needs to be taken away. I don't think there's any food left in the house, a couple of times I slipped a bowl of soup through the veranda door, and when I looked in again it was empty . . ."

The woman led the way through the garden to the back door, which wasn't locked. In the music room broken glass crunched under their shoes, the whole place was full of shards, the drawers had been pulled out of the chiffonier and the contents strewn over the floor. The wall clock had been toppled and the hands torn off. Someone had tried to make a fire in the piano; it was blackened with soot, and several of the keys were missing.

A bald-headed woman was sitting there, leaning slightly forward in her chair. She must have heard them come in, but she didn't look up. She had thrown a blanket over her shoulders. Under it she was wearing a light blue dress, ripped open in front, with an artificial rose pinned to it.

Over her knees lay a quilted coat of the kind worn by *ostarbeiter*. She was mechanically stroking it.

"Halina!"

No response. Anna touched her shoulder. "Halina! Where are the others? The Pionteks? Irma? The children?"

Halina stared at the coat on her lap.

"All gone," she whispered after a while. "Kolya gone too. He took the amber with him."

"Halina! Halina! Pull yourself together. It's Frau Ossadnik from Teuchertstrasse. Don't you remember me? My daughter Ulla used to come for piano lessons, don't you remember? Come, tell us, tell Father Pattas what happened."

Halina raised her face and Anna saw vacant, unseeing eyes.

"All gone," said Halina in a voice that didn't seem to belong to her, all the while cradling an imaginary body on her lap. And then she lowered her face again.

"She can't stay here, we must take her away, but where to? The poor thing . . ." The neighbor woman stuffed her mitten into her mouth to keep from sobbing.

The Archpriest was struck dumb by the look on Halina's face. Then, after a long while, he raised his hand and pronounced a blessing.

"Come, Mamochka," said Kotik. "There's nothing we can do here."

35

THEY WOULD HAVE to leave Ratibor soon. On Sunday they had been given travel rations and a written order to leave within twenty-four hours. And this was Tuesday. If they were stopped for an identity check, they would be shipped under guard to Komotau or Brünn, and people were constantly being stopped by members of the Gestapo or military police on the lookout for deserters. The front had been stabilized east of the Oder and there was even talk of a counteroffensive by the Schörner Army Group.

Moreover, they had no desire to stay there any longer. After a week of searching for Willi the one thing Rosa and Valeska had managed to find out was that he was most probably on the other side of the Oder, where all dispersed soldiers were being rounded up and assigned to new units. And civilians were no longer allowed to cross the bridge in that direction. Little Roswitha's fever was down, so Irma was also ready to leave.

"Let's not get ourselves shipped to Brünn," said Valeska. "From there we'd never get to Dresden."

"I'm for leaving as soon as possible. I only hope the train will be heated," said Rosa, who was massaging her temples. The night on the road had left her with a merciless headache.

"We could go to Marienbad," said Irma, "if Aunt Milka is there with her countess."

Marienbad, those beautiful casinos, Valeska thought. "But how do we know Milka is there? We have no address, nothing. In Dresden at least we have the address of the hospital where Ulla Ossadnik is working."

"It would be quieter in the country," said Irma. "No air raids."

"I'm for Dresden," said Valeska. "I've heard that Oberloschwitz is only a short way from the city. And you know, they haven't dropped any bombs on Dresden. It seems the Allies have chosen it as the new capital after the war."

Another consideration was that Josel also knew Ulla's address. Maybe, when they got there, Ulla would have news of him.

Rosa didn't know anyone in Dresden, not even a bookstore. She thought of her old father, who would no doubt be showing Russian soldiers around his shop and pointing out books on the shelves, Tolstoy and Dostoevski and Turgenev; the Russians were said to be great readers . . . "I'll go to Dresden with you," she said. "Then maybe I'll go on to Berlin."

Herr Leber, who had come back from the First World War minus a leg, was working at the Wolff Bookstore. He wasn't likely to have been drafted. She had wanted to marry him when he was working at the Readers' Corner in Freiburg, but he already had a wife.

"Marienbad sounds so peaceful, so idyllic," said Irma, "and it probably is that way if Aunt Milka and the countess have gone there." Milka always went in for quiet places, she remembered.

"Dresden has such beautiful museums," said Valeska. "Just on that account the English will never bomb it. If only for the sake of Raphael's Sistine Madonna."

"Oh yes," said Rosa, "I've always wanted to see the Sistine Madonna."

They discovered that they were gradually reverting to their old habits. They had even begun to make plans for the future again. Up until then, it seemed to Valeska, they had let themselves drift like a parcel of ground that the current has detached from the riverbank; now she had hopes that the current would someday carry her back again and she would be reunited with the land.

The next morning they went to the station. It was several hours before they found room in a train, and that train went only as far as Troppau. There the cars were needed to take soldiers to the Oder front. The women and children had to spend the night in a school-house. During the night there was more gunfire. Irma's youngest child began to scream and couldn't stop, so that Rosa had to go looking for a doctor in the middle of the night. "It's gunfire," said Irma. "The child can't stand it anymore. We must get away from here."

The next stop was Olmütz, where they had to stay for two days.

The city was unharmed and seemed wonderfully peaceful with its pretty little white houses. The cafés and movie theaters were full. Rosa went to see *The Woman of My Dreams*, a picture she had missed in Gleiwitz. She had enjoyed it, the only trouble being the silly song that kept running through her head: *At night a fellow doesn't like to be alone, 'cause love beneath the smiling summer moon / is extra-luscious if the truth be known / on the one hand on the other and besides* . . .

Rosa stopped a soldier on the street and asked him to buy her some headache pills, there were certain medicines that could be sold only to members of the armed forces. When he came back with the pills, the soldier asked her to join him in a cup of ersatz coffee at the Weisses Rössel. She couldn't very well refuse him, though she knew the others would be waiting for her. She certainly couldn't tell her sister-in-law Valeska that she had gone to see a movie with Marika Rökk in it.

The soldier was a sergeant in the engineers battalion of the 7th Infantry, in civilian life a schoolteacher in Breslau. He was worried about his parents—had they been able to escape from the city which Gauleiter Hanke had designated as a fortress and which would undoubtedly be surrounded any day now?

"It's insane," said the sergeant. "Why Breslau of all places? It has none of what's needed to make a fortress, they'll just destroy everything, everything. Before going into the army, I'd never seen another city, I had no desire to, I was born and bred in Breslau, I'd have been glad to stay there for the rest of my life. I knew every street, I knew all the rivers, I'd often go to watch them flow into the Oder. I played on those riverbanks as a child, it's wonderful to grow up near a big river like the Oder or even a little one like the Weide, that you can wade across in the summer. Of the five rivers in Breslau the Weistritz was the clearest, you could see the trout glistening in the sunlight, I had a friend who used to catch them with his bare hands and sell them to the workers in the suburbs. They'll destroy everything, the cathedral and the Royal Residence, the Elisabeth Church and the old Gothic Town Hall and the Magdalen Church with the poor sinners' bell. You must know Wilhelm Müller's beautiful ballad about the Breslau bell founder: *There was once a bell founder in Breslau in the town, a skilled, respected master, of honorable renown* . . . Have you ever been in Breslau?"

Rosa nodded. She had been in Breslau a few times, she'd gone to Bach concerts there. She had gone to Cathedral Island and to the Jahrhunderthalle, and the zoo in Scheitninger Park, and she had dropped in at the Max and Co. Bookshop on Neue Schweidnitzer Strasse and the East German Bookstore on Albrechtstrasse.

Yes, he had been to all those places, too. "They'll all be reduced to ashes and rubble, all our cities will be reduced to ashes and rubble, there will always be war. From now on. Today all the countries of Europe are fighting one another, but one day Europe will unite against Russia, and before long Europe and Russia will join forces against Asia, and then there will be war between America and Eurasia, and in the end only black Africa will be left . . ."

Suddenly, as though awaking from a dream, he said in an entirely different voice: "Forgive me, I shouldn't talk this way. You can turn me in if you like, just go and find the nearest MP, the railroad station is crawling with them, or tell any officer what I've been saying, they'll string me up, they're hanging people right and left these days, you get a reward, like that East Prussian housewife who denounced Herr Goerdeler, a hundred thousand reichsmarks she got, not to be sneezed at."

"Sh-sh," said Rosa. "Not so loud."

But the soldier seemed bent on attracting attention. She paid for the coffee, tugged at his sleeve, and shouted something or other loud enough to drown out his words. Once on the sidewalk, she left him flat.

"He was a nice man all the same," she told Valeska later. And took two Pyramidon tablets at once. That silly song was still running through her head: *Everybody needs a little bit of love, a statement that I shouldn't have to prove.*

36

THEY SPENT THE NIGHT in Schluckenau. That evening Frau Hauptmann complained of pain in her gallbladder. In the morning there was no improvement, and though it wasn't far to Dresden, she thought it advisable to consult a doctor before continuing the grueling ride in the gasogene. Attracted by the name of the patient, the doctor came quickly. He gave her an injection and advised her to go without delay to a certain hospital in Dresden, where his friend Dr. Hohlwein, whom he had called on the phone in the meantime, would be expecting her. It was decided that the gasogene would stop at the hospital before going on to Oberloschwitz, and Frau Weidner was notified that Herr Hauptmann would be delayed. As they had been at the Weidner Sanatorium several times, Frau Hauptmann knew he would be in good hands. Besides, their son Eckhart, despite the trouble he was having with his Achilles tendon, would look after him.

The roads were deserted and they made good time. Apart from the stretch between Görlitz and Löbau, where they were delayed by columns of refugees, there had been no holdups; there were checkpoints at the bridges, but their Special Authorization was honored everywhere. The gasogene was able to average a good twenty miles an hour on level stretches, and Herr Hauptmann reached the sanatorium by early afternoon. He was so cramped in the backseat, so muffled in robes and blankets that he had seen nothing of the city. Frau Weidner and a lady doctor helped him out of the car. His hat pulled down low over his face, a long muffler wound around his neck, his sable cape over his shoulders, he looked from a distance like a giant bat. At the entrance, he expressed a desire to look out over the Elbe valley and the city he so dearly loved, and they led him to the terrace that offered the finest view. Because of the low cloud cover, he could not see far that day; the edges of the city were lost in dull gray. Below him, the river ran like a black ribbon between snow-covered banks, he saw the tower of the Frauenkirche, the façade of the State Theater, and the Academy, where long ago, as a young student, he had sketched and modeled. He looked eagerly around, as though to fill his eyes and fertilize his soul, to wipe away and repress the old. He knew from long experience that the city would change with the first ray of sunshine.

The women led him to the garden house that had been made ready for him. There, Frau Weidner explained, he and his wife would be able to live undisturbed by the comings and goings in the hospital. A room had been reserved for his secretary, Annie Pollack, in an annex to the main building. Their meals would of course be brought them in the garden house, but they would also be welcome at the the hospital mess, which was held in the lecture hall because the big dining room was being used for the care of the many wounded soldiers. "I'm sure," said Frau Weidner, "that you remember the lecture hall with its magnificent view of the park, because you once gave a reading from your works there."

If Frau Weidner was unusually prolix, it was to get her over her shock at the old man's appearance. His still impressive face was waxen, his eyes were dull, set in an absent stare, his walk was hesitant and uncertain, as though every step cost him an inner struggle. Realizing that he could not be left alone, she assigned one of the senior nurses to his care until Frau Hauptmann should arrive.

In the late afternoon, after a long refreshing sleep, he was examined by Professor Lange, who found no particular symptoms and prescribed hot baths, massages, and Karlsbad salts to stimulate his sluggish intestines. The old man insisted on coffee and cognac after meals; they alone, he said, could overcome the psychological hypothermia from which he had been suffering for several weeks.

In the evening, his son Eckhart and Frau Weidner took turns at his bedside. They had agreed to steer the conversation away from politics and the war news. As Herr Hauptmann asked no questions, Eckhart did not have to tell him that Grünberg and Grottkau, places well known to him from the days of his youth, had been captured by the Russians.

The old man recovered quickly from the fatigue of his journey.

After the first few days he insisted on taking his meals in the main building. The path had been cleared of snow; he might be old, he said, but he was not an invalid.

Professor Sauerbruch, who had just arrived from Berlin, reported what was thus far the heaviest air raid. As he was leaving, fires were still burning in various parts of the city, the Charité hospital had been hit, and a number of patients as well as nurses had been killed. "Why," he roared, "did the British have to terrorize the civilian population; hasn't the war economy brought them suffering enough? The war has gone into its most inhuman phase, they don't even respect the Red Cross anymore. It was different in the last war." At length he simmered down and began as usual to tell anecdotes; he even wove in a few about himself. Those were the ones that made him laugh loudest.

Hauptmann spoke little. Tomorrow, he said, Fräulein Pollack, his secretary, would be arriving, and then he would try to dictate a few things. He still had great plans, of course he would confine himself to completing and revising, but that's how it was at his biblical age, as the Silesians called it. He hoped to finish his *New Christopher*, have another try at his *Winckelmann*, and work some more with Dr. Behl on the Second Part of the Definitive Edition.

When the others had gone, he felt lonely. He missed his wife, who would not be discharged from the hospital for another few days. He couldn't help thinking of the friends who had died recently, of Max Halbe, of Rudolf Rittner and Leo von König. He thought of Goethe's death. He was almost as old as Goethe had been when he died. He figured it out, he would have to live another hundred and twenty days to catch up with Goethe. Had Goethe been at peace with himself when he died? He would look into Eckermann and see what Goethe had been working on at the end. Goethe had an Eckermann. And what had he? A Behl.

"I am not in harmony with myself as Goethe was at the end, but just as helpless," he wrote in his diary. And on a new page: "Leo König painted Meier-Gräfe on his deathbed; he too was marked by death. I would like to think that Goethe died well.

"I have no desire to return to Agnetendorf before I die."

• • •

His shifts of mood, which had been noticeable for some weeks, became more intense and more abrupt. His wife had been discharged from the hospital and slept in the same room because he complained of night fears. Annie Pollack had at last arrived from Agnetendorf. He resumed his daily routine. Holding his wife by the arm, he would take short walks in the small sanatorium park. He did not dictate much, but he enjoyed being read to. On his bedside table lay the Bible; the Poems of Hafiz in two volumes; *Herder's Complete Works. On Philosophy and History, Part Eight; Soul and God.*

After tea, which they took in the garden house, he would go to the main building alone to browse in the library. The library opened out on the lecture hall, and sometimes he heard a young nurse practicing the piano there. The first time he heard her, he sat down at the back of the hall so as not to disturb her. The next day he sat in the same place and noticed that she made a good many mistakes. He went up to her, introduced himself, and complimented her on her talent. Since then he had often sat there. When he stayed too long, his wife and Annie would call for him. Once he suggested to the pianist that she and his wife might give a concert for the wounded. "She, too, is a musician," he said. "She studied with Professor Joachim in Berlin and she still plays the violin very nicely." The nurse, whose nerves had been on edge ever since she found out for whom she had been playing, replied at once in a loud voice: "I studied with Frau Professor Piontek in Gleiwitz."

For some days she had been playing well-balanced programs for the old man. He would rather have had her improvise, it would have been better suited to his dreamy, fitful mood. Her favorite composer, she told him, was Chopin. That surprised him. "I'm not very fond of Chopin," he said. "Too undisciplined, not enough structure. It's just emotional froth. To my mind, Beethoven is the summit of music as Goethe is of literature, Beethoven's settings of Goethe give me a faint idea of the masterpiece that would have been bestowed on Germany and the world if Beethoven had made an opera of Goethe's *Faust.*

"The only thing of Chopin's that I really like is the *Funeral March,* but only when played on the piano, not the usual brass-band arrangement. Could you play it for me some time, just the *Marche Funèbre?*" She had the music with her and sat right down to play. She played from memory without looking at the notes; with the first few measures, the intimations of death, she forgot where she was, forgot her listener, forgot herself. When she finished and looked around, the old man was no longer in his place. She sat there awhile. Then she closed the piano. On her way out, she saw a book on the chair where Herr Hauptmann had been sitting. *The Great Dream.* She opened it and found a dedication, but apart from her name she was unable to decipher the scrawl. A sheet of paper fell out of the book. A poem was typed on it. She read:

The Magic Flower

Far from the wine that you, O Hafiz, gave me,
a coal-black demon held me fast
and pushed the golden skiff that you had
steered
into a sea of plague and murder.
Annulled was all life's meaning
bent into agonizing madness
shot through with bane in place of blessing,
what seemed the truth corrupted into lies.
But through the window, Lo!, a gracious boy
hands me a magic flower,
dispels the blackest of my ghosts,
and God, the good, creates himself anew.

G.H., February 13, 1945, Dresden.

37

On their next visit to Teuchertstrasse the Russians brought an interpreter. Herr Jacob was there too. Like all the Germans he wore a white band on his left arm, but his had something printed on it in thick black letters that Anna couldn't read. All the occupants were summoned to the Mazuras' apartment; when they were all assembled, one of the Russians, accompanied by Herr Jacob, searched the empty apartments. Anna pleaded in vain that her husband was sick; he had to go down with the others, but at least he was allowed to remain seated during the whole procedure, while everyone else had to stand. One of the Russians aroused Anna's suspicions from the first. He had on a light gray coat without braid or epaulets, though the cut suggested a uniform. He didn't say a word, but Anna had the impression that nothing escaped him. From time to time he took out a little black book and wrote something in it. His face was heavily scarred and his heavy, drooping eyelids gave him a tired look; with his chunky build he reminded Anna of the president of the waterworks, whom she had met several times at the Pionteks'. Herr Jacob was now chairman of the Antifa committee; Anna had finally deciphered the letters ANTIFA on his arm band, though they meant nothing to her. All the occupants, Herr Jacob announced, had to be registered again, he felt sure they would understand. New, temporary identity cards would be issued. "Keep your card on you; anyone found without one can expect to be arrested as an agent, a spy, or a werewolf."

Anna had a pretty good idea what an agent or a spy was, but what in the name of all the saints was a werewolf? She didn't dare to ask.

Each tenant had to step forward as Herr Jacob called his name. When the interpreter waved his hand, the name was checked off, and the person crossed to the other side of the kitchen–living room. When it was a man, Herr Jacob asked each male routinely: "Member of the National Socialist Party or any of its subsidiaries?"

Herr Mazura was the first to be called. He replied: "I was a member of the Communist Party until 1933 when the party was suppressed." Here he looked around, surprised that his statement had not made more of an impression. He neglected to mention the fact that he had since then been a member of the National Socialist Party, though everyone in the house knew it.

When Franz Ossadnik's turn came, he hesitated for a moment. Then he said: "German Labor Front."

"You realize of course," his wife added, "that membership in the Labor Front was automatic. Every worker had to join. And an engine driver, you know . . ."

Herr Jacob proceeded to Adolf Zielonka and the interpreter checked off Franz Ossadnik's name, while the man in the gray coat took out his little book and made a note.

When the Russians and Herr Jacob had gone, Frau Aubitzky remarked that the man in the gray coat had given her the creeps. Frau Grochowiak said she could swear he was from the GPU. Anna shuddered. She had seen a movie called *GPU*; that had been quite a while ago, but she remembered how she had cried.

She and Kotik took Franz between them and helped the "sick man" upstairs. When they got there, Franz took a towel and dried the sweat on his face and neck. "Herr Jacob is standing by us," Franz said. "Like a real German." He felt deeply grateful.

Anna patted Kotik on the head. How clever of him to have thought of Franz playing sick. If he hadn't done that, the Russians might have taken him away then and there. Unfortunately, he hadn't been in the Communist Party like Herr Mazura.

Anna left Franz and Kotik alone and went back to the others in Frau Mazura's kitchen. She didn't want them talking about the Ossadniks in her absence. Of course there would be comments about his concealing his Party membership. She came in just as Herr Mazura was saying what a pity it was that he had destroyed his Communist Party book; it would have been a big help to him and probably to the other occupants of the house. But under the Nazis anyone caught hiding a CP book would have been a dead man. Same as a

Nazi Party book today. So he'd burned them both.

Frau Mazura had peeled some potatoes and cut them into thin slices that she roasted on top of the stove. You'd pick one up with your fingertips, blow on it, and put it in your mouth. Old man Bednarz sprinkled his with grape sugar out of his trouser pockets. Frau Zielonka let a slice of potato melt on her tongue like a wafer.

"Antifa," said Anna. Another of those new words. It had been hard getting used to Bakelite, but then they'd started using the stuff for radio sets, and later for clothes hangers, combs, and even summer shoes. And she'd no sooner got used to "evacuation" than a whole new assortment had come along like lanolin and werewolf and Antifa.

"Antifascist Committee," Mazura explained. "People who took up the fight against the National Socialist terror."

"Against what?" asked Frau Grochowiak, who had just put a hot potato slice into her mouth.

"Against Hitler," Herr Mazura explained.

"Oh, I never knew so many people were against Hitler," said Frau Grochowiak pointedly.

She had forgotten about her brother, whom the Nazis had locked up for tuning in on foreign radio stations. Besides, he hadn't really been against Hitler, he just wanted more information. Unfortunately for him, he had talked about it to a fellow worker.

"When you come right down to it," said Frau Aubitzky, "even Herr Jacob wasn't against Hitler. Hitler was against the Jews. That's the long and the short of it."

Frau Jacob was terrified. She held her children close and didn't say another word. When her name came up in the conversation, she hid behind her children, as she had always done.

"Only the fanatics were really bad," said Frau Zielonka. "And there weren't so many of them here in Gleiwitz. The people here are too religious for that."

"Yes, the fanatics were the top Party leaders, they were sent here from the Reich, we didn't want them, nobody asked us. Herr Bracht, for instance, he's no Upper Silesian."

"Who?" Old man Bednarz pricked up his ears.

"You know, Gauleiter Bracht of Kattowitz. He came from Vienna or Graz."

There they stood, eating hot potato slices and passing the time of day, glad to be still together and putting their hopes in Herr Jacob of the new Antifa Committee.

The Russians came back early in the morning, when the whole house was asleep. The thickset man in the gray coat was there and he was holding his little black book. The moment she saw him Anna knew what to expect. He pointed a finger at her Franz and said: "You fascist! You come with!" Those were the only words she was ever to hear him say.

It all went so fast. Anna wasn't even able to give Franz a toothbrush. Kotik sat stunned; he sat there a long while, and he'd have liked to sit there forever, like a stone that's in somebody's way.

Anna went to see Herr Jacob; she stood weeping in the doorway of his apartment, pleading with him to help her; then she ran back and forth between Herr Jacob and his wife, clutching at their arms. Herr Jacob's only answer was: "Order from above. Nothing we can do. You know how it is with orders from above."

For a long time Anna racked her brains about the word the man in the gray coat had used: *fascist*. Why would he say that when her Franzek had never been in Italy?

38

THEY CAUGHT A TRAIN the next day, and finally, after several forced interruptions, arrived in Dresden on the afternoon of February 13. That was the goal Valeska had set herself from the start. The station platform was swarming with people, among them children with bright-colored hats and cardboard noses. "It's Mardi Gras," the people said, as if that were the most natural thing in the world. It had all happened so quickly. Only three weeks ago they had been trudging along the freezing cold road from Gleiwitz to Ratibor, escaping from the Russians. Then one precarious way station after another, and now these merry children with the cardboard noses.

The problem now was finding lodgings in this peaceful city. They would stay here for a while at least, and wait for the others. Rosa, who felt guilty for having dropped the shell-shocked soldier in Ol-mütz, was beginning to think that the war was one of the last great trials to which God would subject mankind. Her Pyramidon tablets were all gone, and her headache had started up again. The first thing she would do in Dresden was to run from druggist to druggist in the hope of getting some kind of headache pills.

How fortunate that they had taken the scheduled passenger train; refugee trains were now being routed around Dresden, where there were already several hundred thousand refugees. An inspector in the train had checked their papers and asked where they were going, but Valeska had offered credible assurance that her daughter in Dresden-Loschwitz would put them up and they had been allowed to proceed.

The Pionteks had a hard time getting out of the train because of the hordes that were trying to get in, though no one knew where it was bound for or when it would leave. All these people had spent several days in Dresden, looking in vain for a place to lay their heads, and now they wanted to get away, it didn't matter where to. According to one rumor, this train would be going back where it came from, to Aussig; maybe the country folk would be more hospitable than these Dresdeners.

"City people are heartless," said a woman from Rasselwitz to Valeska. "Always have been. The Party made a family share their apartment with us, and do you know what they did, they cut off our light and water. I've had enough of Saxony."

She was glad to have found room in the train for herself and her seven children.

At least we have an address to start with, Valeska thought. Ulla will be sure to help us. The three women tied themselves together with scarves for fear of losing one another in the crush. The station was jam-packed with refugees. Two soup kitchens had been set up; you presented your refugee card, and they would stamp it with "lunch" or "supper" when serving your meal. Six stamps were the limit, because refugees weren't supposed to stay in Dresden for more than three days.

Rosa wanted to phone the Weidner Sanatorium at once, but Valeska preferred not to. She couldn't have said exactly why. The truth is she was afraid that if she phoned Ulla might say no. Then they would just have to leave town, and she wouldn't even see Ulla. She simply had to speak to her. And she wouldn't for anything miss the look of amazement on Ulla's face at suddenly seeing her there in the hospital. And now that they had finally got here, a few hours one way or the other didn't matter. She left the others in the waiting room with strict instructions to wait there until she got back.

As Valeska left the station, the city was cloaked in soft, shadowy dusk. But she had no time for beauty, she was too busy fighting for room in the crowded streetcar. No one talked. People got in and out with weary movements and vacant faces. When Valeska asked someone for her stop, she received only a curt, half-whispered answer. At last it was time to get out. After walking a few blocks, she turned into a lonely path, of which she had been given so vague a description that she was suddenly startled to find herself at the gate of the sanatorium. A few steps took her to the main building, which was imperfectly blacked out and cast stripes of yellow light on the snow. She walked in and had gone almost as far as the dining room when an elderly lady asked if she could help her.

"I'd just like to sit down if you don't mind," said Valeska, who was thoroughly exhausted. And without waiting for an answer, she sat down on a wooden bench in the window corner, at the same time pushing aside a vase of ornamental thistles to make room for herself. She would have to catch her breath before she could speak.

"You look rather frazzled," said Frau Weidner sympathetically. "Where have you come from?"

"I'm looking for someone," said Valeska finally. "A Fräulein Ossadnik."

"For whom?" Frau Weidnar was puzzled. Most visitors asked for men, their wounded husbands or sons.

"She's a nurse here," said Valeska, reaching into her handbag for a rather crumpled envelope with Ulla's return address on it.

Frau Weidner didn't even look at it. "Oh, we do have a nurse here who plays the piano beautifully, Sister Ulla, is that the person you mean?"

Valeska stood up. All at once she felt safe. "That's right," she said. "No one plays the piano like her, no one far and wide, and I'm her teacher, Valeska Piontek from Gleiwitz, Upper Silesia, if that means anything to you."

No, Gleiwitz meant nothing to Frau Weidner, but Ulla the nurse and pianist did. Herr Hauptmann had inquired about her in fact. Since then she had played for him every afternoon, and Frau Weidner had noticed that every day he had had his armchair moved a little closer to the piano.

"Do forgive me," said Frau Weidner, who always introduced speeches of any length or importance with an apology. "Perhaps you had better come with me to Sister Olga, the head nurse. She is sure to know where Sister Ulla is at the moment. Then you can go and talk to her. But you mustn't stay too long if she's on duty."

Valeska unbuttoned her fur coat. Excitement brought red spots to her cheeks. She would soon be seeing Ulla Ossadnik after so long a time, and maybe Ulla would have news of Josel, good news . . .

Sister Olga informed her at once that she had given Sister Ulla the afternoon off. Someone had phoned, and Sister Ulla had gone to see a friend, who was a patient in one of the Dresden hospitals.

"A friend?" said Valeska excitedly. "You don't happen to know his name? You see," she tried to explain "I'm not just Fräulein Os-sadnik's teacher, I've also been kind of a mother to her . . ."

In the end, they found out through another nurse that Ulla had gone to the Friedrichstadt Hospital. No one knew when she'd be back, she wouldn't be on duty until tomorrow evening.

"Was this . . . this friend's name by any chance . . . Josel Piontek?" Valeska asked breathlessly. But no one remembered the name.

Valeska would have to go back to the railroad station, it couldn't be helped, but first she would write a short message for Ulla.

At that moment the air-raid sirens were heard, but no one paid much attention. The sirens had howled so often, and the planes had always stopped short of Dresden or bypassed it. Frau Weidner said rather casually to the head nurse: "Make sure the lights are turned out. And plug in the radio. What time is it?"

Valeska looked at her watch. "A quarter to ten," she said.

"You will have to stay here for the present," said Frau Weidner. "The streetcars don't run during an alert. And on foot you wouldn't get far in the dark. If you'll excuse me now, I have things to do. But Sister Olga will take you to the nurses' room. You can write your note, and they'll give you a cup of tea—without sugar," she added with a laugh.

"But what if it is an air raid! I must get back to my daughter. She's waiting at the station. Isn't it especially dangerous there?"

"The people in the station will be sent to the air-raid shelter too. Be patient. It will be over in half an hour. God help us!"

"But the station is packed full of people," cried Valeska. "Where can they all go? There are half a million refugees in the city, *muy Bozhe kokhany.*" Valeska looked around. Then she came closer to Frau Weidner and blurted out: "Couldn't you put us up somehow, my daughter and me? We'll help you with your work. We Silesians are hard workers, you know."

"Yes, of course," said Frau Weidner. "Everybody knows that. But

I'm afraid we wouldn't have room for more than one." With that she vanished into the ward.

Sister Olga and Valeska sat down in the nurses' room, where a dim light was burning, and drank linden blossom tea. Over the radio the ticking of a clock was heard, as usual during an air-raid alert. Sister Olga showed her impatience by looking repeatedly at her watch. Valeska said: "We were told that the British would bomb every one of our cities except Dresden, because they want Dresden to be our new capital after the war. Have you heard that too?"

"Interesting. But isn't it up to us Germans to decide which city is to be our capital?" And after awhile: "You're from Gleiwitz? From Silesia? Did you know that we have the most famous writer not only of Silesia but of all Germany right here in this sanatorium?"

"Really?! You don't say!"

"Oh, this isn't his first visit. He likes it here. He usually comes in the spring. Oh, if only the winter were over! Why just this year did it have to be such a hard winter!"

"Do you think," Valeska asked in an awestruck whisper, "I might be able to get a glimpse of him, I mean, when he's out walking in the garden?"

Rosa would be green with envy when she heard about it. No, she wouldn't dare tell her, or she'd want to stay in Dresden forever.

"Oh yes, that can be arranged. Sister Ulla plays for him every afternoon."

"You mean that Ulla has spoken to him—in person!?" She couldn't get over it.

At that moment the ticking on the radio was interrupted and a slightly uneasy voice was heard. "Attention! Attention! The enemy bomber formations have changed course. They are now heading for the Dresden area. Go to the nearest shelter and stay there until further notice. Anyone seen on the street will be arrested . . ."

As though to confirm the radio announcement, a distant humming of motors was heard. Little by little, it grew louder. The women stood up. Then came the first explosions. They looked at each other, hoping there would be no more explosions. But they didn't stop, they grew louder and more frequent.

Frau Weidner's voice was heard from the ward. "All of you who are able to walk put on warm clothing. You will be taken to the air-raid shelter."

Valeska felt that her strength as well as her memory had drained out of her. There was nothing left in her head but the ticking of the radio clock. Just that ticking. And the explosions outside. Cold air blew in from the corridor.

"Frau Weidner, come and see"—a nurse was running past— "Dresden is on fire."

Valeska buttoned her coat and went down the corridor in the direction from which she had come. Near the door she saw Frau Weidner, Sister Olga, and some other nurses. Looking down, she saw the city silhouetted against the red-glowing sky. Thin columns of smoke were rising here and there.

"They're bombing Dresden!" Frau Weidner cried. "No room for doubt. This raid is against Dresden."

"*Muy Bozhe kokhany,*" Valeska whispered, crossing herself. "Mary, Mother of God, protect Irma and the children. I must go to them. I must go to the station. Can I leave my knapsack here? There are important papers in it. Give it to Ulla Ossadnik, my pupil."

"You stay right here!" Frau Weidner screamed at her. "Wait at least for the raid to be over. You can't run straight into hell!"

39

Ulla Ossadnik was playing the piano. She was playing in the lecture hall of the Weidner Sanatorium, as she did every afternoon. She was playing Beethoven's *Contredanses*, which she had studied long ago with her old teacher but had seldom played since. She was playing for the great writer, for Gerhart Hauptmann, who was sitting behind her; he had asked her to play something by Beethoven, no matter what, as long as it was Beethoven. Ulla was more for the romantics, she preferred to play Schumann and Chopin, and the only Beethoven she could find in her music was the *Contredanses*. Until recently she had played in the late afternoon when it was quiet in the hall, usually improvising or playing whatever came into her head, practicing to keep her fingers supple. She had played certain pieces over and over again for the sake of their technical difficulties, partly to prove to herself that she was still able to play them despite the ten-hour days she was putting in as a nurse. But now she had stopped practicing, she couldn't subject Herr Hauptmann to that. Now she played just for him. Every afternoon she put together a little program.

After Beethoven he asked her, since she was so fond of Chopin, to play the *Marche Funèbre*, no, he wasn't feeling moribund, he was full of life again, it was just that he loved that music, she should just play the one movement, not the whole B-minor sonata. As a token of gratitude he had brought her a book and a copy of a poem he had dictated that afternoon.

When she finished playing, the old gentleman was no longer in the room. But the book was on his chair.

Later, she was called to the phone. A man's voice on the line. Josel Piontek. Josel Piontek? Yes, of course. It was his voice, she hadn't heard it for ages, and never on the phone, she had to get used to it. Josel from Gleiwitz. The first boy who had ever kissed her.

Josel told her he'd been wounded, he was in the Friedrichstadt Hospital, he wouldn't say what kind of wound it was. On the one hand he said it was nothing to worry about, on the other he said he absolutely had to see her that same day. She asked for the afternoon off and told Sister Erika, her roommate, that she was going to see an old friend in the Friedrichstadt Hospital but she wouldn't be back too late, they should save some supper for her in the kitchen.

She took Gerhart Hauptmann's book, inserting, next to the flyleaf with the inscription she had been unable to decipher, a pressed auricula from her album.

She took the bus to Friedrichstadt. It was already dark when she arrived at the hospital and she lost some time in finding the right ward, the ninth, in the enormous hospital complex. On her way from corridor to corridor, she couldn't help thinking of the ninth Station of the Cross, the station at which Jesus falls for the third time.

Josel had lost his left arm in the fighting around Strehlen. Gangrene had set in after an improvised operation, and he had had to be amputated again somewhat higher up. Ulla saw the pain and fear in his face despite the show of good cheer that he put on for her. It was only the left arm, he said, he didn't need it to write with, and he was thinking more and more seriously of becoming a writer some day. At least he wasn't a pianist, that would have been worse.

"Oh," said Ulla, "there are some famous concerti for the left hand."

"Don't say such things," said Josel. He was glad to have found Ulla so quickly. He had arrived in Dresden only the day before, he had phoned this morning, and here she was at his bedside. He could hardly believe it. How lucky that his mother had sent him Ulla's address.

They talked about their families, first hers, then his. Neither had any news of them. They both had conjectures to offer, but they soon fell silent, realizing that they knew nothing and were only trying to keep their spirits up.

Josel leafed through the book that Ulla had put down on his bedside table. A pale pink flower fell out and lay on the white coverlet. "It's an auricula," Josel said. "It reminds me of home."

"I picked it here on the Elbe meadows, last year when I had to stop giving concerts and they made me train as a nurse. But as you see," she added mysteriously, "I still have hopes."

"You still play the piano?"

"Oh yes, whenever I can. And you? Have you been writing?"

"Oh yes, I'm writing a diary. I've got several copybooks full at home in Gleiwitz. God knows what's become of them."

"There's a famous writer at our sanatorium . . ." Ulla whispered his name. "This book is by him, he gave it to me. Imagine . . . every afternoon I play for him. One day he heard me practicing and he came up and kissed my hand. Do you know what he said? He said: The girl is very talented. Herr Hauptmann said that!"

Josel was sitting up in bed. He couldn't see what Ulla was so excited about. Yes, he really was a famous writer. But he was an old man after all.

"He'd like me to play Beethoven the whole time," said Ulla, taking the book from Josel's hand. "But you know, I prefer Chopin. And Schumann."

At that moment they heard the sirens. The alert was not yet over when the lights went out in the ward. Only a dim bulb over the door was still burning. A calm voice came over the loudspeaker: "All please stay where you are. Ambulatory patients, get ready for the air-raid shelter. Don't leave your beds. Wait for further instructions."

"When I'm better," said Josel. "I'll come and see you in your sanatorium. Is it far from here? I'd like to see the famous writer. Face to face. It would be a big thing for me."

The first explosions were not very far away, the blast made the windows rattle and the floor tremble. The wounded men jumped off their beds and ran to the door. Steps and cries were heard from the corridor. Ulla and Josel held hands and didn't move.

"They're bombing the city," said Ulla after a series of powerful explosions. "Can you lean on me? We'll have to go down to the shelter."

They looked around. Only those unable to walk unaided were still lying on their beds. Some were in traction and couldn't have disentangled themselves without help.

"I'm still pretty weak," said Josel. "I can walk, though. But all the way to the shelter . . . ?"

"I'll be needed at the sanatorium if this is serious," said Ulla.

Josel opened the drawer of his bedside table.

"Ulla," he said. "I have a stone, nothing special, a piece of polished anthracite with a cross engraved on it. My father gave it to me. Take it with you."

Ulla felt the stone in her hand. She listened for sounds. What was she to do with this black stone? She put it into her coat pocket.

And forgot all about it.

Someone stood in the doorway screaming: "Dresden is on fire! Oh my God, the whole city is on fire!"

Ulla rushed out. A white light struck her, so blinding that she had to shut her eyes. She smelled fire. She felt it on her face. She ran her hand over her face and discovered that the heat had singed her eyebrows.

40

SHORTLY BEFORE ten o'clock when the sirens started howling, Frau Hauptmann sat reading under the green lampshade. She had given Annie the evening off. Benvenuto had arrived in Dresden and was staying at the Hotel Bellevue. Herr and Frau Hauptmann were going to meet him there and they would all eat dinner together. But then the old man had felt weak and tired and they had put the meeting off till the following day. So his wife had sat by his bedside and read Balzac to him, the scene in which Rafael and Pauline, after a tempestuous night of love, are overtaken by intimations of death: "*Yes, there are chasms that not even love can bridge—it can only be buried in them.*"

Frau Hauptmann saw that her husband had fallen asleep and went on reading for her own benefit. Now and then she cast a glance at him; his regular breathing calmed her. She let her book sink to her lap. This was the first air-raid warning since their arrival in Oberloschwitz. At Wiesenstein she had never heard any sirens, only in Agnetendorf and Warmbrunn, and there they were only being tried out.

She looked at her husband's face and waited for the sirens to stop. He hadn't even woken up. She threw a coat over her shoulders and went to the main building to ask what she should do.

Frau Weidner was in her little office. She hadn't let the air-raid warning interfere with her work, and all was quiet in the building. As far as she was concerned, the alert was mere routine; it might affect people in other parts of the country, but not here, not in Oberloschwitz, or even in Dresden, God help us. There had been several alerts, Chemnitz or Freiberg had been bombed, or the planes had flown on to Hoyerswerde and bombed the hydrogen factory. Dresden really had nothing to fear, there were no munitions factories, no war industry, and the British seemed to know it, because all the other big cities had been bombed regularly for months, while Dresden had had only one raid, on January 16, and that hadn't amounted to much; most people thought it was an error of navigation, God help us.

Frau Hauptmann listened and believed, because she wanted to believe.

If Herr Hauptmann was asleep, said Frau Weidner, she should let him sleep by all means. These alerts didn't usually last long, heaven help us.

A moment later they heard the sound of motors, growing louder and louder, then the thud of bombs hitting the ground, followed by explosions in the city down below. Doors slammed, voices, cries, steps. The two women hadn't budged, but now they ran into the corridor, where nurses were running back and forth, and on to the entrance. In the doorway they stopped and stood staring at the sea of flames down below. Red Christmas trees came floating down, blackening church towers, the dome of the opera house and the retaining walls of the Brühl Gardens. Silver crosses fell from the cloudless sky and descended on the blazing city, followed by a succession of bursting fireballs. White, black, and red clouds of smoke rose up on all sides, came bursting out of roofs, whirled through the streets, rose above the river and darkened the towers.

Frau Weidner turned around and gave orders to move the wounded men to the air-raid shelter. To Frau Hauptmann she shouted: "Stay with him. Nothing will happen up here."

Frau Hauptmann ran back to the garden house and found her husband lying on the bed, still asleep, his face calm and relaxed. His chest rose and fell regularly under the coverlet. She lit a candle, put it on the dressing table in front of the mirror, and switched off the reading lamp. She moved her chair close to the bed and gazed at the sleeper. The dancing, copper-colored light made his features stand out in the darkness. It was still a beautiful face; she bent over it in silence, and every breath revived a memory of the life they had lived together for more than half a century. She stared and stared, her eyes sucked the truth from that face, and she came so close to him that their breaths mingled.

Then cautiously she raised the coverlet, slipped into bed beside him, and pulled the blankets up over their two old bodies. Muffled explosions could still be heard from outside. They came in quicker and quicker succession, but they no longer frightened her.

41

THE AIR RAID hadn't lasted long, no more than a quarter of an hour, but to Frau Hauptmann it had seemed an eternity. The sound of motors was gone and the explosions from the city below came to her only singly. She had heard voices in the park, once right outside the door, but then they too had gone away, there had been no other sound, and the only reminder of the raid had been the red glow on the walls of the room. It came through the rents in the blackout curtains, especially after she blew out the candle.

They awoke at the same time, when an explosion shook the garden house and the blast shattered the windowpanes. At first she heard only a crash practically on top of them, then an icy wind was blowing over her face. It took her some time to find the candle and matches. Then she saw the black hole in the wall where the window had been. She saw her husband, who sat up in bed, pulling the white coverlet almost to his shoulders, his face a rigid mask. She pulled a sweater over his head, threw the sable cloak over him, wrapped a long woolen muffler around his neck, and put his hat on. "Don't be afraid, dear," she said. "I'm with you, we'll go down to the air-raid shelter now, nothing will happen to us, just keep your hands in your muff, oh Lord, why must this happen to us, is nothing to be spared us, but perhaps He wants you to bear witness, oh God, witness to the apocalypse . . ." Her outburst made her feel better.

She opened the top drawer of the dressing table, took out her handbag in which she kept the most important family papers, and slung it over her shoulder. Cold blew in from outside. As they crossed the room, broken glass crunched under their shoes.

They had just reached the door when a bomb burst not far away. The blast threw them back onto the bed; the little garden house trembled, the table turned over, and plaster crumbled from the ceiling. She threw her arms around her husband and buried her face in his fur cape. Then they started out again.

When she opened the door, a fiery glow met her eyes. The city below them was burning. The sky was red. The old man stood staring. The fiery glow fell white and red on his face. His lips moved as if he wanted to say something. His wife bent closer to him, trying to read his words from his lips.

Then Sister Olga and Eckhart's daughter Ingeborg joined the old couple and guided them to the air-raid shelter. There they remained for quite some time surrounded by nurses and wounded soldiers. The explosions in the city had stopped, but the fire had spread and the heat could be felt even up here at the sanatorium.

Suddenly Benvenuto appeared in the shelter. He had come from the city on foot. He embraced his father, who looked at him with expressionless eyes, as though he didn't recognize him. Benvenuto had gone through the first raid in the air-raid shelter of the Hotel Bellevue; the explosions had been so violent that people had been flung from one end of the shelter to the other. When the all-clear was sounded, he had helped the rescue workers; he had seen hundreds of corpses lined up along the walls of the tunnels under the railroad station. All those people had been asphyxiated by carbon monoxide that had been trapped in the tunnels when the exits caved in. The second raid, at about one thirty in the morning, had come so quickly that the alert had not even been sounded, though possibly for lack of electricity. After that he had fled the city and had somehow managed to make his way to Oberloschwitz.

The third raid came the next day, Ash Wednesday, at twelve o'clock. It lasted eleven minutes. One thousand three hundred and fifty American planes, Liberators and Flying Fortresses, which had taken off from the East Anglia base in southern England at seven forty, entered the German air space near Bremen and flew to Dresden via Höxter and Magdeburg without encountering the least antiaircraft fire. They had dropped 783 tons of bombs on the city, giving it the death blow. For five days the sun neither rose nor set over Dresden. The fire was brighter than the sun.

When at length they left the shelter, Frau Hauptmann led her husband back to the garden house. On the way, they saw to their amazement that the snow in the park had melted. Once the old man

stopped on the path to look down into the valley of the Elbe and
the burning city. Frau Hauptmann saw that tears were running down
his face. In their absence boards had been nailed over the broken
windows of the garden house and rags had been stuffed in the chinks.

From then on Hauptmann hardly said a word. When the doctors
came to examine him, they had to repeat their questions several times
before he answered. He wished to see no one but his wife and son,
and even to them he said no more than was necessary. His sciatica
became so severe that he could hardly move. Paul Metzkow's massages were the only thing that helped.

Once Hauptmann said to his wife: "I longed for death, but it
rejected me. Never have I so longed for death as that night. But I
must suffer with my people and my people's suffering is not over."

Another time, he said: "I have been called upon to witness the
death of my beloved Dresden: What a mission! If I were ten years
younger, I would spend the rest of my life writing about it."

One day two radio reporters came and asked him to say something
about the death of Dresden. When they agreed to his stipulation
that not a single sentence must be omitted or modified, he dictated
something to Annie and authorized them to read it over the radio,
as he himself felt too weak. Frau Hauptmann listened to the broadcast. Actually, they had omitted two sentences.

"One who has forgotten how to weep will weep again at the death
of Dresden. That morning star of youth was long a light to the
world. I know there are many good men in England and America
who were not blind to the divine light of the Sistine Madonna and
who will weep bitter tears over the extinction of that star.

"I have lived through the destruction of Dresden beneath the fire
and brimstone of British and American planes. I say 'lived through'
because I regard it as a miracle that I am still alive. I do not consider
myself important enough to imagine that fate selected me personally
to witness this horror in what is almost the most beloved part of my
world.

"Standing as I do on my way out of this life, I envy my dead
comrades-in-spirit who have been spared this tragedy. I am weeping.
Do not chide me with the word 'weeping': the great heroes of an-

tiquity, among them Pericles, were not ashamed to use it.

"From Dresden, that exquisite font as much of music as of letters, great streams have flowed through the world; England and America have also shared in them.

"Have they forgotten that?

"I am almost eighty-three years old and I stand before God with a petition which, I regret to say, I am powerless to back up but which springs from my heart: may God henceforward love, purify, and enlighten mankind more than He has done up to now."

Now he wanted to go back to Agnetendorf, to Wiesenstein, to his refuge. He wanted to die there and to be buried in Silesian ground. That was where he had come from and that was where he wanted to end. And if he had to die somewhere else, let Silesian earth be thrown on his coffin.

42

THAT DAY THE inhabitants of Gleiwitz read new posters on the walls.

> *By order of the High Command the entire German population is mobilized for labor service.*
> *I therefore decree:*
>
> 1. *The entire male population—Germans and German subjects—between the ages of 16 and 50 must report, within 48 hours after publication of this notice, to the*
>   *Labor conscription bureau of the*
>   *Gleiwitz Kommandantur*
>   *where they will be registered and at the same time dispatched to labor duty.*
> 2. *All mobilized persons must bring their identification papers and the following objects:*
>   *at least two complete sets of winter clothing, including shoes and underwear; bedclothes (blankets, sheets), articles of personal use (cooking equipment, mess kit, etc.), and food for at least 10 days.*
> 3. *Persons failing to comply with this order or to report on time will be judged by court-martial.*
>
> The City Commandant.

"But that's tomorrow," cried Frau Zielonka, who was bringing in two pitchers of water.

"*Muy Bozhe*, what do they want of our men?" said another woman, looking anxiously around. "They can't ship them all to Siberia, can they?"

"The Russians need our munitions factories. And they need our men to run them. Skilled workers are always needed." She was trying to reassure herself as well as the other women, as though by saying things she could make them true.

Another woman pulled her head scarf so tight that her face was barely visible. "Every night they come to our house on Raudener-strasse and jump the young women, Holy Mary, Mother of God!" —here she crossed herself—"They've taken everything, even our featherbeds, and now they're taking our men, they're not human, they're devils, devils . . ." And she ran off screaming.

The others looked after her and clenched their teeth. They wouldn't have had the courage to say all that out loud.

"I guess I'll have to go," said Zielonka to his wife after reading the poster. "Noncompliance is punished by court-martial. Do you know what that means? It means they stand you up against the wall. I'm an engine driver. They won't do anything to me. Engine drivers are always needed."

That's what Anna Ossadnik had thought. But they'd taken her husband away all the same, no one knew where to. She had gone to police headquarters where other women whose husbands had been arrested were already waiting. The big gate was closed, barbed wire had been strung in front of it, you couldn't get near it. From the courtyard tinny, pounding music could be heard. Words poured from a loudspeaker, but "MOSKVA GOVORIT" was as much as the women could make out. At the approach of the curfew hour, they went home. It seemed to them that they would never get used to the quietness in their apartments.

"I wouldn't let them take my husband away," said Anna to the other women who had gathered at the Mazuras' to discuss the situation. Yet her husband was the first to have been taken away.

"But what can we do?" Frau Zielonka moaned. "They threaten us with court-martial."

"Hide them. I never thought they'd arrest a plain man who'd been forced into the Party. I'd have hidden my Franzek if I'd known."

"What difference does it make? They took your husband this morning. Ours have to go tomorrow morning."

"At least you can give yours warm underwear," said Anna. "There's some comfort in that."

Frau Mazura quietly put underwear, blankets, a pillow, a mess kit, a chunk of bread, and a bit of margarine on the table. Old man Bednarz contributed a package of grape sugar.

"I don't think they'll do anything to us," said Mazura. "Proletarians of all countries, unite. That's what the Communists say. And what are we? We're plain workers, that's what proletarians means. The Soviets are against capitalists and against the big landowners, but not against the little man. So give me my stuff, Mama, I'm going to the Kommandantur right now, I'm not afraid, 'cause the Bolsheviks are for the little man."

Frau Zielonka prayed aloud: "Our father who art in heaven, hallowed be thy name, they kingdom come . . ."

Anna Ossadnik decided to go and see Father Pattas, the Archpriest, at the Peter and Paul Church. When Kotik refused to go with her, she burst into tears. At that he relented and promised to meet her there. On the way he went to Miethe-Allee to see what had become of his villa. He stood outside it and saw the shattered windowpanes, the smashed door, the furniture strewn about the front garden, the mangled dressmaker's dummies, the phonograph minus its player arm. For a while Kotik stood just where he had stood a few days ago, before jumping over the fence. Then he went slowly away without once turning around.

Outside the presbytery Mamochka was waiting. She didn't scold him for being late; he wasn't a child anymore.

Kotik saw to his surprise that the main portal and the side doors of the church were boarded over, but he said nothing. Mamochka pretended to herself that nothing could be more natural. They had to wait in the anteroom along with three other women, who told them why the church doors were boarded up. On Sunday the Archpriest had held a silent mass in the Lady Chapel. At the Sanctus— imagine!—some Russian soldiers had rushed in, fired shots at the ceiling, driven the worshipers out of the church, and taken the Archpriest away. They had kept him overnight at the Kommandantur and released him the next morning. Reason for holding him: Gatherings of more than five persons were prohibited.

Anna had the impression that the other women had come to see

Father Pattas on the same business as herself. They were mumbling prayers and their eyes were red from weeping.

"I suppose the church will have to be reconsecrated," said Anna to the Archpriest when she and Kotik were at last admitted.

Father Pattas looked at her and said: "Thank the Lord, nothing has been destroyed."

The Archpriest made a note of the name and the circumstances of the arrest, and promised that if he was admitted to the Kommandantur, he would bring up the case of Franz Ossadnik. And he pointed at a thick briefcase.

"I know," he said, "that it won't do my parishioners much good if I try to console them with a Bible quotation. But the word of God stands truly . . ."

". . . the word of God stands unduly . . ." Kotik interrupted.

"I beg your pardon?" The Archpriest looked at the boy, whom he hadn't quite noticed before. Then he want on: "The misfortune that has befallen my congregation is so great that words fail me, and yet, my dear Frau Ossadnik, we have no alternative but to trust in the Lord God, for God is our strength. He makes darkness into light, the ways of God are strange, the word of God is pure, He is a buckler to all who trust him, as it says in the eighteenth Psalm." And Father Pattas blessed the two of them.

Kotik took his courage in both hands and said: "Just a moment please. Zarathustra says: They knew no better way of loving God than to nail men to the cross . . . they inscribed bloody symbols on the path they trod, their folly taught them that the truth is proved with blood . . . Blood taints the purest doctrine, transforming it into madness and hatred . . . You've read *Zarathustra*, I suppose?"

"Kotik! I beg you, not here!" said Anna, turning up the collar of her son's coat.

"Why not?" Kotik protested, putting his collar down again. "I'm sick of pious sermons. We must bear our cross with patience! I've been hearing that ever since Mamochka started dragging me to church. I don't want a suffering God, I want a God who rebels."

Anna was aghast. "What are you saying, child? And in a holy place!" She pushed him in the direction of the door. "Praised be

Jesus Christ," she said aloud and kissed the Archpriest's hand. He still has his ring, she thought. From us they've stolen everything. When Frau Aubitzky didn't want to give up her ring, the Russian threatened to chop off her finger with an ax, and Frau Aubitzky's ring wasn't nearly as beautiful or as valuable as Father Pattas's.

"Does the boy still read so much?" the priest asked in a tone of forbearance.

"Oh yes," said Anna, prepared to put her hand over her son's mouth if he started saying anything blasphemous. "He reads everything he lays hands on, and just now it's this *Zarathustra.*" She didn't know whether to feel proud or ashamed of him.

"Reading is always a good thing," said the Archpriest. "But in times like this prayer is also necessary."

"So you think," Anna asked, "that I can bring the crosses and holy pictures up from the cellar and put them back on the wall? You don't think the Russians will come and smash them?"

"No, they won't do that. Stand by your religion. The Russians will respect you for it."

Kotik had tears in his eyes, tears of rage because he had let his mother interrupt him. He wasn't a child anymore, far from it, and he didn't understand why he had let her get away with it. Something in this presbytery had struck him dumb. Was it the heat of the room, the priest's vestments, that unctuous voice, the holy pictures on the walls? He would have preferred the walls to be white as they were at home since Mamochka had taken down the crosses, though anyone could see what had been there before. On the way home he clenched his fists in his pockets with helpless rage. When his mother asked him some harmless question, his only reply was "Leave me alone! Just leave me alone!"

At home they learned that Frau Zielonka and Frau Mazura had taken their husbands to the Kommandantur and seen them disappear behind the green doors. More men had come, carrying old suitcases, and they too had disappeared behind the doors, in front of which sentries with submachine guns had been pacing back and forth. How, the women wondered, would they ever find room for all those husbands in there?

Some days later Anna Ossadnik and her fifteen-year-old son Kotik were summoned by the chairman of the Antifa Committee, Moishe Jacob, the former Joseph Jacob, and assigned to dismantling work. They were put on the night shift at the VOH Wire Works behind the railroad station. There they were given a meal and allowed to take home some soup in a pail. It wasn't quite enough for Frau Aubitzky and her three sons, but Frau Grochowiak, who had been assigned to dismantling the railroad repair shop, also brought home soup, so no one went hungry in the house on Teuchertstrasse. In addition, old man Bednarz had hidden a few pounds of flour, semolina, dried peas, and grape sugar so well that even when the house was looted for the eighth time they hadn't been found. And to think that Herr Mazura had always insisted that old man Bednarz was a little soft in the head.

Anna was also put on dismantling. With hammer and chisel she would detach machines from their concrete base. The machines were then wrapped in oiled paper and loaded on flatcars. Kotik, who with his fifteen years was thought not to be strong enough for such heavy work, was made to stencil the words HE KAHTOBATb (Handle with Care) on crates. I must get out of Gleiwitz, he kept thinking. As soon as the war was over; he'd go to Persia, where Zarathustra came from, or to America, where Lubarski had become a millionaire.

On Sunday there was a change of shifts. The Peter and Paul Church was still closed. Anna made a fire in the stove, sat down beside it, took her rosary, and started her Sunday devotions with the sorrowful mysteries.

Kotik sat down with this *Zarathustra*.

"I'm going to pray for your father," said Anna. "Wherever he may be. He's been gone for four weeks now and still no news."

"Mamochka," said Kotik after watching her pray for a while. Touched by his affectionate tone, Anna broke off her prayers. "Yes," she said. "Yes, my Kotichek."

"I made a big mistake," he began. For a long time he had wanted to get this off his chest. "I should have escaped with the others when I had the chance. I don't belong here. I've got to get out of here. Whatever happens in the next few years, I'm leaving. I don't know what it is, but I can't go around hanging my head all the time, I can't keep kneeling, beating my breast, suffering in silence. It's the Church that teaches us that, but I also think it's the soil here, this Silesian soil that says to us: kneel, bow your head, let yourself be beaten, suffer, it's God's will. I don't believe it anymore. What might save the people here is rage, rebellion, but they haven't the strength, because the priest keeps talking about the cross. But the cross isn't meant for everybody, I just don't believe it. Jesus, the son of the Christian God, took the cross on himself so mankind wouldn't have to bear it; otherwise what would be the point in his sacrifice? Believe me, Mamochka, I'm getting out, and I won't be the only one, maybe we've got to leave here because this soil keeps dragging us down into an orgy of suffering—no, let me finish, I didn't read that in *Zarathustra*, as you seem to think, this has been going on inside me for a long time, it has nothing to do with the Germans, Russians, Poles, or anyone else. As long as we keep our hands folded in prayer, some supermen or other will come and oppress us, we must learn to unfold our hands and embrace our friends and stand up to our enemies. I don't believe God wants us to kneel to Him and bow our heads, He wants us to look up, to look at the sky and the stars, because that's the face of God . . ."

"Kotik," said Anna, raising her hands to high heaven. "Is it you saying these things? Holy Mary *Matka Bozhe* . . ."

"Yes," Kotik screamed. "Unfold your hands, Mamochka, pray if you must, but clench your fists, rebel . . ."

Glossary and Notes

Here, as in the translated text, German words are spelled as in German and Polish words as in Polish. Upper Silesian and Russian words are written roughly as they would be in English.

page 6. *Moja siostrzyczko* (Polish). Vocative of "my little sister."

page 7. *Bozhe muy* = My God. Corresponds to Polish *Boże moj*. More usual in the order *Muy Bozhe*. "Zh" is pronounced like the French "j" in *jour*.

page 8. *Ostarbeiter*. German plural *Ostarbeiter*. Workers imported by force or suasion from occupied Russian and Polish territories to relieve the German manpower shortage.

khakhar = bastard, no-good

page 10. HY = Hitler Youth. German HJ, *Hitlerjugend*

page 11. *kapusta* = sauerkraut

page 12. *żur* (Polish). A sour soup made from cabbage, cucumbers, or sourdough.

page 13. *hoppek* = kid, also guy

Pyerunnish, the adjective or adverb of *pyerunnye*, the standard Silesian expletive. Here "lousy" or "rotten," but according to the tone and context it can be almost affectionate, as "damned nice."

page 21. *zygana* = gypsy

kachka = (lame) duck

ogura = pickle

chapla = loony

zebulla = (stinking) onion

hadra = bitch

dupa = asshole

tuleya = idiot

klekota = hatrack

tepshlag = idiot

page 26. *Pani* (Polish) = Mrs. or lady. A respectful way of referring to the boss.

muy Bozhe kokhany = My holy God

święta Maryja Matka Boża or *Boska* (Polish) = Holy Mary Mother of God

page 43. The Annaberg is regarded as the holy mountain of Upper Silesia. On March 21, 1921, a battle was fought there between Polish insurgents and German "self-defense" troops. According to the Germans, the Poles withdrew in defeat. According to the Poles, they were forced back by the troops of the Interallied Control Commission.

Freikorps, or Free Corps. An army secretly and illegally organized in 1919 by the German Army High Command to combat communism. Consisting largely of demobilized soldiers, the *Freikorps* murdered thousands of political enemies in 1919 and the early twenties. Many of the founding members of the National Socialist Party came from its ranks.

page 46. "Where danger threatens salvation grows apace." A quotation (familiar to many German readers) from *Patmos*, a poem by Friedrich Holderlin.

page 87. Eichendorff's Good-for-Nothing. A reference to *Die Geschichte eines Taugenichts (The Story of a Good-for-Nothing)* by Baron Josef von Eichendorff (1790–1857), a Silesian by birth. A charming romantic tale, which begins exactly as in the present passage.

page 90. *galoty* = trousers

page 95. Korfanty. Adalbert Korfanty (1873–1939), Polish politician. Worked for union of Upper Silesia with Poland.

page 98. *gowno* (Polish) = shit

powinność (Polish) = duty

page 123. poor Fallada. See *Grimms' Fairy Tales* "The Goose Girl."

page 127. *platzek* = (under normal circumstances) potato pancake

page 132. *utopletz* = water sprite

page 144. *gorolik* = naughty child

page 147. (Polish) God, we thank thee for what thou hast done for us. Thou providest food for us and blessest all that grows.

page 159. (Russian) The winds blow, the storm rages
The trees bow down to the ground
Oh, how my heart aches,
But the tears won't come.

page 185. *dyobok* = devil

page 203. *pyolter* = brandy and soda. Word coined by Gerhart Hauptmann.

page 240. The quotation is from Balzac's story *La Peau de Chagrin (The Wild Ass's Skin)*.

Horst Bienek was born in Gleiwitz, Upper Silesia, in 1930. He began his literary career as a journalist in Berlin, where he studied with Bertolt Brecht at the Berliner Ensemble. Arrested on a political charge in 1951 in East Berlin and sentenced to twenty-five years' forced labor, he spent four years in the Vorkuta prison camp in the northern Urals before being freed by an amnesty. Since 1956 he has lived in West Germany and continued his career as a poet, essayist, and novelist as well as an accomplished filmmaker. He is the recipient of numerous literary prizes, among them three of Germany's most coveted: the Hermann Kesten Prize, 1975; the Wilhelm Raabe Prize, 1980; and the Nelly Sachs Award, 1981.

Ralph Manheim has been translating since the late thirties. Born in New York and educated at Harvard, he later studied in Munich and Vienna. At first a specialist in philosophy, history of religion, and history of art, he branched out to fiction with Günter Grass's *The Tin Drum* in 1961, for which he won the P.E.N. Club Prize. A prolific translator of both German and French, he has won numerous other awards, including the National Book Award in 1970 for *Castle to Castle* by Céline, the Goethe House–P.E.N. Prize in 1975 for *Sorrow Beyond Dreams* by Peter Handke, and the Schlegel-Tieck Prize in 1979 for *The Flounder* by Günter Grass. He is also the 1988 winner of the P.E.N. Club's translation medal.